SPACE: 1975

SPACE OPERA STORIES WITH A 1970S TWIST

Edited by

ROBERT JESCHONEK

CONTENTS

SPACE: 1975
Published by IE Books, an imprint of Pie Press Publishing

Cover and interior design copyright © 2021 Pie Press Publishing
Cover and interior illustrations copyright © 2021 by Ben Baldwin
www.benbaldwin.co.uk

Ebook ISBN-13: 978-1-7361687-0-7
Paperback ISBN-13: 978-1-7361687-1-4

Published in January 2021 by arrangement with the authors.

www.piepresspublishing.com

INTRODUCTION

BARBARA BAIN

The stories in this book are inspired by the "space operas" of the 1970s. Such stories have a connection to my own life's journey, as I appeared as Dr. Helena Russell in the TV series *Space: 1999*, which first ran from 1975 to 1977.

It is rewarding to find that some of the work I did many moons ago still has resonance. The universal themes in *Space: 1999* did indeed reach 180 countries in its first release.

Most meaningful was the unexpected journey in which our characters found themselves, thrust into outer space, unarmed (as our base was scientific, not military), by an explosion caused by Earth's mindless storage of atomic waste on the Moon.

Our Moonbase Alpha family spent the various episodes with the ever-burning hope to find a home. This theme drove the stories (and the technology of the time gave my space-based medical practice some fun toys, some of which have since appeared in current, everyday life).

In the collection you're about to read, the stories have similar themes, plus twists straight out of the 70s. Sometimes, the twists involves the music of the 70s, or the fashion, or the fads; sometimes, they involve the history, or the attitudes, or the styles of those years. In one story, "Good Vibrations," two 70s teens fly a spacegoing VW Beetle into an adventure with some music-loving aliens; in another story, "The 1970s Must Die!", the actual decade of the 70s is stolen by a rogue time bandit on the run. This is a fun read.

I suspect that Dr. Russell—and Commander Koenig, and Captain Kirk, and all the rest—would very much agree with me.

Los Angeles, California, January 1, 2021

THE SEVENTIES – SCIENCE FICTION'S GOLDEN AGE?

MARC SCOTT ZICREE

Were the 1970s the Golden Age of Science Fiction? That's for you to say.

The science fiction we're exposed to in our youth holds a special place in our heart. Partly this is because, as has often been quoted, "The Golden Age of Science Fiction is thirteen." And also because, as I myself have noted, "Kids have no taste."

But that's not a bad thing. I simply mean that kids love to be entertained and don't give a damn if the production is cheap, the acting bad, the writing sub-par. They love it because they love it.

Or as Guillermo del Toro once told me, as a child in the Seventies he was so entranced by *War of the Gargantuas* when he first saw it in a theater in Guadalajara that, even after a kid poured a full cup of piss on him from the balcony, he still stayed until the end of the picture.

I myself was a teenager in the first half of that decade, but for me, the real transformative moment came in 1966, when I was ten and *Star Trek* debuted. Again, to quote myself (the most reputable source I know), "Some people find heroin, I found *Star Trek*."

But for many, their first exposure to *Star Trek* was in the Seventies, when it entered syndication and played every day in the afternoons rather than late at night on the network—a perfect time for kids coming home from school.

The Seventies was a transformative time for science fiction. In 1968, *2001: A Space Odyssey* had premiered, a game-changer that we thought was a postcard from the future showing all the wonders we would have by then. In 1969, Neil Armstrong and Buzz Aldrin landed in the Sea of Tranquility. But by the Seventies, space travel was passe, with astronauts playing golf on the Moon and getting low ratings from bored viewers. Clearly, science fiction would have to find other ways to beguile us.

But a miraculous sea-change was occurring. In the early decades of the century, you were lucky if you got one standout sci-fi picture every ten years. For the Twenties, it was *Metropolis*, for the Thirties, H.G. Wells' *Things to Come,* for the Forties...well, World War II took pretty much everyone's attention; for the Fifties, *Forbidden Planet,* and some might argue *The Day the Earth Stood Still* or *The Thing*. Printed science fiction was read by a small minority of (mostly male) oddballs who bought pulp magazines, dime paperbacks, or Science Fiction Book Club hardbacks. Writers got a penny or nickel per word for a short story, as little as a thousand dollars for a novel.

But all that started to change when *2001: A Space Odyssey* became the top-grossing film of 1968 and *Star Trek* went on to make billions. In the Sixties, the focus in science fiction in both films and TV was to *say something*. Shows with profound meaning in their DNA included *Twilight Zone, Outer Limits, The Prisoner,* and *Star Trek*.

By the Seventies, many of the most successful movies and TV shows were proving to be science fiction, and the top SF novelists were turning out bestselling titles making them millions.

The major tropes of science fiction were still popular—dystopian futures, travel in space and time, alien invasion, genetic and mechanical manipulation of human beings and the natural world—but in general, there was a lighter, more escapist tone than there had been in the Sixties. You might get a movie like *Logan's Run*, in which everyone was executed at age thirty...but they were all dressed in pastels.

A bit of a technology check here. Telephones were plugged into the wall, not carried in your pocket, most films were made by major studios and shown at movie theaters and drive-ins, and there were three major networks generating most of the drama and comedy series, with reruns and cheaper shows airing in syndication on local stations. You could listen to recordings on LPs or cassette tapes (or 8-tracks, if you were a weirdo), but until late in the decade, there were no VHS or Betamax machines to record your favorite TV shows or movies to watch later. Books and magazines were physical objects made of paper, and if you wanted to look something up, you went to the library. Computers were something scientists had, and if you tried to pick one up, you'd get a hernia.

That said, if you were a sci-fi fan, the Seventies were hog heaven.

This was the decade when Spielberg and Lucas utterly changed the nature of cinema, to something that to this day defines a blockbuster as popcorn entertainment that, if successful, generates breathless thrill rides, a cornucopia of merchandising, billions in revenue...and endless sequels.

In television, Glen Larson made a name for himself with *The Six Million Dollar Man*, *Battlestar Galactica*, and *Buck Rogers in the 25th Century*. British producer Gerry Anderson, whose marionette-starring sci-fi shows such as *Supercar* and *Fireball XL5* were hits both in the U.S. and UK in the Sixties, turned his talents to human actors in the Seventies, with such popular shows as *UFO* and *Space: 1999*.

Comic books, which had been derogated in the Fifties as degenerate material that transformed kids into juvenile delinquents, had gained a shaky legitimacy in the Sixties, and over those decades, both Superman and Batman had seen fruition as rather cheesy TV shows. But in the Seventies, these spandexed, bemuscled men and women proved major moneymakers, with Christopher Reeves' *Superman* on the big screen, and such shows as Lou Ferrigno's *The Incredible Hulk,* Lynda Carter's *Wonder Woman, Shazam!,* and *Super Friends* on TV.

In reality, you couldn't look at a TV or movie screen without seeing science fiction all over the place. Many of the same writers who'd defined the sci-fi of the Sixties adapted to the needs of the Seventies—Richard Matheson with *Duel* and *Kolchak: The Night Stalker,* George Clayton Johnson and William F. Nolan with both the film and TV versions of *Logan's Run,* and the great Rod Serling with *Night Gallery.*

The Brits also contributed to the TV landscape, with the previously mentioned Gerry Anderson shows, and also *Blake's 7* and the Tom Baker *Dr. Who.* Even Nigel Kneale of *Quatermass* fame added John Mills' *The Quatermass Conclusion,* in which the hippies' bizarre behavior was laid at the feet of malevolent aliens.

Visitors both from and to lost localities made their mark on Seventies television with *Man From Atlantis* and *Land of the Lost.*

TV and movie hits of the Sixties saw themselves rejiggered into the *Planet of the Apes* TV show and *Star Trek: The Animated Series,* while at the same time, the decade saw further big-screen iterations of both with *Star Trek: The Motion Picture* and *Beneath the Planet of the Apes, Escape From the Planet of the Apes, Battle for the Planet of the Apes,* and *Conquest of the Planet of the Apes.* Comedy was well-served by Woody Allen's *Sleeper,* Paul Bartel's *Death Race 2000,* Dan O'Bannon and John Carpenter's *Dark Star,* and *The Rocky Horror Picture Show* (and also in radio and later books, TV and film, Douglas Adams' singular and superb *The Hitchhiker's Guide to the Galaxy*).

Novelists also saw their works transformed into movie and TV hits. Martin Caidin, whose novel *Marooned* had been made into the pretty-decent 1969 Gregory Peck film of the same name, struck it rich when his book *Cyborg* was transformed into *The Six Million Dollar Man* and its spinoff, *The Bionic Woman.* And in film, Michael Crichton scored big with *The Andromeda Strain, Westworld,* and *Futureworld,* years before his *Jurassic Park* would seize the world in its dinosaur jaws. *Rosemary's Baby* author Ira Levin would chillingly explore human duplication with both cloning and androids in *The Boys From Brazil* and *The Stepford Wives.* And long before Steampunk was even a concept, *The Seven Percent Solution*'s Nicholas Meyer wrote and directed the delightful H.G. Wells time travel pastiche, *Time After Time.*

And the movies! Charlton Heston, who had been so iconic in 1968's *Planet of the Apes,* continued his tradition of sci-fi hits with *The Omega Man* and *Soylent Green* (based on novels by Richard Matheson and Harry Harrison, respectively). Years before James Cameron's Skynet would take over the world in *The Terminator,* D.F. Jones' novel and film would roll out an equally world-conquering computer in *Colossus: The Forbin Project.* And flying saucers got a terrific showcase with Spielberg's *Close Encounters of the Third Kind.*

These were mostly light entertainments, good for an evening or Saturday matinee's diversion. Which is not to say you didn't have the occasional darker or heavier cinematic experience. Certainly, there were films like Douglas Trumbull's *Silent Running*, Andrei Tarkovsky's *Solaris* and *Stalker*, Kubrick's *A Clockwork Orange*, George Roy Hill's *Slaughterhouse-Five*, Harlan Ellison's *A Boy and His Dog*, Norman Jewison's *Rollerball*, Nicholas Roeg's *The Man Who Fell to Earth*, Philip Kaufman's *Invasion of the Body Snatchers*, and John Boorman's *Zardoz*. But while some of these films were successful, they weren't really part of the *zeitgeist* of the decade, and didn't seize the public's imagination in any substantive way.

But one of these filmmakers created a dystopic feature-length version of a short he'd made in film school whose lukewarm reception caused him to shift his aesthetic gears toward a more broad-based entertainment. This would result in a film that, like *2001* in the Sixties (a clear inspiration) led him to create the game-changer of the Seventies.

The dystopic film was *THX 1138*. And the film that George Lucas followed it up with was 1977's *Star Wars*.

And if you don't know what *that* did to the world at large, you clearly need to get out of your bomb shelter more.

The other major medium of Seventies science fiction was, of course, the printed one. As opposed to TV and film, which had for the most part chosen a lighter path, sci-fi novels, novellas, and short stories were enjoying a time of great experimentation and profound expression. The Old Guard of writers who had established the modern genre of science fiction from the Thirties on came directly in collision with the *enfants terrible* of the New Wave. The four great writers of SF—Heinlein, Asimov, Bradbury, and Arthur C. Clarke—were still very much alive and actively writing, as were such stalwarts as Jack Williamson, Poul Anderson, Alfred Bester, Frederick Pohl, Jack Vance, Theodore

Sturgeon, Roger Zelazny, Cordwainer Smith, Keith Laumer, Clifford D. Simak, Robert Silverberg, and many more.

A list of the notable books of that decade would be on pretty much anyone's must-read list: Larry Niven's *Ringworld,* Jack Finney's *Time and Again,* Clarke's *Rendezvous With Rama,* Ursula K. Le Guin's *The Lathe of Heaven,* Joe Haldeman's *The Forever War,* Philip K. Dick's *A Scanner Darkly,* Octavia Butler's *Kindred,* Philip Jose Farmer's *To Your Scattered Bodies Go,* James Tiptree, Jr. a.k.a. Alice Sheldon's *Ten Thousand Light Years From Home,* and Harlan Ellison's *Again, Dangerous Visions.*

And we mustn't forget our brothers behind the Cold War's Iron Curtain, including Stanislaw Lem, whose masterpiece *Solaris* and *Memoirs Found in a Bathtub* were first published in English during the decade, as well as Arkady and Boris Strugatsky's eerie and atmospheric *Roadside Picnic.*

But despite its widening popularity, print SF would never equal the broad exposure of sci-fi in film and TV. Even if you didn't read a single novel or short story, if you were around in the Seventies, you *definitely* watched a number of these TV shows and movies.

Given the broad scope and tone of these myriad expressions of speculation, each person will definitely have his or her unique definition of what Seventies sci-fi means to them.

And that's exactly how it should be. As Damon Knight, author of the classic, "To Serve Man," once said, "Science fiction is what I'm pointing at when I say science fiction."

So now we present *Space: 1975,* an anthology of stories that, should we succeed, will give you some of that warm fuzzy feeling you got way back when.

Or maybe not so fuzzy. Because the *other* game-changer of the Seventies got in just under the wire in 1979.

Earlier in the decade, two college students wrote, directed, and starred in a little sci-fi comedy film they hoped would launch their careers. But once they graduated and tried to sell it, they were informed it was too short for a feature film and they'd have to shoot another sequence to complete it.

So Dan O'Bannon came up with a truly ludicrous idea—that the crew's alien pet (made up of a beach ball and two *Creature From the Black Lagoon* hands) escapes into the bowels of the ship, where Sergeant Pinback (played by O'Bannon) tries to capture it, the creature trying all the while to kill him.

Silly stuff, but it rounded out the running time. And so *Dark Star* was released.

But O'Bannon couldn't get the notion out of his head. What if a spaceship crew encountering a malevolent alien *wasn't* done for laughs? What if it were truly horrifying?

O'Bannon got together with his pal Ronald Shusett and wrote the script. Then, he hired political cartoonist Ron Cobb to paint ten concept paintings for the princely sum of $1,000. Twentieth Century Fox bought the script and hired a newbie director who'd previously only shot commercials and one artsy historical feature that was very much an acquired taste.

Fortunately, that director was Ridley Scott, and the movie was *Alien*.

I remember seeing a preview screening of that film at Worldcon, with no prior knowledge of what was to come. Harlan Ellison was sitting in front of me in the audience, and when the chest burster erupted out of John Hurt's chest, he jumped a foot—as did everyone else.

So whether your favorite alien is the Xenomorph from *Alien* or the boneless wonders from *Close Encounters,* whether your robot pal is C-3PO or Twiki, and your best-loved sarcastic Princess is...well, that could *only* be Princess Leia...we hope you love these new stories from those of us who came of age in that long-ago time, and hold it dear.

And by the way, do you know when the Golden Age of Science Fiction *really* was?

It's always right now.

Los Angeles, California, December 2020

PROFESSOR FUTURE VS. THE TITAN OF SIRENS

JIM GOTAAS

CHAPTER ONE

Professor Future was living in the past.

Temporarily.

And temporally. He'd supersaturated his body with antichronons, sending him backward against the inexorable increase of entropy.

He was incognito, wearing a coruscating silver and blue jumpsuit and thigh-high golden boots with six-inch platform heels. Even without the heels, his muscular six-foot eight-inch form would have towered above most of the crowd. He was flinging his arms asunder, wildly kicking out, jumping from one garishly illuminated floor square to another, singing at the top of his voice with perfect diction and pitch.

He was striving to be inconspicuous.

He'd succeeded.

The air was filled with a billowing mist of sublimated dry ice, enriched by the smoke of dozens of cigarettes and joints. Harmless decorative red laser beams cut through the smoky atmosphere, crisscrossing the room, mostly above the heads of the hundred humans desperately trying to have fun.

Despite his physical exertions, despite being surrounded by heaving bodies, migraine-inducing, strobing, colored lights, and the deafening roar of people screaming over the underlying musical cacophony, he still managed to keep his mental focus on solving the equations describing the eventual collapse of the physical universe back into a spacetime the size of a small pea. He'd reached the fifth-level solution when a young woman stumbled into his arms and hugged him, trying to plant a wet kiss on his cheek.

Even for Professor Future, it was just too much. His multidimensional visualization of the cascading equations shattered.

Damn. The combination of simultaneous physical and mental exercises was crucial to maintaining his superb fitness and capabilities, and he hated losing focus because of a mere minor physical distraction.

Without losing his balance, he grabbed the amorous assailant in one arm, whirled around, and handed the writhing female off to another body of indeterminate gender.

Then, he cleared his mind and body with a stupendous leap six feet into the air, somersaulting as he slapped his ankles with his hands, landing softly to balance on his toes before rocking back on his Cuban heels, without missing a beat. He was about to start the mental derivation again when his wrist monitor emitted a brief, sharp, coded electrical shock. The specific frequency combination told him it was an alert from his Portable Probability Prognosticator, or P^3. He quickly tapped the precise required combination into his wrist controls, and all the sounds and lights and people around him froze into a real-life diorama as he shifted outside the ordinary temporal flow.

Another quick set of taps, and the P^3 set up a virtual display in his field of vision. The warning message was clear. A triple-Z-star emergency was looming back in his own time, and it was likely to be something only he could deal with.

He popped a chronon booster into his mouth and waited just outside time until his chronon/antichronon balance was reset. With a final glance around the disco floor, he sang goodbye to the twentieth century, then vanished, leaving behind a mildly disrupted reality flow as the marijuana-laced air rushed to fill the temporary vacuum.

CHAPTER TWO

In literally no time, he was once again in his Laboratory of Space and Time—or LoST, for short—in high orbit around the Earth, fully stealth-shielded so it was invisible to all normal instruments of the twenty-fifth century. The Main Probability Prognosticator was blaring alarms that rattled energized furniture assemblages and the transparent bulkheads.

"Absolute silence," he ordered, and the alarms fell silent. Then, "Full display!"

Every wall became a screen, filled with equations flickering, numbers dancing, and projected future images wavering as probability flows were analyzed and turned into less abstract symbols.

Professor Future's head whipped back and forth over a three-hundred-degree span, taking in all the information, adding his own brilliant intuitive powers to the more mundane probability calculations of the googol-plexed quantum computers that sat in the core of his laboratory station.

It was clear. Catastrophe loomed, not just for the Earth, but for the entire Assembly of Sapient Systems and Electronic Symbionts, the organization that maintained lawful order among the various species and polities of the galaxy.

Unfortunately, it wasn't clear just *what* that catastrophe could be!

He automatically sent a warning message to the Headquarters of the Assembly Space Patrol orbiting safely outside the massive black hole at the center of the galaxy. But as brave and intrepid as the multi-species members of the Space Patrol were, he knew it would be of little use without more details. They had their limitations, which is why they relied on Professor Future to provide the important lead in crucial situations.

He commanded the LoST to turn off gravity and adopted a lotus position, his preferred condition and posture for deep thought. His fingers danced in a frenetic but precise blur in front of him, triggering virtual controls that modified data filters and reset probability triggers. He studied the results, looking for any clue as to where the danger was coming from.

He spent an incredibly long thirty seconds on this task.

At the end, the conclusion was clear!

The danger was coming from an adjacent pocket universe, a spacetime that Professor Future himself had set up to contain the monstrous evil that was Galactopus: the Creator, Ruler, Chief Orchestrator, Program Director, and Publicity Agent of the Choir of Sirens of Bewilderment.

Galactopus, who preferred to be called the Titan of Conquest and Destruction—but settled for Titan for convenience—had come dangerously close to conquering the entire Milky Way galaxy only months ago in the main time stream using only the mind- and mood-altering songs of his trillion-strong chorus of sirens!

It had taken all of Professor Future's intelligence and powers to stop that evil plan. As was his invariable custom, dictated by his absolute code of integrity and morality, he'd spared their lives. It had been one of the most difficult decisions of his long life. For during the battle across the galaxy, Galactopus had managed to take control of Future's closest confidante, the only person he'd even been tempted to call a friend, the smartest and bravest woman he'd ever met.

Captain Guinevere Frost had been turned as a weapon against him. She'd come at him, blasters blazing, snarling oaths that had never crossed her lips before. She'd been trained in sixteen different forms of lethal combat, skilled with a hundred different weapons, able to face death with a song on her lips. She was possibly the only person who had any chance of claiming victory in single combat with the Professor.

So when she'd come at him, he'd made a mistake. He'd inadvertently reflected some of the energy blasts back at her. They'd hit her head, completely annihilated it. Galactopus hadn't even allowed her the safety of a personal defensive screen.

Accident or not, Professor Future was responsible for the death of Captain Guinevere Frost, and he would never forget it.

Nor would he ever be able to forget that the Titan had been ultimately responsible.

CHAPTER THREE

Somehow, Professor Future had still managed to stick to his code. Galactopus and the sirens would be spared, but spend their remaining existence locked away where they could do no more harm.

But Future had been well aware that no Space Patrol prison world would be able to hold them, so he'd simply placed them in effective quarantine in that pocket universe, safely isolated from the inhabitants of the galaxy.

Now, they were trying to return and resume their monstrous quest for galactic dominion.

Worse, the probability configurations indicated they had a 62.9981% chance of succeeding.

He pulled in a deep, determined breath and straightened up. Time to change into his multi-configuration Powers Amplification Skin Tights. But he'd barely finished ordering the PAST to appear when he was enveloped by a complex sound of a cappella humming.

He didn't have time to don his PAST or fully activate his Multiply Aggressive Space Cruiser, or MASC.

Before he could do anything, he felt a familiar wrenching, his mind twisting away from a confrontation with a brain-numbing pseudo-reality, as his body was literally turned inside out.

Professor Future was snatched out of his laboratory, helpless to intervene!

The only trace left in his lab was a dash of stomach acid and a few drops of blood, the residue of his almost superhuman body being turned inside out.

CHAPTER FOUR

Professor Future reentered spacetime, turned back right side in, and stumbled a step forward, where a normal sapient would have collapsed into a disorganized heap. He straightened up and looked around.

He'd arrived in a black circle in the precise center of a circular white marble floor, with a hemispherical surface extending hundreds of feet above him. He was surrounded by a phalanx of sirens who continued to hum at him. He could tell that the space was designed to focus all their sounds on the place where he stood.

He was familiar with the physical nature of the sirens—all identical, absolutely white, three feet tall, totally naked, betraying no gender, lacking eyes, but with huge ears. He knew they "saw" through a form of sonic echolocation, which allowed them to effortlessly focus their songs on any part of their surroundings and interpret the complex waveforms that bounced back to them.

He'd expected as much, having recognized the distinctive character of the voices that had surrounded him and drawn him across into another universe before he could act.

Finally, he turned his gaze on the one aspect of the room that wasn't absolutely white: Galactopus!

Its form was also familiar—taller even than Professor Future—but its surface was an absolute absence of light, except for a thousand huge eyes, with black pupils embedded in dark crimson irises within bright yellow sclera. Beneath each eye grimaced a mouth filled with jagged teeth. A million squirming tentacles spread out for hundreds of feet in all directions, each containing a million organic tuning forks, the method by which it communicated with and commanded the legions of sirens.

The thousand mouths spoke in unison, deep voices echoing across the room, speaking standard Galactic Universal Language Forms. "Surprised, Professor Future?"

"Just a bit," the Professor answered in kind. "A very little bit. At first. No longer."

The tentacles of the Titan writhed in petulant annoyance. "Don't pretend you can understand what's happened to you!"

Future smiled thinly. "But I can, of course. When I placed you and your minions here in this small pocket universe, you managed to record my voice, which is ultimately unique because of my special mental and physical capacities and genetic enhancements. Using the ultra-high sonic harmonics that your sirens can generate, you were able to twist spacetime and reach through to me. But only me. And only to bring me here. You are still trapped."

Even as he spoke, Professor Future was rapidly considering the necessary equations that would describe the spacetime wrenching action of the sirens. He was bluffing, of course, since his Probability Prognostications had identified a serious threat to the galaxy. Somehow, Galactopus either had found or would soon find a flaw in the isolation of the pocket universe, which would allow him to escape and wreak havoc across the galaxy once more.

Unless Professor Future could stop him!

Without the precise knowledge of what action was required, Future fell back on physical distraction. Even as he analyzed the myriad possibilities this moment in time could lead to, he leapt in the air, removed his boots, and slid them over his hands. He fell back into a crouch, as the boots transformed into gloves, molded precisely to the contours of his long fingers. They responded immediately to his thumb twitches, firing a combination of pulsed high-energy packets and hypersonic stun darts at the evil form of Galactopus.

Unfortunately, faster than the speed of light, his monstrous opponent erected an impenetrable shield. Professor Future saw the energy pulses simply absorbed and the darts fall harmlessly to the floor.

Worse, the voices of the sirens altered their frequencies and intensities, and he felt himself immobilized, unable to move a muscle, as Galactopus generated a thousand renditions of maniacal laughter!

CHAPTER FIVE

"Your petty weapons can't affect me, Professor Future. Without the resources of your LoST, PAST, or MASC, you are little more than a nuisance. You can't even speak unless I permit it!"

Future stared impassively at his captor. He was unable even to move his tongue and lips to offer a crisp rejoinder to Galactopus's taunt. But he still had a means of communication, buried deep at the base of his superbly shaped skull: his Translation and Language Consolidation Unit and Receiver.

He triggered this device, the TaLCUR, directing the modulated and modified telepathic stream at his adversary.

You underestimate my abilities.

Galactopus snarled wordlessly and waved a dozen angry tentacles at him.

Professor Future continued his deep analysis of the pattern and quality of the sounds that assaulted him and the mathematics of the actions that had brought him to this pocket universe. Simultaneously, he continued to goad the monster.

Even without my external resources, I am still powerful enough to defeat your clumsy attempts.

"Not this time! You were simply lucky to defeat me last time. Without your artificial aids, you are no match for my choir of sirens! And now you will accept my mastery and join me."

With that pronouncement, the tenor and form of the sirens' voices changed.

At the front of Future's mind, strange and alien thoughts appeared: it would be *good* to allow the Titan and his creations to go back to the home universe. What harm could it do? They were ready to transform all sapient life for the better!

But in the deepest part of his mind, Professor Future realized immediately what was happening. They were attempting to control his mind, to use their alien powers to make him their puppet.

But they underestimated his spirit and resilience. Professor Future was more than just the tools he had, his LoST, PAST, and MASC. At the core of everything he was and did, it was his fundamental strength of mind that enabled him to carry out his lifelong fight against evil. That inner core had never failed and never would.

So, dismissing that external compulsion, he forced out the words he felt, rather than the words Galactopus wanted to hear.

Never! I stand against you, now and forever.

Galactopus snarled incoherently in his rage. A single tentacle whipped out across the gap, aimed at Future's face, landing a terrible glancing blow that rocked his head back.

But Professor Future simply sent a *mental smile* at the monster.

"Then we will do it the hard way. I have discovered the one way that will allow me to return to our normal universe, where I will complete my conquest of the galaxy. It will unfortunately require your death. However ..." Galactopus paused and formed every mouth into a leer before narrowing each of its eyes in a hideous wink.

"I am generous and willing to give you one more chance. To spare you, but only if you yield of your own free will and return me and my choir to the galaxy. You will remain my prisoner, but you will survive. You will be my first trophy, and I will enjoy seeing you suffer the spectacle of my ruthless conquest of the hundred billion stars."

Professor Future pretended to consider the proposal, all the while systematically continuing his analyses. After a few seconds, he finally reached the inevitable conclusion. He knew how Galactopus planned to return to the normal universe. And he knew that he couldn't allow it.

The massed ships and troops of the entire Assembly Space Patrol would fight bravely to their deaths but would have no chance against the cruel weapons of the sirens. Their voices generated not just sound waves, but also hypergraviwaves that could penetrate any normal wall or shield. The sapient crews of the Space Patrol would be just as helpless this time as they had been during the first assault. Not even those species that were totally deaf were able to withstand their attacks.

The entire Assembly of Sapient Systems and Electronic Symbionts would fall under that assault!

Professor Future would willingly die to prevent that.

Unfortunately, he now knew that his death wouldn't prevent that assault.

He had to find another way!

He thought his defiance at Galactopus: *I will never willingly assist you in returning to our Milky Way galaxy.*

The thousand mouths roared at him. "Then you will die! And you will die knowing that your very doom allows me to resume my conquest!"

CHAPTER SIX

Immediately, a dozen more tentacles stretched out toward Professor Future's immobile form. As they wrapped tightly around his body, they blocked the effects of the sirens' voices, and he regained the ability to move. He took hold of several of the tentacles and used all his strength to push them away from him. But even as those reluctantly yielded to his superhuman strength and released their hold, another pair gripped him even more tightly.

Even Professor Future's strength was insufficient against the pull of those dozen tentacles, and he was dragged inexorably across the floor toward Galactopus.

The tentacles held him in front of the Titan. Another dozen wove patterns around him, extruding razor-sharp shards of neutronium alloy, deadly and precise. With surgical precision, they cut away his boot gloves, then every stitch of his clothing, leaving him naked. It would have daunted most men, but Professor Future was unaffected by being forced to confront the Titan. Even more, the removal of the clothing revealed his mighty thews, the exceptional sculpted musculature that he'd developed through years of diligent exercise, controlled intake of vitamins, and a carefully-balanced diet. Only his wrist control was left, a band of bioelectronics that was actually grown from his own flesh.

"You have one last opportunity, Future. Yield to me, and you will keep your miserable life."

Professor Future stared into the abysses of fifty eyes. Then, he smiled.

"No."

It was a simple word, spoken firmly, without hesitation, but with all the force of his total resolve and immutable dignity. It dismissed the threats thrown at him without bravado. He had always lived by a code of honor, a code so strong and inviolable that it could have been given the physical form of ultimate diamond, unbreakable, totally clear, without a hint of a flaw.

He had lived by that code. If necessary, he would die by that code.

Galactopus raged on. "You simple human fool. Do you know what torture awaits you? Can you comprehend the pain that will send you screaming to your death? You have no concept of what I must now do."

"Of course I do. I have calculated the one approach that would allow you to escape from this prison universe. You intend to vivisect me, embedding one of your sirens within my body, then gradually replacing my own nerve paths with neural filaments from your creation, using my own life force. If allowed to finish, I would be dead, and my body would simply be a puppet for you. Then, you would send that puppet back to my laboratory and start the process of transferring yourself and your minions back to the normal universe."

Even past the monstrous shape of the Titan's eyes and mouths, Future could read the amazement and shock the other felt.

"How...?"

"In the end, it was a simple calculation. Your efforts to defeat me here made it more difficult, but not impossible."

"Yet knowing what hellish pain awaits you, you still refuse to cooperate?"

"Do you think you're the first adversary who has threatened me with pain and torture? I have the ability to simply switch off my pain receptors. You may do what you will, but I will feel no pain."

Galactopus writhed. "A shame you will not actually feel my fury. But I will still escape this prison and be free to carry out my plans."

Professor Future, however, had taken advantage of the Titan's distraction and managed to press a finger against a stud on his wrist controls. A crucial mistake by the other!

CHAPTER SEVEN

In an instant, Future's body was encased in an invisible protective shield that no ordinary physical object could penetrate—including Galactopus's tentacles and the sound waves of his sirens. It even partially blocked their hypergraviwave influences, leaving the Professor free to act.

Every one of the Titan's mouths howled with rage. Its tentacles lashed at Future, but without effect. Its tentacular tuning forks emitted sonic commands, and the sirens in the room rushed toward them. Simultaneously, sections of the wall disappeared, allowing thousands more of the creatures to enter. They hoped to overwhelm the Professor with their sheer bulk, effectively imprisoning him even as their blows fell harmlessly against his body shield.

But in allowing his sirens to assault Future, Galactopus had released him from the embrace of his tentacles, and the Professor took advantage. He climbed up the backs of the bottom rank of minions, and with a contraction of his massive leg muscles, he leapt away from the mass attack.

Before they could respond to his movement, Future pressed another control. Suddenly, his PAST was with him in the room, and with a quick action, he'd donned the powerful suit that enhanced his already incredible physical abilities. A second later, there was a massive shock boom of air as his MASC appeared just behind him.

He immediately took remote control of his craft and used its blazing weaponry to encase Galactopus and all its sirens in a stasis field that held them locked in a single moment of time, unable to do anything.

Finally having a spare moment, Professor Future paused and looked around.

Even with all his abilities, this had been a close call. If he restored the status quo in this pocket universe, could he be certain that Galactopus wouldn't find another method of escape? The Professor had a profound understanding of his abilities, including their limitations. No sapient was perfect. Even *he* could make a mistake, fail to recognize a remote possibility of failure. Did he dare take that chance?

The stasis field would hold them for a while, but eventually, it would decay.

Was it time to accept his limitations? To accept that there was a moment when his code of honor needed to bend? To end the threat of the Titan and his sirens forever?

There was a small part of his soul that ached for revenge, that wanted desperately to destroy the evil that had led to the death of his closest ally, Captain Guinevere Frost. And he knew she would approve. Even the noble Space Patrol accepted the occasional necessity to take deadly action against its enemies. And Guinevere had always had a dark edge, a willingness to take that final step, to issue the ultimate punishment to those who had themselves stolen lives. It had been their only disagreement.

No!

He carefully locked away that weakness of the spirit that tempted him. He wouldn't dishonor the memory of the finest woman he'd ever known. He would remain true to his code.

Future would ensure that Galactopus couldn't repeat this approach. He would add extra barriers between the pocket universe and the home universe. And he would rely on his Probability Prognosticators to give him sufficient warning of any form of escape attempt.

He entered his Multiply Aggressive Space Craft and returned to his home universe and the comforts of his Laboratory of Space and Time.

Just in time to hear alarms ringing again. The next threat to galactic civilization was already looming!

But Professor Future was ready. As always. At and in all times!

Jim Gotaas is a retired physicist, born and bred in Chicago but now settled into Carlisle, England. A long time ago (actually in the last millennium, 1971), but still in the local galaxy, he published a novelette in *Worlds of If*. Having resumed writing, he's had a story in *Daily Science Fiction* and multiple appearances in *Pulphouse Fiction Magazine*. He's also published nonfiction posts in Dan Koboldt's blog, "Science in Sci-Fi, Fact in Fantasy", of which the first two were published in the *Writer's Digest* collection *Putting the Science in Fiction*. You can catch up with Jim at www.jimgotaas.com.

GOOD VIBRATIONS

RON COLLINS

It had taken about an hour to install, but the tape deck was now officially the most beautiful thing Cody Swanson had ever seen. A brand-new Motorola eight-track player. A TM226S. Almost top of the line, bolted onto the undercarriage of the dashboard and sitting there like it was Mick Jagger himself, sleek in its black casing, cool, calm, and full of promise, fixed by a metallic bracket so thick Cody could already feel waves of hammering decibels.

The deck felt huge, too. Bigger than life itself. Wider than the freaking universe.

And it loved *him*, too. He could feel the thing whispering to him as he finished the installation. Literally. *I'm going to take you places you've never been*, it said as he'd pulled it from its electro-static packaging. *I'm going to show you things you've never seen,* it added as he'd connected it up.

He and that tape deck were already sympatico.

"*Stereo, right and left,*" the sales rep had crooned. "*Digital program indicator. Sliding controllers for volume, balance, and tone.*"

"Precision-mounted head," Cody said to Matt Lamb, who

was bent over the passenger seat, gazing at the machine with rapture.

Matt had been his best friend since freshman year. They were juniors now. Next year, they would rule that damned place.

Cody's Disco Sucks button dangled from the rearview mirror. It was late afternoon, and, after a hot summer, leaves had started to turn. The temperature was September crisp. The smell of dust hung over the garage where Cody had been working. Matt had come to hitch a ride to a scuba class they were taking at the YMCA. (Cody said he was thinking about being a marine biologist, so his dad paid for it. Matt just wanted to do something fun.)

After the class, they'd double date with the girls again.

Everything was working according to plan. Cody had not told Matt about the tape deck before he came over *specifically* because he had wanted to experience this very moment. Matt's curly brown hair fell over his brown eyes, but no one could miss the copious drool he was dropping.

Cody loved the smell of a great plan in the morning.

He'd been worried the deck would look wrong attached to his car, a 1963 VW Beetle painted a bright British green that had faded to dull matte several years ago. Its wheels were balding. Each of its four fenders had been dented at least one more time than they'd been pounded out, and you could see road through the rusted-out floorboard on the passenger side. The engine ran, though. Even though the odometer was stuck at 25,763.9—a number Cody was sure represented at least one time through the rest of the revolving gauge—the engine would get to rocking every time he turned the key.

He'd been wrong to worry, though.

It's tubular, man, their other friend, Willy, would say. *Totally tubular.*

Nobody really liked Willy, but he could play "Wish You Were Here" on the guitar, so he was okay to hang with.

"You know the first tape, right?" Matt said. His gaze flitted to the vinyl case of tapes Cody had already wedged into the tiny backseat underneath the tanks, regulators, and other scuba equipment they would be using later tonight.

Cody smiled.

Matt gave the proper nod. "RHPS, baby," he said, "RHP-bleeping-S!"

"Get in, dude," Cody said as he slid into the driver's seat.

Dad would give him shit for leaving tools out, but that was a fight for another time. The game was afoot now. There were tunes to play and neighborhood windows to rattle.

Cody turned the key, and the tiny engine rumbled to life. He ignored the fact that the sound was more go-kart than Ferrari.

"Let's rock this taco stand," he said as he backed down the driveway.

Cody, Angela, Matt, and Vickie had first seen *The Rocky Horror Picture Show* three weeks ago.

Three weeks later they'd seen it twenty-one times.

A buck a show and worth every penny.

The soundtrack was as good as the movie. "Science Fiction/Double Feature." "Dammit Janet." "Over at the Frankenstein Place." Cody knew them by heart. The order on the eight-track was different, of course. At least on his copy it was. Each of the four programs (two "tracks" for each "program") could carry about eleven minutes. Rather than cut songs in the middle, groups usually just rearranged them. So RHPS on eight-track started with "Science Fiction/Double Feature" like the movie and the album, but went to "I Can Make You a Man," and then "Hot Patootie Bless My Soul." There was a release that played the order straight through, too, but it sucked to cut songs.

To know the difference in these things was to be cool, though, and to be cool was...well...to be cool was to be cool.

There was a whole system of pecking orders to check when it came to being cool. Cody's dad was into country and western, and still played Elvis and all those tinny old records. Definitely not cool. He had an entire *album* of storms, for crying out loud. Leo Sayer was too soft. Captain and Tennille, Jesus H. Christ no. Just no. Seals and Crofts were borderline, Jim Croce too touchy-feelie.

There was more. Layers and layers more.

When it came to RHPS, though, Matt knew the orders. Willy did not.

With the girls, it was different. Being absolute "stone cold" on the fox meter gave them a head start, but being cool with him and Matt put them even farther ahead. Angela really was great, though. First girl he'd felt comfortable with—though she liked to dance and was getting into disco. Most definitely also *not* cool. To be honest, he was trying not to feel betrayed. It was like she'd played bait and switch.

If it wasn't for that, Angela would be perfect in every way.

It was just him and Matt for now, though.

In anticipation of the deck's maiden voyage, Cody had pulled the RHPS cartridge in the middle of track two, right after "Dammit Janet."

~

Rattling down the street, Matt held the cartridge in hand. "I see you shiver," he said, "with antici..."

"Pation!" Cody replied.

He cranked the volume slider, and Matt slapped the cartridge into the deck.

A single beat. *Boom!* ... then that sublime guitar riff, choppy and low.

da-da-da-da-da-da-da-da ... da-da-da-da-da-da-da-da ...

"Time Warp, baby!" Matt screamed, throwing a fist out the open window.

Cody kept time with the beat by slamming his hand on the bleating horn. He grabbed the clutch, put the car into gear, and mashed his foot to the metal. The engine *wheeeeeeed* as all forty horsepower shot the car forward.

The frame wobbled with speed and sound.

Riff Raff's voice was a warbling purr.

The world spun as he drawled the word "astounding."

Something's different, Cody thought as he gripped the wheel. His entire body tensed to press even harder on the accelerator. Riff Raff sang of madness. A vortex built ... *Something's odd ...*

Riff Raff sang on.

Ahead, the street became a whirlwind of darkness. A blanket of stars formed.

The Beetle's little speakers felt like they might shred. The Disco Sucks button bounced on its string. Wind rocked the car left, then right as flares flared.

Riff Raff's voice changed as he hit the chorus in full note. The band played hard—it was a sound like nothing that had ever been made before, gravelly, screaming now, mixing in with Matt's voice, too, as Cody's friend also screamed.

... something's wrong ...

In a distance that might have been another dimension, Cody felt the tape deck speaking to him, whispering, calling, pleading, even promising ...

The Beetle lifted off the road.

An explosive *whomp!* ripped through space.

Then there was only silence.

There is a train of thought that says a human being left exposed to deep space will explode into a globby mess. That vacuum will suck all the air from a person's body, and that the body will shred itself.

This is not true.

Here are things Cody experienced, in the order Cody experienced them.

Dead silence.

Pitch black.

Frigid cold.

A column of light bleeding through the floorboard.

Vibration through his seat—the speakers still pumping "Time Warp" into the cosmos.

His skin frying with raw cold.

Cold! Cold! Cold!

Rubbing his arms.

Fingers aching at the joints.

The cracked vinyl seat breaking into pieces.

They say freezing is the best way to go. The thought died before it finished, though. *They*, Cody decided, *are full of atomic-grade shit.*

Instinctively hitting the contact heater on the dash.

Turning to Matt. Unable to make sound beyond a grunt.

Matt, reaching to the back.

Floating.

A field of stars outside the VW.

Holy shit, were they in ... space?

Gulping for air and feeling like he was trying to suck down a slab of cement.

Lungs burning.

Jesus H. Christ, he couldn't breathe!

He tried to scream but, again, nothing came.

This was it. He was going to die. An image of Mom and Dad flashed over him. His brother. Then Angela. Sweet, sweet Angela who despite her dalliance with disco would never hurt a flea. He would never see her again. Would never feel the touch of her fingers on his hand, would never ...

Then Matt punched him in the mouth.

Sonofagodamned bitch. He was sitting here dying and his best friend punched him in the goddamned mouth! ... then there was air. Sweet God, pure, clean air. It rushed into his lungs, oxygen racing through his blood. The heater kicked on, too, and radiated a ripple of warmth over his toes.

He realized he was grinding rubber between his teeth.

A scuba mouthpiece! Matt had grabbed a tank, kicked it on, and shoved the mouthpiece into Cody's mouth. Jesus, he could kiss the guy right now. This is why they were such a good team. Matt was the action guy—see problem, fix problem—and Cody was the planner. Thank God Matt had been here.

Hollow sounds of breathing traveled through the regulator hose that ran from the tanks in back—the tanks themselves were floating in zero-g.

Blinking, Cody realized they were *actually* scuba diving in space.

Take that, Jacques Cousteau.

He pressed his toes into the vent, and warmth flowed up his foot.

He'd have to thank his dad for replacing the coil last winter as well as encasing the blower. Sometimes, a wonky engineer comes in handy. It was still rugged cold though, and he wasn't stupid enough to think the Bug's heater coil was going to win against the vast vacuum of space.

Not without a little help, anyway.

He grabbed the crank and rolled the driver's window up. If they could lock the compartment down a bit, maybe the heater would save them. For now, anyway. Then they could figure out just what the hell was going on.

Matt was no dummy. He did the same.

Cody's gaze went to the hole under Matt's feet.

A planet below that was definitely not Earth reflected orange light, probably from the sun behind them. Of more importance now, however, was that Matt was turning far too blue for his tastes. The hole was seeping heat.

Something hard hit his head, and he thought his skull was going to shatter.

The tape case!

Big and boxy, the case was full of all the best music made on Earth. He shoved it under Matt's legs. Matt got the hint, and managed to position it on the floorboard, then press the hole closed with his feet.

Cody cranked the heat and tried to relax so his brain would work.

The heat was fading fast. In vacuum, and with the engine dead, even if they captured most of the heat inside the cabin, once radiated, it would be gone forever.

His Disco Sucks button floated on its tether.

Maybe he was hallucinating; maybe he and Matt were really just sitting stoned at some gas station. Yes, that made more sense.

He pressed the accelerator, but nothing happened.

This is when a Mack truck plowed into the bottom of the car.

At least that's what it felt like.

The entire vehicle shuddered, and Cody whumped downward like he'd hit the bottom of the steepest roller coaster in the universe. Every disk in his back compressed. His head thrust forward and back. The button straightened on its tether and, from the back seat, Cody felt both scuba tanks crash into the seat with a metallic clang so harsh it travelled through the VW's frame and up his backside. Cody thought he heard a muffled cry from Matt, but that couldn't be right.

Then it was silent again.

The pressure of his seat grew normal.

He sucked air from the tank.

Matt, now even more wide-eyed, flashed the underwater symbol for "What the hell was that?" In tandem, they both noticed the green spotlight that was now bathing the car. As if on cue, they edged forward to look up through the VW's windshield.

The spaceship was big and sparkly.

Its expanse was likely white or silver, but the light gave it a green cast. A hole gaped open in the middle of the spacecraft's body, and suddenly Cody realized it was shaped like a big-assed Stratocaster guitar, with a tail end that could have been a fretboard if there'd been machine heads bolted onto it.

Matt pointed with one hand and pounded on the dashboard with the other.

The ship was drawing closer.

No, Cody realized. It was them that was moving.

The Stratocaster had the VW in a tractor beam.

He clamped onto the mouthpiece and looked at the door crank. Nothing good could happen if he opened it now.

Cody sat back, defeated. Matt joined him.

At least the cabin was warming up, he thought as they waited for the ship to take them prisoner.

∿

Later, Cody would remember the Beetle rising into the bay area. The door closing and a hiss of air buffeting them like an automatic car wash. The sound of Tim Curry singing "I Can Make You a Man: Reprise" faded in, which meant no more than five or six minutes had passed since they were zooming down his street. He spit the mouthpiece out and felt the pure joy of sucking fresh air. Never before had a single breath meant so much.

Noting the officially dead engine, Cody turned the ignition off.

The tape stopped in mid-song, which hurt. "Never turn good music off," Matt said.

He would remember all that.

Aliens dressed in multiple colors circled the Bug.

They were mostly taller than either Cody or Matt, who were both too short for basketball but tall enough to avoid getting bullied too often. Some of the aliens were squat, some not. They had four arms like something out of a Dungeons and Dragons manual. Big eyes, small eyes. Some black, others gray or green. Hair seemed to come in as many colors as their skin. Some had scales—though maybe those were more like holographic tattoos.

They were, Cody would say later, a total smorgasbord of a group.

The only thing the aliens had in common, it seemed, was that each pointed some kind of weapon at Cody or Matt as they extracted both from the car. Once so extracted, one alien pressed a button on a device they all seemed to wear mounted on their chests. Lights flashed in a random sequence, then flared in red and green.

"Hello, Icanmakeyouaman," it said, "Follow me."

Only the presence of what might well be a horrible death ray pointed in his general direction kept Cody from laughing out loud. The alien must have heard the song before he turned off the engine.

He looked at Matt. "Should we go?"

"Hey, a nice guy in a spaceship just said he can make us a man," Matt replied with a shrug.

If they could parrot *Rocky Horror Picture Show*, maybe it would work out.

Or not.

Breathers can't be choosers, though, and it wasn't like they had many choices.

"Do I look like I have time for this?"

The leader was clearly busy, and just as clearly unhappy with having been interrupted.

The aliens had led Cody and Matt on a long expedition through corridors and lift tubes that would have made Gene Roddenberry proud. Now they stood, mouths agape, on what appeared to be the outer surface of the spaceship but was instead a huge observation and control deck. The "ceiling" was a domed bubble that exposed the entire bowl of deep space. Cody looked right, left, up and then down, orienting himself by noting the way the guitar's tail led off to his left. There was a planet in view. Breathtaking, really. The workspace was maybe half a football field in diameter, filled with aliens who gave a constant chatter while scuttling this way and that. A cacophonous wall of sound seemed to pulse in waves that were a mix of dirge-like anticipation and intense concentration.

Cody was no expert at alien relations, but something was going down.

The leader stood with an annoyed hand on his hip, tall and thin, dressed in a skintight outfit that would have been right at home at a David Bowie show. To that matter, the leader could have been an impersonator, though his red hair was more shag than glam, and his body type was more wide receiver than scarecrow. His face was powder white and lined with patterns of red makeup, the angles and curves of which made Cody reassess whether said leader was actually a "he" or a "she." A hollow-cheeked scowl seemed painted on, too.

Yes, Cody thought. Very Bowie.

"We've just retrieved them from the tractor ray," their escort said to the leader. "Doctor Zanze says they may have some importance."

From the deepening scowl, it was obvious he/she/they/what-the-hell-ever did not agree with the good doctor.

"What are you doing here?"

"We have no idea," Matt replied.

The leader looked at Cody.

Cody shrugged. A darkness outside the dome gave a purple flash.

"They were carrying this," one of the aliens said. It handed the leader the eight-track cartridge. "It carries music."

"Hey," Cody said. "That's ours!"

The leader accepted the cartridge, then turned it right and left with his long, graceful fingers. His expression went through an array of contortions.

"What does it sound like?" the leader said.

The alien's lips contorted, and it broke out in a perfect

rendition of program one, song one "Science Fiction/Double Feature's" intro, including interplay between the low piano, the bass, and Riff Raff's voice—all a cappella. It stopped after a line or two.

"Holy crap, Batman," Matt said. "That was cool."

Brows knit, the leader turned the cartridge in his hand, examining the photos of Dr. Frankenfurter, Riff Raff, and Magenta front and center, then lingering on Brad and Janet and cute little Columbia.

"I've got to think about this," he said.

Cody cleared his throat. He felt a tingle at the base of his skull that reminded him of the quiet moment when he was alone and installing the TM2226S. He wasn't sure what it was, but there was something here.

"You seem to be having a problem," he said after noting all heads turned his way. "Tell me what's happening, and maybe we can help."

The answer to that question, it turns out, was complicated.

The *Glam*—which is the name of the ship they had been "collected by"—was a Maintenance ship, one of a fleet of spacecraft that the leader said served to hold the universe together. Yes, their whole "we save the world every day" flavor seemed a bit strong for Cody's tastes, too, but who was he to argue?

The leader's name sounded like Duggan, but had a soft "t" in there somewhere that neither Cody nor Matt's tongue could ever get quite right.

And, yes, there was a problem.

It had to do with string theory, a bit of science magic that was suddenly becoming more popular, but that Cody only knew about because of the simple fact that his dad was a nerd who made him watch shows on PBS. There was no other way Cody would be caught dead turning the dial to that channel—except for the one time their fund drive included a Don Kirschner thing featuring Steppenwolf in concert. String theory, it seemed, was the Farrah Fawcett of academia. Physicists loved to gaze at it longingly.

Dad's program used terms like "quantum gravity" and "dark matter" and other things that made Cody want to roll his eyes. Mostly, though, what he came away with was this: string theory said the universe was made of stuff that vibrated in some other-world dimension, and that those vibrations made the world Cody lived in.

So, vibrate there, change here.

Whatever, right?

And your Chia pet can do tricks.

Anyway, it all sounded fishy to him. A bunch of grown men playing with comic book science. He could get that with the X-Men.

Luckily, Duggan was able to put things in a way that even Matt and Cody could understand.

"Think of a plane of existence outside yours in which every-thing is music," the leader said.

"You mean, like if you could eat a song?" Matt said.

Cody scowled at him.

"What?" Matt said. "I'm getting hungry."

Duggan ignored them. "More like if a string on that other dimension was on a guitar, and if that string played a song, it could take part in creating a ham sandwich in your dimension. If it played a different song, perhaps the sandwich here would be bologna."

"Cool."

Now Cody was getting hungry.

"You're saying the whole universe is made of songs from this other plane?" Cody replied.

"What is sound, after all, if not vibrations." Duggan said, eyes wide and bold against his ashen-white face. "Everything you see. Everything you hear. Every thought you have comes as a result. The universe is a collection of all the songs mixed together into one big soup. Remove one, and you change everything else."

"A melting pot," Cody said, remembering the TM226S earlier that afternoon, cold in his hands. He could almost hear its voice again, whispering though time and space directly into his mind. He was starting to piece an idea together. Was it talking to him again? If Duggan was right, this memory itself originated as a plucked string in the other world. Could they be related? Could the feelings he had this afternoon and this memory itself come from the same place? Was this a message?

"A million songs played on a million instruments," Cody said, his voice growing distant. Another thought hit. "We need them all."

"Indeed."

The idea bothered Cody for more reasons than he could say.

The world needed music to make it what it was.

All of it. Rock. Jazz. Soul. Gospel. Rhythm and blues. Classical.

The Beatles, and the Mamas and the Papas and Alice Cooper and Otis Redding and Lawrence Welk and Bill Moody and the Monkees and even Pat Freaking Boone. John Coltrane. Elvis. The Stooges. Bill Haley, Chuck Berry. Chopin. Mozart. Janis Joplin. The Doors, the Stones, and the Who. Even Angela's Donna Summer.

What would it mean if even one of them hadn't been there, or if one was suddenly gone?

An image of his Disco Sucks button flashed in Cody's mind, and he felt even more uneasy.

"So, what's the big deal?" Matt said.

"The big deal is right there," Duggan said, pointing to a huge darkness in the dome of space opposite the planet.

"A black hole," Cody said before Duggan could elucidate.

Now that he was looking at it, Cody didn't understand how he'd missed it to begin with.

"That's right," Duggan said. "They connect the dimensions."

Cody's brain engaged. Patterns fell together like dice in a cup. He remembered parts of the programs his dad made him watch. "Discarded material from our universe flows into the music-verse so it can be made into something new."

"Yes. Think about black holes as controller channels."

"Or amplifiers?" Cody said, suddenly feeling like he understood the issue. "Something's wrong, though. Something's missing," he said before Duggan could reply. "There's a feedback loop and you can't damp it."

Matt caught on. "It's going to run away."

"Like putting a microphone too close to the amplifier."

Duggan replied. "Usually, resetting a black hole is a simple scrub, but we've done everything we know to do. There's a hole in the fabric, though, and increasing the pressure just makes it worse. If we can't reset this black hole, the universe will wind itself into a completely unstable meltdown.

"The world as we know it will cease to exist."

Now, Cody understood the intensity that had covered the crew.

His eyes strayed to the cartridge that was still in Duggan's hands, and he remembered the thrill of installing his tape deck earlier this afternoon. He thought about vibrations in other dimensions and remembered the thrill that rolled over his skin as he touched the tape deck.

He understood then. Felt it as sure as he'd felt anything in his life.

His anticipation earlier in the day had been a message from the plane of music.

Vibrations speaking to him through the deck.

Somehow.

His skin crawled again. He heard crooning, then snarling, then laughing. A vibration that was Riff-Raff's voice...fresh, new, and different. He heard Meatloaf's voice, Susan Sarandon's.

The tape. The sound that moves something so strongly inside him. It meant something.

It could fill a hole.

"I think I know what to do," he said. "But I'll need some help."

Cody strapped into the driver's seat. "You good?" he said to Matt.

Matt put his thumb in the air. "All systems go, Houston."

He had given Matt the option to sit this one out, but Matt wouldn't take it.

That's a thing about being cool, too. Friends are friends.

They rolled up the windows again. The new sealants squeaked against the glass. Cody glanced at the floorboard and saw the new baseboard that Duggan had had his aliens install along with the sealants.

Both Cody and Matt chomped down on their mouthpieces. The air in the cabin would only go so far, and the fact was, they'd rather not breathe it anyway; having more air in that compartment, hopefully, would conduct heat better.

Cody turned the ignition and cranked the heat.

The engine roared to life. It was no longer a rat-a-tat little thing, but instead some kind of quantum-foam pile drive that Cody knew better than to think he'd be able to let his dad see.

It was going to be fun to see what this baby would do on the open road, though.

Assuming he got home, anyway.

Which he was pretty sure he would, but, you know...space, right?

He thought about Angela again, then forced the image away.

He pressed the accelerator once more, then gave the thumbs-up to the alien controlling the bay door. It opened to reveal the expanse of the black hole that now lay below them. From behind the control panel, Duggan, decked out in his full Bowie regalia, gave a final, crimson-headed nod.

"We're going in," Cody said.

He turned the wheel, crammed the Bug into gear, and hit the accelerator. The drive tilted, sending them on a direct path to the black hole. He wondered how this baby would handle on asphalt. *Question for another day*, he thought.

As they flew through space in their tricked-out VW Bug, Cody pulled the mouthpiece.

"Ready Chamber One."

"Chamber One prepared," Matt replied, pushing the cartridge into place.

It was set to "Time Warp" again—set to the chorus, to that one moment when the voice of Riff Raff combined with guitars, a driving drum set, and an old-timey, almost ragtime piano to create a sound that did not exist in any other place or any other time.

The black hole loomed closer.

A frying rose like the sound of fire.

They had to hit the right moment if he was going to retune the string on the other side, had to fill the hole with just the right vibration to reset the fabric of the universe. Otherwise, tidal forces would mash them both into atom-sized particles of space meat.

He glanced at the beautiful TM226S.

I'm listening, baby. Don't treat me wrong.

"Three," Cody said to Matt through his mouthpiece.

The car bucked and moaned.

"Two."

He mashed the throttle. Metal squealed. The smell of burning rubber filled the cockpit.

"One!"

Matt slammed the tape into the player.

"Time Warp!" Matt screamed.

The return was anticlimactic.

The vortex was six inches above the street. The VW hit hard enough to throw sparks as its chassis hit the ground. They were lucky that (1) no other cars were on the sleepy little street, and (2) none of the tires blew.

The tape deck played on.

Later that night.

Or rather, something past two o'clock or so the next morning, Cody dropped Matt off at his house. They said goodbye to Vickie ten minutes earlier, which meant Cody and Angela were alone for the first time. The compartment was quiet now, and he could still smell the faint aroma of her perfume.

Whatever vibration created that smell was his favorite vibration of all time.

"I've been meaning to ask," Angela said, pointing at the chunk of stone that dangled from the Beetle's rearview mirror now. He'd replaced the Disco Sucks button shortly after they'd made it back home. It was a black stone, rough and heavy. Duggan had given it to him before he and Matt had left the Glam.

"Something to remember us with," the alien had said.

Like that was necessary.

He smiled.

"It's my pet rock," he said.

"Far out," Angela replied, adding one of those smiles he found so dazzling.

He wondered if she listened to more than Donna Summer.

"Hey," he said. "The clubs are still open. You wanna go dancing?"

Ron Collins has contributed stories to many premier science fiction and fantasy publications, including *Analog, Asimov's*, and several issues of the Fiction River series. He is the award-winning author of *Stealing the Sun*, a series of space-based SF books, and the fantasy serial, *Saga of the God-Touched Mage*, which sat at the top of Amazon's Dark Fantasy best seller lists for several months. His work has garnered a *Writers of the Future* prize, and a CompuServe HOMer award. His short story "The White Game" was nominated for the Short Mystery Fiction Society's 2016 Derringer Award. Find current information about Ron at typosphere.com or follow him on twitter at @roncollins13.

THE 1970S MUST DIE!

ROBERT JESCHONEK

No sooner had Agent Lyssa Bonne Nuit darted through the hail of dial telephones and cheese whiz than her chrono-bike raced into a blizzard of Saturday Morning Cartoons.

Instantly, the lilac-skinned woman in the black carbon mesh jumpsuit was engulfed in churning waves of bright primary colors and limited animation. Images of snickering dogs, teenagers, and superheroes moved stiffly around her as she worked the bike's controls with all six hands, fighting to catch up with her quarry...and the treasure she'd chased halfway across the time-realm of When, all the way from the Everarium.

Suddenly, the giant image of a singing cartoon duck and rabbit appeared in front of Lyssa, jarring her attention...but she didn't slow down. The duck's orange bill seemed to swallow her whole as she squeezed the accelerator and bolted through it.

Zipping out the other side, she saw the burst of speed had been worth it. Pyre Ransom, the object of Lyssa's pursuit, was up ahead, hurtling through a rippling curtain of colorful characters—everything from cartoon bears to cavemen to cats and mice.

Pyre zoomed through it without ever looking back. The

fugitive—a gold-skinned female android—was focused only on getting away with her prize: the decade dubbed the 1970s by the extinct species known as humanity.

Agent Lyssa was determined to take that prize away from her at any cost. Its containment cartridge was steadily leaking Saturday Morning Cartoons and other sociocultural flotsam from the 70s, causing havoc in the skies and streets of When.

One more burst of speed, and Lyssa tore through the last rippling curtain of cartoon characters in Pyre's wake. This time, she emerged in a storm of streakers—images of naked human beings sprinting through the silvery mist, body parts bouncing wildly with each loping step. Every one of them was grinning, an expression Lyssa had come to associate with human joy or pleasure...though she had never met a human and never would.

Because every human being had died out ages ago.

The human race lived on only as echoes in the Yesterplex of the Timekeepers—hyper-rez snapshots of life on ancient planet Earth captured at intervals throughout human history. These flawless log files recorded every detail of entire decades on compact cartridges like the one in Pyre's pack.

These decade backups—known as decalogs—were stored in the vaults of the Everarium, a repository considered impenetrable until Pyre's daring heist. Decalogs were priceless beyond all words, especially in the case of a species like humanity that no longer existed.

As the streakers bounded past with organs flopping, Lyssa fought to stay on track. She lost sight of Pyre up ahead because the gaggle was so dense—also because she was distracted by seeing so many life-size humans in one place. Over the years, Lyssa had studied humans at length and formed a special bond with their long-gone species. They had something in common, something she connected with on a very deep level.

As a final surge of virtual streakers poured past, meaty

bodies jiggling, Lyssa saw she had a clear shot at Pyre, who was less than fifty meters away.

Yanking the Was-Gun from the holster strapped around her thorax, Lyssa pointed it at her golden target. Quickly taking aim, she squeezed the trigger, unleashing the weapon's payload.

The barrel of the gun disgorged a deadly Past-Blast—a roiling mass of temporal detritus sucked from multiple eras of a chosen species' history. As always, Lyssa's own sidearm was set to tap the past of humankind, the object of her greatest fascination.

The ejected mass hurtled through the mist, a cyclone of ancient Roman swords, World War II machine guns, furiously kick-stomping boots, and exploding Molotov cocktails. The mass was moving so fast, it looked as if it would consume Pyre's bike at any second.

Before that could happen, though, Pyre dove from its path and swooped away. The Past-Blast spun harmlessly off through the mist, its howling/booming/clanging growing fainter with each passing second.

Cursing, Lyssa dove after Pyre, pouring on as much speed as she could. Still staying out of reach, Pyre dropped into a bank of crimson clouds, kicking up bright red wisps in her wake.

Only when Lyssa plunged through those same clouds and burst out the other side did she realize where the thief was headed.

"Oh no." The violet antennae and feathery pink cilia on her head flickered madly. "She's heading for the *Yesterplex!*"

When you lived and worked in When, as Lyssa did, the past, present, and future blurred together. Memories, current experience, and premonitions intermingled, because When existed outside normal spacetime.

It was a phenomenon you had to learn to block or at least manage if you wanted to live anything like a normal life...but there were some things you could never narrow down to present sight alone. Some things were so filled with power and importance, they *forced* you to see them from all time angles. They *intruded*, they *insisted*, they *expanded*.

Which was exactly how the Yesterplex was to Lyssa. Gazing down at its lofty silver spire in the present day, she also remembered the first time she'd seen it, the first time she'd come to When as a child.

Welcome to the place that is both of and beyond all time. Those had been the words of Skulk, the red-scaled spider-thing who had brought her here from her home planet of Hinjeri VII. *It is here you will be cared for and learn to care for all the ages in turn.*

The whole time Skulk had talked, Lyssa had simply stared at that giant spire jutting skyward, a tower that had seemed to her to symbolize the end of everything she'd known.

Her parents had been so proud when she'd been chosen to study at the Yesterplex to become a Timekeeper. Lyssa had been so excited when Skulk had come to Hinjeri VII to get her... but it hadn't lasted. Near the end of the journey to When, terrible news had come in over the radio; Lyssa had learned her entire world had been destroyed by a catastrophe. That was when her excitement had turned to anguish, her hope to fear, her dreams to nightmares.

Because, for the rest of her life, she'd be known as the last survivor of her extinct species, the Hinj.

These are the halls of the Yesterplex, she remembered Skulk saying, pointing at the vast figure eight structure sprawling around the base of the silver spire. *The Timekeepers dwell within, preserving yesterday, today, and tomorrow.*

Years later, Lyssa had become a Timekeeper herself. She had poured herself into it, giving it everything she had to make up for what she'd lost. She had never regretted it, either—except when she'd discovered the limits of her commission. Except when she'd discovered the true depths of hopelessness into which she could fall.

When Lyssa touched down at the base of the great silver spire, she saw Pyre's chrono-bike discarded on the golden pavement there. Pyre herself was nowhere to be seen...but the route she'd taken was obvious.

The ground-level doors to the Yesterplex gaped nearby, blown open by something that had left scorch marks and shattered glass in its wake. The bodies of dozens of armed and armored Timekeepers lay all around it, unmoving—victims of the golden-skinned android's great strength, blinding speed, and arsenal of weapons. The security here had been no better able to resist her than that of the great repository of the Everarium.

Leaping from her bike, Lyssa hurried forward, stopping only to check the pulse of one of the Timekeeper guards. He was unconscious, not dead, which was a relief—but she knew she didn't have time to check all the rest. Her most important task right now was catching up to Pyre, then finding out—and stopping—whatever it was she intended to do next.

The nature of Pyre's plans was still a mystery to her, though. All Lyssa knew for sure was it was no accident that Pyre had gone straight to the Yesterplex after stealing the 70s decalog from the Everarium.

Drawing four sidearms, Lyssa charged inside the building,

right into the aftermath of another battle. Dozens more Time-keepers were scattered across the floor of the vast lobby, every one of them battered, still, and silent.

Red emergency lights flashed, and sirens shrieked at deafening levels. Though Lyssa knew there were many more Time-keepers in the complex, they hadn't arrived yet to pick up where their defeated comrades had left off in stopping the intruder.

Lyssa wasn't about to wait for them. Guns at the ready, she ran into the central corridor dead ahead, dodging the bodies of guards that were strewn underfoot.

~

As she raced down the gleaming central corridor, Lyssa tapped a lump on one wrist and called up a virtual status map to guide her. The blinking red blip that represented Pyre was only a few turns ahead and registered as stationary, holding position at least for the moment. Maybe she'd finally been cornered by Time-keeper security?

Heart pounding, Lyssa raced toward her target, resolving to fulfill her two-part orders from Timekeeper Command: to stop Pyre from attaining whatever goal she had in mind and to retrieve the decalog intact.

The second part could prove to be tricky, as the decalog cartridge was already damaged and leaking flotsam. Yet again, as she closed in on Pyre, bits of the 1970s sailed around her. Cans of Billy Beer pelted past like they'd been shot from a cannon, then Richard Nixon heads and platform shoes with towering heels.

As she rounded the final corner, fingers twitching against the triggers of her Was-Guns, the image of a platoon of Viet Cong soldiers, all in black, came howling toward her, firing away with Kalashnikov rifles. The troops were just temporal backwash, a trick of the light, but they startled her, and she hesitated.

That was just enough time for Pyre to unload a blast from her Was-Gun. A howling cyclonic bolus of barbarian axes, rabid wolves, berserker warriors, and laser-equipped airborne drones came spinning after the Viet Cong, punching straight toward Lyssa.

As that raging plume of death bore toward her, Lyssa felt again the sense of doom and horror she had known on the day her species had died...and the day they'd died a *second* time, all because of her.

As a child and then a young woman, Lyssa had been fascinated by the decalog repository of the Everarium.

You see before you the archived eras of every sentient species in the galaxy, alive or dead. On Lyssa's first visit there, Skulk had swept one bristly black leg from side to side to encompass a seemingly endless vault with all its sky-high ranks of crystalline drawers. *The past and present of intelligent life is preserved here for all posterity.*

Even my own people? little Lyssa had asked. *Even the Hinji of Hinjeri VII?*

Of course. Skulk had skittered to an access kiosk and typed on a keyboard there. A virtual image of Lyssa's home planet had spun to life above the kiosk, then zoomed in to show the long-dead populace going about their daily business. *As long as this recording exists, their legacy will survive.*

Another day, Skulk had shown her around the Yesterplex, introducing her to the multitude of sophisticated devices there—like the Chrono-Rebooter, which could restore a decade from a decalog backup if the timestream for an era became corrupted.

This powerful instrument can undo the damage of warped or ruined time by rebooting an archived era from the Everarium, Skulk had explained. *Yet it can only be handled by the most experienced of Timekeepers in the most delicate of ways. To do otherwise risks a chain reaction that could ravage all eternity.*

Lyssa had nodded with an expression of full understanding, but all she'd really heard was the part about rebooting an era from the Everarium.

Starting that day, she'd worked out a plan, always keeping it to herself. If she'd said a word to Skulk, she'd been sure the great spider would have turned her in to the Timekeeper authorities.

But months later, Lyssa had found herself wishing that Skulk had known about the plan after all. Maybe then, someone would have stopped her from "borrowing" a few key decades of Hinji history from the Everarium, then sneaking them into the Yesterplex. Maybe she wouldn't have used the Chrono-Rebooter to try to reboot Hinji history into the spacetime continuum and restart her dead species.

Maybe then, Lyssa wouldn't have made a drastic miscalculation that destroyed the stolen decalogs, wiping out decades' worth of backups that could never be recovered.

And a chunk of Hinji history would not have been forever erased and all hope of resurrecting her people as she'd known them extinguished because of something she had done.

～

Six arms whirling, Lyssa battled her way through the Past-Blast from Pyre's Was-Gun, repelling every axe-hack, wolf bite, laser blast, and sword slash with speed and grace.

By the time she was done, the blast components were scattered and defused, bleeding out on the floor or skidding along the walls or ceiling. Tossing away an axe she'd seized, she spun to face Pyre, only to find she was long gone by then.

Cursing, Lyssa pulled up the virtual map and broke into a run. According to the map, Pyre was already deep in the tunnels leading to the core of the Yesterplex.

Knowing Pyre was heading for the core was enough to make Lyssa run faster. She could only imagine the kind of damage someone like Pyre could do in there with a loaded decalog in her possession.

Pyre certainly knew her way around the Yesterplex and its array of instrumentation. A former Timekeeper, she'd gone rogue for reasons unknown, putting her skills to use in breaking into the Everarium, stealing the 70s human decalog, and bringing it here.

Rounding one bend after another in pursuit of her quarry, Lyssa kept four Was-Gun pistols in hand and ready to fire. She kept her antennae and cilia focused ahead, probing the air for any scent, vibration, or chemical reaction that might signal danger.

But when the danger finally came, she wasn't ready for it.

Racing into an open intersection centered on a statue of Hojo Cahoot—founder of the Yesterplex and Timekeepers— Lyssa was struck by a sudden wave of future sight. She foremembered a distant tomorrow in which the spot where she now stood was a barren plain with the smoking rubble of the Yesterplex scattered across it.

Stunned, she staggered to a stop, overwhelmed by the smell of death and the shrieks of the dying all around her. Carrion birds wheeled overhead, their great wings beating, and scavenger vermin scampered among the corpses.

Would *this* be the result of whatever grand plan Pyre had in mind? Would the destruction of the Yesterplex and the slaughter of the Timekeepers be her masterstroke?

Suddenly, Lyssa heard a familiar voice from somewhere nearby, begging for death. Even before she turned to see the source, she recognized it all too well.

She recognized it as *her* voice...and in that instant, she knew the forememory was false.

Pinching her eyes shut, she shook off the vision. Trained agent that she was, she knew a fake when she saw one and how to fend it off. Future memories were always experienced through your own senses, from your future self's point of view. If, when experiencing a foremembrance, you heard your voice as part of the mix, but you weren't actually doing the talking, it was never the real thing.

It was nothing but an *aftermine* in action, a device that generated false visions of the future.

Opening her eyes, she saw the nightmare future was gone. Looking further, she saw a mirrored sphere, no more than four inches in diameter, tucked between the webbed feet of the statue of Hojo Cahoot.

Sprinting forward, she crushed the aftermine sphere with the heel of her boot, smashing it to tiny pieces. Then, hoping she hadn't been too long delayed, she bolted down the corridor that led to the core.

As Lyssa charged into the core—the cavernous central chamber underneath the spire of the Yesterplex—she came upon another dozen unconscious Timekeepers on the floor. Apparently, they'd made a last stand against Pyre...and failed to stop her.

Beyond the bodies sprawled concentric rings of alabaster white partitions and alcoves—the mazelike command complex of the core. Searching those convoluted warrens for Pyre could take hours...if not for the very clear sign of her exact location that Lyssa instantly spotted.

A giant yellow circle rose like a sun near the middle of the core, its massive face marked with a simple smile in thick, black strokes. Student of humanity that she was, Lyssa instantly recognized the classic smiley face symbol of the 1970s.

Weaving through the command complex, she no longer needed to watch Pyre's blip on the virtual map. The place was like a maze, but the enormous smiley face was easy to follow.

Lyssa braced herself as she closed in, expecting another trap or trick. Her last few turns were uneventful, though, and she reached the open plaza at the middle of the core without incident.

At the plaza's center, a massive machine hung from above, a silver-plated cone extending high into the cavity within the Yesterplex's spire. The cone was covered in twinkling, multicolored lights and tapered to a fine point ending a meter or so from the floor. Standing there, operating a virtual control console encircling the cone's tip, was Pyre Ransom herself.

Seeing her there like that sent a shiver through Lyssa's body. She knew that machine well—*too* well—from past experience.

Pyre was using the very same Chrono-Rebooter that Lyssa had used to accidentally gut the recorded history of her people so many years ago.

Lyssa slowly approached, but Pyre didn't look up from her work. Her golden fingers flickered over the virtual controls, causing changes in the patterns of blinking lights on the cone-like device.

When Lyssa was ten meters away, however, Pyre told her

not to come any closer. "I'll put you down, I swear," she said calmly.

Lyssa stopped and lowered her guns. "So you like humanity's 1970s period too, huh?"

As she said it, red, white, and blue streamers and fireworks exploded in midair above them, residue of the United States of America's Bicentennial celebration in 1976.

"Sure," Pyre said without looking up. "Just not in the way you think."

Lyssa knew she should take a shot at gunning her down; the potential danger of letting her keep working on the Rebooter was high. But part of her was holding back until she understood better what Pyre's plan was. "So are you going to try bringing them back? The 1970s of humankind?"

"Maybe you should mind your own business." Pyre's fingers flew through a complex sequence of controls, and all the lights on the Chrono-Rebooter ignited at once.

"Are you sure you don't want any help?" asked Lyssa.

"*You* wouldn't be much help. You lost your user rights to this thing *ages* ago."

Lyssa scowled. Pyre was right; the Timekeepers had permanently revoked her rights to use the Rebooter after the Hinj incident. It was the one piece of equipment in the entire Yesterplex that she wasn't allowed to use.

"Pretty sure *you're* not supposed to have user rights, either," said Lyssa. "The Timekeepers deprovisioned you from all systems as soon as you quit the corps."

"True," said Pyre, "but I was smart enough to buy an access hack from an unscrupulous insider."

"Good for you."

Suddenly, Pyre reached into her pocket, and Lyssa tensed. Pyre drew out a cylindrical cartridge the length of a cigar, made of a clear material and churning inside with red, yellow, and green mist.

Lyssa knew instantly what it was, what it had to be—the 1970s decalog—and she guessed Pyre was ready to deploy it.

Leaping into action, she charged Pyre. Shooting would have been too risky; she didn't want another destroyed decade on her conscience, especially from the history of humanity.

As Lyssa sprang, Pyre whipped out her Was-Gun. She got off one shot, but it was wild, and Lyssa put hands on her before she could fire another...*five* hands, to be exact.

Her sixth hand landed on Pyre's hand that was wrapped around the 70s decalog. Maybe she squeezed too hard, though, or the shock of the impact triggered a reflexive contraction of Pyre's grip.

Because as soon as Lyssa made contact with the cartridge, a blinding white light flared, and she was gone.

Lyssa blinked away the white light and the black spots it had left raging in her eyes. Little by little, her vision cleared, and she was able to make out the details of her surroundings.

It was then she realized she wasn't inside the Yesterplex anymore. She was somewhere different, somewhere unfamiliar, somewhere...

Grander.

She stood on a hilltop, gazing out at a valley below. The valley was filled with trees, a carpet of emerald rippling in the warm breeze of a sunny summer day.

What interested Lyssa the most, though, were the occupants of the skies overhead. Massive crystal spheres hung high above the valley, glittering in the midday sun. Through the skin of these colossal objects, Lyssa could see the dance of light and movement that signified life—sentient life capable of building such grand structures and miraculously keeping them aloft.

"Spectacular, aren't they?"

At the sound of Pyre's voice, Lyssa jerked her head around to see the android standing behind her.

"The cities of paradise, circa 1975," said Pyre, smiling serenely. "Each one full of people living to their maximum potential."

Lyssa scowled. Her instinct was to grab and restrain Pyre, but she held herself back...for the moment, at least. "Where *exactly* is this? Where are we?"

"Inside the 1970s decalog," explained Pyre. "Our *minds* only. Think of it as a peek inside the cartridge I stole."

"The 1970s *where?*" asked Lyssa. "Because it sure isn't the *Earth* of *humanity.*"

"Oh, but it is." Pyre chuckled and stepped away, moving forward on the hilltop. "I assure you, it very much *is.*"

Just then, a low-flying aircraft buzzed the hill, and Lyssa ducked. The craft zoomed away without making a sound, its oval fuselage tipped with a long, pointed nose like a needle. Vents on its backside glowed bright blue and shimmered with what looked like heat ripples.

"That is *not* a human-built aircraft from 1970s Earth." Lyssa stared at other ships in the distance, zipping around and between the crystalline spheres. "*None* of them are."

"*All* of them are." Pyre spread her arms wide to take it all in. "Every last one of them."

Lyssa frowned, struggling to understand. Airborne craft of many shapes and sizes swooped and darted among the spheres, threading from one to the next across the busy blue sky. Little satellites revolved around the spheres as well, often narrowly avoiding collisions with each other, with aircraft, with birds... and with human beings engaged in unaided flight.

Humans flew in and out of the spheres with grace, banking and looping and soaring as if they'd been born to it. As far as Lyssa could see, there were no signs of jetpacks or antigravity tech anywhere on them.

Lyssa was amazed...then annoyed. "This is some kind of elaborate illusion. You've trapped me in a multisensory deepfake."

"But I haven't," Pyre said calmly. "This is recorded reality from Earth in the 1970s...the 1970s *as they were meant to be.*"

Lyssa's frown deepened. "Enough of this. End the simulation."

"It's no simulation," said Pyre.

Lyssa grabbed Pyre's gold-skinned arm. "You can't *save* yourself with *trickery.* You are going to *pay* for your *crimes.*"

"Haven't you ever wondered?" Pyre shook off Lyssa's grip and sat down on the grassy peak. "Haven't you wondered why humanity died out so soon? Why things went downhill so fast for such a promising species?"

It was indeed a question Lyssa had asked herself many times, though she wouldn't give Pyre the satisfaction of knowing that. "Species die out. There isn't always a sensible explanation."

"But there is this time."

"What do *you* know about them?" snapped Lyssa.

"Everything." Pyre looked up at her with a grim smile. "Humans *made* me."

Lyssa gaped at her, surprised.

"Human built me, and those like me, to outlive them," said Pyre, "and I have. And now I will correct an injustice that was visited upon them millennia ago...because I can.

"Because all I need to do is replace the 1970s as they happened with the *rightful* 1970s...whatever the cost may be."

~

Lyssa well remembered when she'd first discovered the human race of planet Earth.

As a young trainee Timekeeper in the Everarium (before her ill-fated attempt to resurrect the Hinji), she'd been obsessed with viewing the decalogs of extinct sentient species. She'd made the most of her access to the archives, poring over preserved eras of vanished species for hour upon hour at the expense of her trainee assignments.

So many extinct species had been so much like her own, their tragic stories brimming with lost potential. She'd been fascinated by the multitudes of unsolved mysteries associated with them, the many unknowns left behind in their wakes.

But no species had captured her imagination quite as much as humanity. No species had been so colorful, passionate, and unbridled or had touched her so profoundly with their arts and struggles.

No other species had made her think, if she had to be something other than Hinji, that she would choose to join their ranks.

And no human era had spoken to her so clearly as the 1970s. The thrilling music, flashy fashion, and larger-than-life celebrities had excited her. The search for meaning in an off-kilter world was much like her own search for identity in the realm of When.

The 70s had been such a big deal to Lyssa that they had figured prominently in her own rogue scheme with the Chrono-Rebooter. Originally, she'd planned to bring back humanity after raising the Hinji...and she'd known all along, if she'd gotten that far, that she would have started with the 70s.

It was an obsession she had never grown out of. It was why she had pursued Pyre with such determination when other Timekeepers had fallen by the wayside. It was why she'd come so far and fought so hard.

And it was why now, instead of taking swift action to do her duty upon getting an inkling of Pyre's true intentions, she listened to what the android was saying.

A light breeze wafted over the peak as Lyssa sat cross-legged beside Pyre. Paradise went on around them, its wonders amazing to behold...but Lyssa found her gaze locked on the android's, attached as if by magnets.

"How can there be a *rightful* 1970s?" asked Lyssa. "How can there be anything but history as we know it?"

"Long ago, history was sabotaged," said Pyre. "By those who feared humanity would *surpass* or *destroy* them. A decade was removed from human history, the decade of humankind's greatest renaissance, the ascendance that should have come on the heels of the age of idealism and creativity in the 1960s."

"The 70s were removed?" Only among Timekeepers of When would such a question be asked so matter-of-factly.

Pyre nodded. "And replaced with a very different decade in which a renaissance never happened. An era of selfishness and silly obsessions, a time of conflict and crisis and drift. A flawed decade that gave rise to the forces that robbed humanity of its golden age and accelerated a doom that should never have come."

"That's not true!" snapped Lyssa. She hated hearing her precious 70s denigrated like that. "The 70s may not have been perfect, but *no* decade ever is."

"They weren't what they *could* have been," said Pyre. "What they *should* have been."

Lyssa felt the urge to punch her in the face. "According to whom?"

"According to the one person who *lived through* the original version, came to When before the timeline changed, and still survives to *this day*." Pyre tapped her chest with an index finger. "According to *me*."

~

Lyssa felt her anger draining away. She gazed at Pyre as if seeing her for the first time.

Now she knew—if Pyre was telling the truth—how she could be so certain that an alternate 1970s had replaced an original version populated by an enlightened humanity. Now she knew—again, if Pyre wasn't lying—how the promising human species had died out so prematurely.

It was all thanks to the Timekeepers and their technological wonders.

Still, Lyssa had trouble wrapping her head around it all. "But the Timekeepers are sworn not to tamper with the timelines. It's our greatest oath."

"Certain circumstances may supersede that oath," said Pyre. "Such as whispers of the threat one species may present if allowed to reach full bloom. The *status quo* must *always* be preserved." Pyre grinned and held out her hand, where the mist-filled cylinder of the decalog cartridge remained—or at least a mental manifestation of it. "Unless someone is stupid enough to keep a *backup* copy of the overwritten *original*."

Lyssa frowned. "But I thought the stolen decalog was from the *accepted* 1970s. The whole time I chased you, it was leaking smiley faces, streakers, Viet Cong soldiers—all sorts of 70s odds and ends."

Pyre shook her head. "That was all virtual trickery, projected by me to hide the true nature of my mission." She pressed her chin, opened her mouth, and the image of a 70s game show host with shaggy brown hair, a long microphone, and a powder blue leisure suit with white buck shoes appeared in midair between them. When Pyre closed her mouth, the image disappeared. "The decalog only ever contained the essence of the *rightful* human 70s."

"Which you want to use for a reboot?"

"To overwrite the replacement 70s, yes." When Pyre smiled, her bright red eyes sparkled. "Make the golden age a reality again as it was meant to be. Give humanity a second chance to overcome its premature extinction."

Lyssa's antennae twitched with strong emotion. What Pyre was saying—she didn't hate the idea. But there were issues the android hadn't mentioned yet.

"If you do this—it'll change more than *human* history, won't it?" asked Lyssa. "Assuming humanity is reborn, the ripple effects will affect everyone the resurrected human species comes in contact with. Will the Chrono-Rebooter even let that happen?"

"I believe so," said Pyre. "With the right *minds* injected into the mix to guide the process." She grinned. "Say, a human-built synthetic who can interface with the rebooter's A.I. and a female organic who can convince it that rules are made to be broken."

Lyssa's eyes widened. Pyre was talking about *her*.

For a long moment, Lyssa just stared at Pyre, wondering if this was what they'd been moving toward all along.

Did Pyre know how she felt about humanity? Was it possible the android had been pulling her in this direction from the start, for just this purpose?

Either way, a proposition had been made that could change everything—a proposition with an extremely uncertain outcome —yet Lyssa found she could not dismiss it out of hand.

"I still don't understand what makes you think I can help," she said.

"Using my own computerized mind, I have calculated that the rebooter's A.I. will more likely respond favorably when interfacing with someone like you," said Pyre. "Someone who knows what it's like when you don't *have* a chance to bring back the people you've lost. Someone who understands from first-hand experience that the *absence* of those who matter can send out just as many ripples as their *presence* can.

"Someone who once used that very rebooter to try to bring someone else back—and now wants to give both of them a chance to make up for that failure."

"I see." Lyssa was surprised at how sensible it all sounded, though one question kept nagging at her. "So how do I know you're not lying?"

Pyre frowned. "About what?"

"About everything," said Lyssa. "How do I know that any of this is the truth?"

"Because of all this, of course." Pyre gestured at the scene stretched out before them—the great glittering crystalline spheres hovering over the emerald forest.

"Which could be nothing but an illusion," said Lyssa.

"But listen." Pyre leaned toward her, one golden index finger raised instructively. "Can you take the chance that's all it is? If I'm right—which I am—but you let me fail, can you bear it? Can you live with yourself, knowing you could have brought back humanity but didn't?"

Lyssa didn't answer. Pyre's story was strangely persuasive, appealing to her longtime love of humanity and her desire to resurrect that species—but part of her held fast, refusing to be convinced of anything by the fugitive thief. No Timekeeper worth her salt would fall for a line of bullshit like the one she was hearing, and she knew it.

At least that was how she felt before the next question Pyre asked.

"Also, can you live with yourself if this is all true, and you let it fail...knowing success could have led to more than one change?" Pyre folded her hands together, her fingers interwoven. "What if humanity's destiny is connected to *another* destiny that is not at first obvious?"

"Another destiny?"

Pyre shrugged. "Who's to say that bringing humanity back won't bring back someone else?"

Lyssa's heart pounded as she considered the implications. Her doubts and fears began to melt away.

"Do you...do you know this for a fact?" she asked. "That someone else could be restored by such a change?"

"I do not know it for a fact," said Pyre. "But can you bear to take the chance that it won't happen?"

Lyssa turned away, thinking and watching the view of paradise. Multicolored beams of lights blazed from the city-spheres, splashing over the emerald forest and sapphire sky. Music like wind chimes and whalesong played from speakers unseen, echoing in the distance.

It was beautiful. Was it worth leaping into the unknown for, though? Solely on its own merits? She couldn't seem to make that argument to herself.

But that last thing that Pyre had said, she could not ignore. It kept running through her mind, again and again.

Can you bear to take the chance that it won't happen?

"If we do this, what will happen to us?" she asked suddenly. "After it's all over, whatever the outcome...what happens to us?"

Pyre shrugged and reached out with the decalog cartridge in her hand. "Does it matter? Will it change your answer?"

Just like that, Lyssa realized she had made up her mind. It was not lost on her that it was the most impulsive decision she had made since trying to reboot the history of the Hinji three decades ago. "No." Smiling, she folded all six of her hands around the cartridge in Pyre's grip. "No, it won't."

Then, she felt Pyre squeeze tightly, crushing the cartridge, and the glorious vision of the rightful 1970s dissolved in whirling clouds of phosphorescent vapor.

~

Elsewhere, Elsewhen:

Silver and sleek, the star-skiff full of humans swooped into the atmosphere of the pink-and-purple planet. Gleaming in the light of the planet's triple suns, the little craft swooped gracefully toward the surface, approaching the celebration of a momentous occasion.

"This is the Earth skiff *Impresario*." The little craft was just as lovely on the inside, its bright cockpit fitted with silver consoles studded with blinking, multicolored controls. The pilot, Murphy—a willowy woman with short red hair and a pale blue uniform with silver piping—spoke into a mic that floated in front of her lush red lips. "Requesting permission to land."

"Only if that *admiral* of yours isn't aboard!" the man on the other end of the call said teasingly. "Though Todd Chamberlain's so *old* and *frail* these days, I'll bet he had to stay in orbit on the *mothership* and take his *nap!*"

Grinning, the gray-haired man in a navy blue uniform who shared the cockpit with Murphy leaned over from the co-pilot's seat to speak into the mic. "You think I'd miss out on *today*? Forget it, Mr. President!"

The man on the line chuckled. "It's only our five-hundred-year anniversary, Todd! No need for a big man like yourself to come down off your high horse and mingle with us *little people*."

"I wouldn't miss it for anything, President Prine," said

Admiral Chamberlain, who looked middle-aged though he was much, much older. "Any chance to rub your nose in what I did for you, I'll *jump* at it."

"*You?* It was all *you*, now?" Prine said with mock outrage.

"Who's gonna say any different?" asked Chamberlain.

"Have you forgotten my people can live to be a thousand years old?" said Prine. "You *humans* are lucky to live *half* that!"

"Whatever." Chamberlain winked at Murphy. "You people have a funny way of acting grateful, don't you?"

"We won't kiss your asses, if that's what you mean." Prine laughed. "But come on down anyway if you like. We won't stop you."

With that, the communication ended.

And Chamberlain and Murphy howled with laughter.

"What a character!" said Murphy.

"I love that guy!" Chamberlain slapped his knee. "He's just as hilarious as he was 500 years ago when we saved his goddamn planet!"

Later, after the skiff had landed and the ceremonies had begun, Chamberlain marched solemnly over the purple ground of the planet, flanked by several human dignitaries in their best formal attire. Up ahead, a dais waited, adorned with pink, violet, and lilac colored flowers.

Flickering video panels hung in midair, replaying scenes from the historic events of half a millennium ago. On one, Chamberlain saw his old vessel, the Earthship *Intensity*, descending to the surface for the first time. On the next panel over, Chamberlain's science team worked with an array of elaborate equipment on the planet's surface, confirming the ominous readings they had first detected from orbit.

On the next panel, Chamberlain and his crew made one of the least auspicious first contacts ever with the local inhabitants, informing them of their findings. *Hi, nice to meet you! By the way, your world is about to explode.*

Then, on the final panel, the humans and locals were working side by side, constructing a gargantuan device that would stop the explosion and save the world. All thanks to the high-tech ingenuity and altruism that had thrived on Earth since the start of humanity's golden age in the 1970s, two thousand years ago.

Chamberlain felt a surge of pride and nostalgia as he approached the dais where the leading lights of the planet waited to mark the great occasion. Before he could set one foot on the dais, however, his old friend, President Prine, ran forward.

And threw his six purple arms around him in a bear hug.

"It is so *good* to see you, my friend!" Prine leaned back, his beaded violet antennae bobbing with pure joy. The feathery pink cilia on his purple head and neck fluttered and danced as he beamed. "You have been away from Hinjeri VII and the Hinji people for far too long!"

"Tell me about it!" Tears rolled down Chamberlain's cheeks. People were watching—whole planets of them, via the media— and he didn't give a damn.

"Thank you again, my friend," said Prine. "If not for you, this place would not exist. None of us would."

"I've always had a feeling," said Chamberlain, reveling in the embrace of his Hinji friend as the galaxy looked on. "I've always had a feeling that somehow, it works both ways."

∽

Robert Jeschonek is an envelope-pushing, *USA Today*-best-selling author. His stories have appeared in *Galaxy's Edge, StarShipSofa, Escape Pod,* and many other publications. He has written official *Star Trek* and *Doctor Who* fiction plus comics for DC and AHOY. He has won an International Book Award, a Scribe Award, and the grand prize in Pocket Books' Strange New Worlds contest. His young adult slipstream novel, *My Favorite Band Does Not Exist,* won the Forward National Literature Award and was named one of *Booklist's* Top Ten First Novels for Youth. Visit him online at www. robertjeschonek.com. You can also find him on Facebook and follow him as @TheFictioneer on Twitter.

BRINGING DOWN THE MONA LISA

IAN DOUGLAS

With apologies to the Honorable Edward Bulwer-Lytton, it was a dark and stormy decade. My God...the 1970s were when terrorism became big business. It was the decade of the Munich Massacre and the Yom Kippur War, of Jim Jones and Jonestown, of the Arab oil embargo, gas rationing and endless waiting lines in gas stations. It was the era of "I-Am-Not-A-Crook" Nixon's resignation under a cloud, and we found ourselves with the first U.S. president *ever* who hadn't been elected.

Some said we were maturing, that we were growing up at last. But then...hard rock, bell-bottom pants and, God help us, *disco?*

They said the 1970s were a decade of transition, the Summer of Love giving way to the Winter of Our Discontent. Post-war prosperity became stagflation and recession, with the worst global economy since the Great Depression. Johnson's Great Society bogged down in the muck of Vietnam. America's love affair with science—*better things through chemistry!*—shifted into a dark and deeply rooted mistrust of the scientists who'd given us environmental pollution and thermonuclear weapons.

Above all else, Watergate taught us one lesson: *never trust the government!*

Bitter? Yeah, you're damned right I'm bitter. I remembered the Seventies as the decade when we stopped going to the Moon, when Americans spent more in a year on *pizza* than NASA spent on space, and the D.C. bean-counters decided that even that was too much for a bag-full of rocks. It was the decade when Kaysing wrote *We Never Went to the Moon* and set off a firestorm of conspiracy theories, falsehoods and anti-science idiocy calculated to con Americans into thinking it was all a sad lie. Damn it, somehow Armstrong's immortal "one small step" gave way to budget cuts, short-sighted bureaucratic self-service, and, above all, to a despairing failure of *will*. The Moon was within our grasp, and we turned our backs on her.

At least...so it seemed. So it still seems today, at least to most people.

But then, things aren't always what they seem...*especially* when the government is involved.

My name is Dick Gordon. With over 4,500 hours of flight time logged, I was a fighter pilot, a Navy test pilot, and eventually one of NASA's Group 3 astronauts. I was the Command Pilot of Apollo 12, orbiting the Moon 45 times on board the *Yankee Clipper*, while Charles "Pete" Conrad and Alan Bean bounced around on the Ocean of Storms. Between Gemini 11 and Apollo 12, I logged 315 hours and 43 minutes in space, with almost three hours of that spent in EVA. I was proud of what I did, proud of my record, proud of *NASA*, though the bureaucratic aspects made me gripe at times. I was chief of advanced programs there in 1971, and I helped work on the Space Shuttle.

But I remember the kicked-in-the-teeth feeling in

September of 1970 when word came down that Apollo was getting the ax, that Apollo 17 would be the final flight in the program. Damn it, I was in line for the mission commander slot for Apollo 18. I wasn't the only one outraged by the budget cuts, of course. Something like thirty guys were lined up waiting for a chance to fly to the Moon, and none of us would be going.

Or so I thought.

I'd been retired for three years, since January of 1972, when the men in black suits and dark glasses showed up on my front porch, one of them carrying a briefcase. They showed me credentials alleging that they were from the CIA's Directorate of Science and Technology. To this day I don't know if that was true. I suspect that they worked for someone way more rungs up the intelligence ladder than anyone in the Central Intelligence Agency.

But they had me sign my life away with nondisclosure documents before they told me anything. Breathe a word about *anything* I was about to hear, and I would end up in a federal prison for a very long time to come. They had me pretty curious by that time, so I signed. I'd signed NDAs before, both for NASA and before that, in the Navy. I had to know...what the hell did these clowns want?

By this time, I'd privately labeled them Tweedledee and Tweedledum. They wouldn't tell me their names.

"Captain Gordon," Tweedledee said, "We'd like you to return to the Moon."

"Haven't you heard?" I asked. "Apollo is dead. They killed it. *No* one goes to the Moon anymore."

Tweedledum smiled, an emotionless showing of the teeth that chilled me. "Well, Captain Gordon...as it happens, that's not entirely true."

And that's when I learned about Operation Darkside.

The photos they took from the briefcase were what caught

me first. Back in July of '71, Al Worden had spotted the anomaly as he orbited overhead in *Endeavor*, the Apollo 15 Command Module, and snapped off a number of pictures. They showed *something* lying on the rim of a crater ten miles below...cigar-shaped, something pointed at both ends, with barely discernable features that looked like sponsons and streamlined equipment housings emerging from a curiously etched hull. Whatever it was, it looked artificial, something *made*.

I was told it was an alien spacecraft crashed on the lunar farside. The Darkside mission would be touching down next to or, possibly, directly atop the wreck, and they wanted me to find a way inside.

The shock left me reeling. There'd been plenty of rumors around NASA about stuff we never talked about—of mysterious objects following our spacecraft, of anomalous radio signals...even rumors that Aldrin and Armstrong had had some kind of up-close-and-personal sighting on the Lunar surface. This, however, was the first solid information I'd seen that there *was* intelligent life of some sort out there, that other civilizations perhaps thousands of years older than us might be out there watching us. My first thought was *It's true! We're not alone in the universe!* My second carried a sharp stab of paranoia: *Why is the greatest discovery of all time being kept top secret?*

"This information," Tweedledee told me, "is classified well above top secret. You will divulge this to no one." He tapped the papers I'd signed sitting on the desk between us. "We have your signature, your *agreement* right here."

"It would be *extremely* unfortunate for you if you told another soul," Tweedledum said.

"Look, I get it," I told them. "I can keep my trap zipped. But *why?*"

"Ever hear of the Brookings Institute report?" Tweedledum said.

"Of course."

The report had come out in 1960, saddled with a gosh-dreadful mess of an unwieldy title: "Proposed Studies on the Implications of Peaceful Space Activities For Human Affairs." Commissioned by NASA, it had been presented to Congress in 1961. For the most part, it had discussed a range of possible future studies and technologies that might be expected to arise from the space program—space-based communications, weather forecasting, space industry. Every astronaut read it during their training.

But one very short section had discussed the implications of our encountering life in space—anything from mosses and lichens on Mars, to godlike, super-intelligent beings that might not want anything to do with us. It mentioned the possibility of discovering the technological detritus of an advanced civilization as we explored the planets, or even our own Moon.

And, it seemed, that is exactly what had happened.

"The Brookings Report," Tweedledum told me, "recommended that the public not be informed of the discovery of intelligent life...at least not right away. It cited the possibility of a collapse of the stock market and our economy, of religious institutions, even the destruction of civilization itself as panic took hold and people rioted in the streets. *That* is why this stuff is secret."

Privately, I thought they were badly underestimating the human capacity for absorbing new information. But I nodded and said nothing.

"One more thing," Tweedledee said, replacing the photos, snapping the briefcase closed, and standing. "Do you believe in God?"

"Eh? Why should it matter?"

"Answer the question," Tweedledum said.

Hell, what *did* I believe? I'd been raised Presbyterian and never considered myself religious...but did I believe in God? An old man with a flowing white beard living in the sky...no. But a higher power guiding our destiny, maybe creating us in the first place? That was tougher to answer.

And complicated. I wasn't about to get into a theological discussion with these two, so I shook my head and said "No."

"Good," Tweedledee said. "If you were a believer we would have had to drop you from the program."

"Why?"

He'd already slipped the photographs back into the brief-case. He patted it. "Because we have evidence of a truly advanced civilization here, Mr. Conrad. "Maybe even godlike in its scope and knowledge. It's important that your objectivity not be...adversely affected by religious convictions."

Tweedledum stabbed a finger at me. "Remember! You won't say a word about what you've seen, right? Not even to your wife!"

I knew how this worked. If I leaked a word, my life would be over, I'd be labeled crazy, and I might end up in Leavenworth for the rest of my life. That wasn't worth it. Nothing was.

But...my God...*a chance to walk on the Moon....*

Training took place out in the desert, and I wasn't sure where. I heard that it was Nevada, but one pile of sand and gravel out there looks pretty much like another. We called the base "the Ranch," and were kept too busy to think much about sightsee-ing. That's where I met my crew...and when I got another shock. My lander pilot was a Russian.

And not just any Russian. He was Alexei Arkhipovich

Leonov, and he was the first man to walk in space. That had been during the Voskhod 2 mission in 1965, and the word was he'd been first on the list of cosmonauts slated to land on the Moon. When the Soviet Moon landing program was cancelled, he'd been given command of the Soyuz capsule during the Apollo-Soyuz docking, the famous "handshake in space." He'd just returned from that flight and, it seemed, now he was going to the Moon with me.

Also on the crew was a woman—Doctor Sandra Davis. She was not an astronaut and had never been in space, but before a merger had turned North American Rockwell into Rockwell International back in '73, she'd been an engineer on the Apollo capsule design team, and she knew the spacecraft inside and out. I'd met her, worked with her during my training for Apollo 12, and knew her to be steady, cool, and competent. Alexei I knew only by reputation.

I wondered if Alexei's presence had something to do with the secrecy as well. I mean...we'd been in an all-out race against the Soviets, right? The Cold War...the missile gap...all of that.

Then détente had come along, highlighted by the most expensive propaganda photo-op of all time, with Americans and Russians shaking hands in space.

And there was more. We wouldn't be flying an American LEM—the Lunar Excursion Module—down to the lunar surface. We had some leftover hardware from the program that was built before it was cancelled...but apparently we had no new LEMs available. We would be taking a Russian lander down, the *Lunniy Korable*, or LK for short.

"Originally, LK was designed for one cosmonaut," Alexei told us as we explored a mockup of the craft. "It flew in orbit twice, but without crew. This model is redesign, with room and fuel for two plus cargo, not one."

"You were only going to put one man on the surface?" I asked.

"At first, yes. Later designs were...uprated."

"What I don't get is how we're supposed to dock the CSM with your lander," Sandra said. She pointed at the top of the ugly little spacecraft. "The hatches are incompatible."

"And how was Soyuz mated to Apollo in Apollo-Soyuz mission?" asked Alexei.

"A special docking adaptor that—oh."

"Which we tested for first time in Apollo-Soyuz mission, *da*?"

I laughed. "You don't think that stunt in orbit was just for a *photo op*, do you?"

"I suppose not." She sounded chagrined. She might have been angry that they hadn't told her everything about the mission.

"So the Apollo mission profile remains the same?" I asked Alexei.

"*Da*," he replied. His English was quite good—he'd learned it as preparation for Apollo-Soyuz—but he sometimes lapsed into Russian when he was stressed. "Except for one thing."

"What's that?"

"We will have...*them* looking over our shoulders."

He said it lightly, but I could tell it bothered him.

We didn't have much in the way of actual training. We'd all already been through the survival courses, the emergency escape procedures, navigation, communications, and all the myriad other schooling they gave to both astronauts and cosmonauts. Even Dr. Davis had already been through most of that, and our stay at the Ranch was dominated by practice with our

moon suits, practice egressing and entering the LK, and communications protocols. They'd already launched a constellation of
comsats into Lunar orbit. One would always be above our horizon, so we would be able to communicate through secure channels both with Sandra in the command module orbiting
overhead and with mission control.

It wouldn't be Houston we were talking with, though. We
never learned where mission control was located. Its call sign
would simply be "Control," which naturally evoked memories
of a TV spy-comedy cancelled just a few years before—*Get
Smart.*

The command-service module was *Constellation.* The LK
lander was *Phoenix.*

We launched from Vandenberg Air Force Base, near
Lompoc, California, on August 16, 1976, rather than from the
Cape. Vandenberg, subject to tyrannical security measures, was
used to put military missions into space, but had never sent a
manned mission there. As we thundered skyward on a shud-
dering pillar of flame, I wondered if our rushed orientation at
the Ranch had been enough to cover all eventualities.

Then I decided...who the hell was I kidding? They were
sending us into space cold. Sandra hadn't even been to space
before, though she reportedly had several thousand hours of
flight time. And none of us had ever worked together on a space
flight, forming the trust and cohesion vital to any mission. *Any*
manned spaceflight is an incredibly complicated affair, with a
million things that could go wrong and ten million ways we
could screw things up.

But everything unfolded perfectly and by the book. We
achieved orbit, then four hours forty seconds later we lit the
Saturn S-IVB stage a second time, putting us into TLI—trans-
Lunar insertion. Transpositioning went smoothly, as we sepa-
rated the command and service module from the S-IVB, the

SLA adaptor module panels jettisoned, and we flipped the CSM end-for-end and docked with the LK.

Life on board settled into a smooth routine. There's less room inside an Apollo capsule than there is inside the typical American car. I was surprised at how well Sandra took the stink, the crowding and the complete lack of privacy. Within hours, the first American woman in space was just another astronaut, one very good at her job. Alexei made some wry comments about how it had been the Russians who'd put the first woman in space—Valentina Tereshkova, back in 1963—and Sandra merely grinned and replied with a snide "*da,* comrade. And what has your boy's club done for us lately?"

We passed the 330,000 kilometer point without incident. Not that we were *superstitious* or anything...but even now the Apollo 13 incident made people a touch nervous. One of 13's O_2 tanks had blown at the 330K mark...on April 13th, after launching at 1313 hours three days before.

No, of *course* we weren't superstitious.

But I think even Alexei breathed a bit easier as we hurtled past that magical waypoint.

The Moon ahead grew huge. It glared at us in half phase so that every crater along the terminator was crisply defined in dazzling white and shadowed black. The flight so far had been completely nominal; we only needed to make two of a planned three midcourse corrections before sliding into Lunar orbit. Both Alexei and Sandra were hypnotically entranced, pressed against the CM's tiny windows watching the brilliant surface slide by below. For me, it seemed strangely like coming home. The timing of our mission had been set so that the landing zone on the far side was in late afternoon. We wanted to be able to see...but not be broiled by the solar radiation of the Lunar midday.

That landing zone was a rather bland and featureless stretch of terrain. Our objective was the inside rim of Guyot Crater, at 10 degrees South, 117.5 degrees East, a thousand kilometers southwest from the Mare Smythi, which is right smack on the horizon of the Moon as seen from Earth. As the Soviets found out back in '59 when they snapped the very first photos of the Lunar far side from Luna 3, the *far* side—*not* the "dark side," since it receives as much sunlight as the side facing Earth—the far side is rugged and heavily cratered, with only the tiny Sea of Moscow and the dark floor of Tsiolkovsky to break an otherwise vast and monotonous sameness.

We orbited the Moon with a perilune of just twelve kilometers, performing a careful photographic survey of our area of interest. Damn...even from seven miles up we could see the thing—a tiny, gray rice grain against the unending gray of the surface. Five orbits...and Alexei and I crawled through the docking adaptor tunnel and entered the LK.

"Luck, you two," Sandra said. She sounded...taut. Not scared, exactly, but decidedly under stress. "You come back, understand me? I don't like being alone."

I knew how she felt. I'd watched Pete and Alan crawl into the LEM *Intrepid* and leave me to circle the Moon alone.

"Keep a light burning in the window, Sandra," I told her. "We'll see you very soon."

The descent to the Lunar surface was uneventful...and it left my heart pounding. The lander was unbelievably claustrophobic, making the Apollo CM seem luxuriously spacious by comparison. Alexei and I could barely squeeze in shoulder to shoulder, standing at the controls...and this model had been enlarged to accommodate two. The one-man model must have been a flying spacesuit.

The deorbit burn passed without incident, as the Lunar surface swept by beneath. An unmanned Russian *Lunakhod* rover was already at the LZ, moving about on *top* of the alien ship, checking conditions, looking for dangers, and broadcasting a beacon to home us in. Alexei, as LK Pilot, was at the controls, while I filmed through one of the windows with a 16mm video camera. He was as familiar with the flight characteristics and handling of a Russian lander as Sandra was with the command module and was a true virtuoso at the controls.

Below us, a ship nine times the size of the Empire State Building lay on her side, 3.77 kilometers long and half a kilometer thick, her elegantly grooved and dusty upper surface pocked and cratered. My God...how long had she been there? Scientists would be able to make a guess by counting craters, but from here I was guessing at *least* a million years.

"*Sorok metrov,*" Alexei said, speaking quietly, almost to himself. Forty meters. He must have been nervous....

"*Tridtsat' metrov. Chetyre s polovinoy vniz.*"

"English, Alexei."

"*Da...da...*Four and one half down. Eight forward..."

The surface below was flat...*artificially* flat, flat enough that we'd elected to home in on the Russian rover and land directly on the thing.

"*Vpered tri...*"

Ahead three...a delicately executed adjustment.

"*Desyat' metrov....*"

Ten meters.

"*Dreyfuyet vpravo. Der'mo!* Sorry! Drifting right."

"I see dust," I announced.

"*Pyat'....*"

"Contact light," I told him. A meter-long probe reaching down from one of the lander's footpads had just touched the surface.

"*Dva...adeen...*"

There was a jar.

"Engine off!" he said, flipping a line of switches. "Out of

detent. Mode control...auto. Descent engine override...off. Engine arm...off."

"Control," I announced, "Darkside Base here. The *Phoenix* has landed."

"Copy you down, *Phoenix*," the anonymous voice of the mission director replied, slightly delayed by the time-lag to Earth. All very matter-of-fact and businesslike, with none of the excitement and banter that had marked other Moon landings.

I wanted to lighten the mood. I was jubilant, my heart pounding in my chest. "Would you believe...we're down?" I added in my best Don Adams impression, an homage to the old *Get Smart* show.

My attempt at humor fell flat. "*Phoenix*, Control. Com security."

Sorry about that, Chief...

But we'd made it. I felt buoyant—partly because I was feeling only one-sixth of a gravity, of course, but mostly from the surge of adrenaline burning through my system.

On the surface of the Moon...

An hour later, I'd squeezed through the tiny egress hatch and descended the ladder, the thirteenth man in history to set foot on the Lunar surface. I noticed the boxy little Lunakhod nearby, recording me, I suppose, just in case this episode was ever released to the historical record. I hoped it would be...not for the sake of fame, but because the Moon landings were part of the shared heritage of all Mankind. It was criminal to keep it hidden...

Alexei joined me a few moments later, moving cautiously to ease his bulky PLSS backpack through that narrow hatchway. "Welcome to the Moon, Alexei," I told him.

"Is good to be here," he said. I could see him grin through his helmet visor. "Is good to be number fourteen...not unlucky *thirteen...*"

"I'll pretend I didn't hear that."

Superstitious? Nonsense.

The Lunakhod had already found a way inside. We followed the small, wheeled vehicle across a dusty surface already crisscrossed by its tracks, as Control gave us a running commentary. "Phoenix, Control. You're almost there. We think it's an emergency escape hatch, something like that. It's rectangular, and about three meters wide."

"We see it, Control. Somebody left the barn door wide open." I switched on my lights, rigged on my suit special for this mission. "I can see the inner airlock door from here. It's open as well."

Exploring that vast and alien vessel would have taken an army months to accomplish. What could two men hope to accomplish in a few hours? The interior was pitch black, illuminated solely by the dancing glare and shadows of our lights. The interior was in hard vacuum, too.

In 1973, Arthur C. Clarke, a favorite SF writer of mine, had written a gripping tale called *Rendezvous with Rama* about an immense alien cylinder fifty kilometers long sweeping in through our Solar System out of interstellar space. Inside was an entire, inside-out world, and the tiny crew of Earth scientists who'd penetrated it had had only hours to explore its mysteries, few of which were revealed.

One interesting coincidence: the fictional Earth ship that carried them there had been named *Endeavor*...like the Apollo command module that had discovered this craft.

And I recalled another oft-quoted line by Clarke: "Any sufficiently advanced technology is indistinguishable from magic."

What magic might we find within these dark and tangled passageways?

But we found no magic, none beyond the obvious fact of this

vessel, its size, its mass. The ship was dead, its inconceivable power plant inert, its chambers empty, dark, and lifeless.

Eventually, we found the control room.

At least, we assumed it was the control room, for it contained two bodies reclining on couches, and they were hooked directly to some sort of panel by slender metallic devices like spider legs attached to their eyelids, nostrils, and foreheads. Metal probes held their mouths wide open in eternal, silent screams.

She was human...sort of. Her facial features under the hardware were exotic, her eyes and lips too large for her face. Six-fingered hands. Black hair. She was completely nude, but she was encased in something like transparent wax, a protective coating of some sort. Between the wax and her pale skin, she looked like a porcelain doll...or possibly a geisha, her face heavily caked in makeup.

Her companion, also nude, was male...but the body had been savagely mutilated; by what, we couldn't tell.

The male was definitely dead, his internal organs long since desiccated by the vacuum. The woman, though...it was tough to tell. Alexei thought she might be alive, preserved for the eons by some kind of suspended animation.

And Control agreed. "Bring her back with you, Phoenix," the anonymous voice told us after we'd televised images to them. "Unhook them both and bring them back. You should have space in your rock box."

"Are you sure, Control?" I asked. I hesitated. "This is a gravesite, after all. Maybe we should—"

"Don't argue," the voice interrupted. "Secure those bodies and get them back here! This is a matter of national security..."

So we did what we were told. The woman's face seemed more relaxed, more natural, more serene after we removed the spidery device that held her mouth wide. We dubbed her

"Mona Lisa." The spider device might have been for control or navigation. I could imagine feeding visual data directly into her nervous system through the eyes. Her nostrils were plugged up with wax, so the tubes there could have been for breathing. The probe attached to her forehead left a deep mark when we pulled it off...like the bindi mark worn by Hindu women.

But, Jesus! What an ungodly way to travel!

Definitely third-class.

Alexei and I made the trip back mostly in silence. What more was there to say? I think we both were unwilling to broadcast our thoughts back to Control over the secure communications net. The state of those two bodies had been both horribly grotesque and deeply disturbing. The male body, what was left of it, we packed into a vinyl storage bag and gently placed it atop the woman's body in the compartment intended for Lunar rock samples. We waited until *Constellation* was in the correct spot in her orbit, then lifted off.

The Russian LK operated the same as the American LEMs, using the lower descent stage as a launch platform for the insect-like ascent stage. Mona Lisa spent part of the three-day trip back to Earth on our laps, much to Sandra's disgust, because that CM was simply too small for four. It seemed...undignified to cram her into the CM's storage locker with her male counterpart, though we managed to get them both in and locked tight for the reentry and splashdown in the Pacific.

They told us very little afterward. The woman, they said, was in some sort of suspended state, neither alive nor dead, and her body was carted off to "an undisclosed location" for study. The male would be autopsied; they never told us the results.

It's been over twenty years, and I know less now than I did then. Among those I spoke with after the mission, the assumption was that Mona and her companion were the alien pilots of a spacecraft that crashed on the far side of the Moon. Crater counts gave the ship an estimated age of one and a half million years.

But...I have doubts. Deep, persistent, *nagging* doubts.

Was Mona Lisa truly alien, the member of a species evolved in another star system? Look at the incredible diversity of form and shape and function within Earth's biosphere—with creatures as varied as octopi, slime molds, dragonflies, and humans. Could creatures evolved on an alien world look even remotely human? Minor cosmetic differences—six fingers, large eyes—those don't count. *Star Trek's* Mr. Spock, human but for pointed ears, upswept eyebrows, and a devotion to logic, is ludicrous. Any being we encounter walking among the stars will be so alien we might not recognize it as life at all, and so advanced that its technology will seem like magic. Thank you, Mr. Clarke.

If she's not alien, the Mona Lisa must be human.

A million and a half years ago, humans as we know them today didn't exist. *Homo erectus* was just barely recognizable as genus *Homo*, his face flat and apelike, his braincase small, and he was just beginning to figure out how to use fire. The thought that Mona was the member of some ancient, long-vanished human civilization seems unlikely at best.

Time travel, then? Perhaps Mona hailed from the far future, when humans had evolved a sixth finger and built star-traveling time vessels four kilometers long. But...surely people from that remote future would have other ways of guiding their ships than metal spiders wired into their faces.

I have a different thought. I wish I did not.

The UFO literature today is filled with accounts of alien abductions, of aliens examining and probing living humans, of cattle mutilated for obscure reasons, of unseen Masters lurking in the shadows. Suppose aliens abducted a couple of humans—perhaps from the future to explain that extra finger—

And took them away into the depths of time to...study them?

Or better...suppose aliens *created* humans in the first place, genetically altering *Homo erectus* into something more advanced, bigger-brained...and every few thousand years, the creators stopped by to check up on their creations?

The organizers of Apollo 20 might not want people who believed in God to face such thoughts.

The organizers of Apollo 20 might not want the public at large to learn of a future—or a past—where human captives were vivisected in the name of alien science.

The organizers of Apollo 20 never did tell us what happened to Apollos 18 and 19.

Perhaps the abductions continue.

Perhaps They are right, and it's better that the world never know what took place on the very dark side of the Moon.

Perhaps those obscene conspiracy theories swirling about the Apollo Project were deliberately planted. *There* were *no Moon landings. There's nothing to see here. Move along...*

I swore to keep what happened at Guyot secret...but I'm old, now. What are they going to do if I talk? Kill me?

I think of the words of another writer, arguably science fiction, though perhaps as distant in tone and theme from Clarke as it's possible to get. H.P. Lovecraft, an American writer of horror and so-called weird fiction, wrote: *"The most merciful thing in the world, I think, is the inability of the human mind to correlate all its contents."*

But Lovecraft was wrong.

I remember it all.

And I wish I could forget...

∾

New York Times bestselling author **Ian Douglas, a.k.a. William H. Keith**, began his career in the RPG industry over 30 years ago, first as an artist and then as a writer. His work encompasses geopolitical technothrillers, young adult fiction, alternative military history, military science fiction, detective science fiction, comedy, horror, and fantasy. As the author of over 170 titles, including games and game modules, short stories, non-fiction, and 100 novels, he occasionally lifts his nose from the grindstone long enough to attend SF cons and Mensa gatherings, hike in his beloved Laurel Mountains, and pet the cats.

SHOT THROUGH WITH SHARDS OF LIGHT

CAT RAMBO

blue and green and violet, shot through with shards of light, colors bright as music, sounds as sharp as blades

Since she was five and had seen it on a documentary, Lucy had dreamed about Scintilla Five, the space station shaped in the oddest way, built around an ancient, enigmatic corpse, the space station where the rich and elite came to dance and dream and gamble and most importantly, spend money in a public way.

Scintilla Five (the fifth, and grandest iteration, of its concept) was the place that you dreamed about if you were a particular kind of person, the sort of person who loved glitter and sparkle and sought it out, who would always be dazzled by a flash of light in the darkness, the gleam of holiday lights, or the glittering scintillations that lay in the hearts of diamonds and other, more mysterious gems. And Lucy was that kind of person, through and through.

The strength of that allure was, perhaps, because Lucy was born on Adora, a muted planet, a place of placid blues and serene greys and dove brown, where there was placidity and serenity. A contemplative place, a sanctuary nestled in one of the larger civilizations dedicated to spiritual practice. Adora devoted itself to the mandates of Hector Allende, a prophet of unknown provenance, whose sayings had melded enough wisdom and practicality that he had acquired sufficient following for a colony to be dedicated to the practices that gradually solidified into social structures over the decades. The planet that had produced Lucy Voss, age 22 and a half, not quite sure what she wanted from life, but very sure that she wanted something, and by preference, something glittering.

Lucy was not particularly spiritual by her planet's standards, and intensely so by anyone else's. Despite her parents' protests, she had gone off-planet for the final years of her schooling, to a university willing to offer her a scholarship in modern music theory. While she had in fact been very interested in that subject at first, she had been convinced by a particularly charismatic instructor to become a xeno-archaeologist specializing in the Forerunners, those precursors to everyone else whose leavings and gleaning the current Known Universe subsisted on. She studied the gates that led between the stars, whose technology no one entirely—or even more than fragmentarily— understood, and the corpses of the star moths that floated in the empty spaces between worlds, once living starships and now just husks inhabited by a multitude of dangers.

Lucy had visited two star moths in her time. Not gone inside; very few people were brave enough to try that sort of thing, and an even smaller fraction of them emerged intact from the trip. No, she had done two internships, first helping monitor the inactive corpse from one of the study-stations hovering near the one closest to her planet.

And now this second one at Scintilla Five, which had made its moth a tourist attraction, cupped itself around the ancient corpse, creating a core that no one dared enter, and an industry built around those who came to gape at the entrance, those who came to die in a very spectacular way, and those who simply came to gamble and enjoy themselves and be seen at a place where so many of the universe's more prominent tourists came to relax.

Lucy had grown skilled to the point of boredom in maneuvering robotic drones along the vast outer structure, picking at the outer scales. On rare occasions, she was allowed to maneuver one inside the corpse and then review the video files of the few moments that they lasted inside the structure before being torn to pieces by unknown forces.

She was coming to the end of her internship—only a few more weeks to go. And finally, three free shifts in a row! She'd dreamed the previous night of her childhood imaginings of Scintilla Five, *spark of actinic blue and laser white jitterjagging gems*, and it made her whimsical in the morning, enough to abandon the reports she should be spending her free time writing up.

Instead, she took a skiff from the academic section, a set of utilitarian modules anchored near the moth's rear, and went over to Scintilla Five proper, where the casinos and hotels and game-units and entertainment spheres clustered, visiting someone she had met through VR space, who had turned out to be a pleasant enough companion. After a few hours in bed together exploring various things that she hadn't had a chance to explore since starting her internship, they decided to head down to one of the food courts. Lucy had been eating paste for the past few months; something with some sizzle to it sounded just the thing and sent an anticipatory crackle along her nerves.

So many people, so many smells and rustles and footsteps! Buskers working the entrances, singing and clapping and turning cartwheels, others weaving songs and lights together, still others melding and separating, flowing together in dance. Lucy would have stopped and gawped, but her companion touched her wrist, pulled her along. He had been unremarkable, and she was already regretting her decision a little, because he seemed as mildly pleased but overall unimpressed as she was, and that was damaging to the ego. He said, "I know those two over there," and they stooped beneath a constellation of flares and musk and past three stalls, and sat down at one of the public tables with the people he had pointed to.

There were three of them all together, all bartenders at the main casino. The youngest, Pam, was very new, and very ready to compare notes with Lucy about what she had experienced so far, and what were the things that one shouldn't miss, where celebrities were prone to unexpectedly appear; the food court they were sitting in was one, she insisted, despite her companions rolling their eyes.

"It's been swella good," Pam said when they were getting ready to go. She fished a couple of chits out of a belt pouch and slid them on the table over in Lucy's direction. Lucy felt a flush of satisfaction; the other woman had been flirting hard with her all through the meal, to the amiable amusement of Lucy's companion, who was clearly about ready to head back to their own employment and leave Lucy to hers. "My shift's starting soon. Come over if you want to see me at work."

Another of them snorted. "You only been at work here two weeks and already handing out the coax-chips," they said wryly.

Pam ignored them, eyes fixed on Lucy. "Say you'll come," she said, with just enough breathlessness to sound enticingly flustered. "Just stop in, at least." She was small and amber-skinned, compact and of indeterminate age, her eyes a grey reminiscent of an Adoran dawn.

Lucy demurred. She wasn't sure she wanted to linger longer

on Scintilla Five itself. She had work to get back to on her own substation, each report full of data to note, algorithms to enter, commas to be corrected.

But the sparkle of that chip chimed to her somehow, a little fishhook of *blue-white light glitter tempt gleam*. No surprise there, manufactured by a marketer who knew the heart of those who might be tempted to come to the casino.

But even though she knew that, knew that the lure that felt so tailored was the opposite of personalized, somehow, a cold calculation of effects—even so, Lucy let herself be seduced by that. It had been a good day, and she had been on the substation studying for months, letting others get away for escape by taking their shifts. It wasn't like she minded, she told herself, most of them had people they were making plans with. But now, she thought with a touch of pride, she'd had someone waiting for her, someone to make plans for. Even if that person seemed all too ready now to amiably pass her along. This new assignation, though, maybe they'd be the sort of person one made long-term plans with.

In a casino, there were gambles, risks. She might as well throw the dice. What did she have to lose?

Still, she hesitated, hoping her companion would say something like, "Won't you stay an extra day or so?" and show a touch of regret that she might not. But he said, instead, "You were right, Pam. That guy over there's from that band you like, Lucy, the Three Bensons. That's their coordinator, Robert Battle, over there." They pointed across the food court to where a trim, dark-skinned man stood talking with someone.

"What's he doing over here?"

"The Bensons are playing here next week. Usually, bands come a few days early, enjoy the place. And like I said, best spicy dumplings here, better than any over on the corp-side. We'll try it sometime, maybe." Pam leaned over to touch a fingertip to the back of Lucy's hand, a little kiss of skin that might have seemed practiced, if Lucy had been more experienced. But Adorans are not known for being a forward people, and the direct admiration of the approach disarmed Lucy. Made her feel like a special star being coaxed into blooming. And so she nodded and later that afternoon even bought a new tunic for the occasion, and tights spangled with lights that made her look like she was dancing, even when she was standing still.

∼

Oh the casino. *Glitter gleam sparkle dazzle scintillate emerald blue laser diamonds.* Colors and lights bursting everywhere, dancing like the music that throbbed through the air. You couldn't help but twitch along with it, let it dance through you. It was loud, but careful sonic engineering ensured never so loud that you couldn't hear someone talking directly to you, and all the old slot machines pulsed and whistled in tempo, lights chasing themselves along their trim, the sentient ones hooting and whistling like carnival barkers to try and entice new customers. A few shouted at Lucy, but she didn't entirely understand everything they were proposing, and so she blushed her way along through the crowd.

She was wide-eyed; those around her much less so. Scintilla Five attracted both nouveau riche and old currency. Empresses and war leaders came to gamble here, the heirs to thrones and the stars and starlets and sycophants that made up their entourages. They played games with cards like razorblades whose numbers went up to the thousands, dealt by dealers whose eyes had been replaced with lenses and dice, and if there was something to be bet on, you could do it there.

She breathed in deep of the musk of mixed atmospheres and mingled body aromas. A walking tree brushed past her, scattering golden pollen in its wake, and she inhaled the honey-and-apple chamomile scent recklessly, without wondering what effect it might have. Surely, the casino would mitigate any dangers. At least, any that were not the subject of bets.

Pam had told her which way to go, and so she went along through the glittering corridors of machines amid the hum and bustle and whine and click and squeak and moan of the crowd around her. Adora was not a frequent tourist attraction, and those pilgrims that did make their way to it were not the sort to stand out in a crowd, but rather the sorts who tried to blend in and not call attention to themselves.

Every being that she saw here, by contrast, seemed to want to occupy the center of all attention. The clothes were often much more noticeable than the person, although sometimes it was hard to tell where clothing left out and alien began. Jewelry glittered around her that would have funded revolutions or corporate takeovers, and some of the beings that wore it did so with studied nonchalance about its cost, as though it had fallen on them when they got dressed in the morning.

Others were dressed to showcase it, making it the focus of their outfits. Some daring souls wore nothing but painted circuitry on their outer layers, paints that flashed and glowed and hummed and sometimes showed art that had been specially commissioned to accentuate their bodies, and sometimes showed old artwork. Was that the Mona Lisa that had swayed past on the body of a tall, dark man?

She caught a glimpse of one of the Bensons, she thought, through the press of people, and got the rest of the way to the bar in a happy glow. One person, and then another, a pair of assignations....what might not come next? What if she met a Benson? What if they said something to her about staying another few days? They had toured her planet once, back when she was a child, and she had been smitten then. The dream was a happy one, even though she knew it was adolescent and overly romantic in her heart, and she let it spin out a little, and it made her smile even wider at her new friend's grin where their eyes met.

Without asking, Pam poured her a drink that swirled red and blue in the glass, and in which golden bubbles rose like eyes winking, one by one, from the surface of the drink. It tasted like fiery fruit with an undertone of sulfur.

"Having a good time?"

Lucy nodded. "Thought I saw a Benson," she said happily.

Pam grinned even harder. "Well," she said, with a happy little purr even more seductive than that finger touch, more warming than the drink she'd poured, "Look over there and you'll see another."

Lucy followed the direction of the pointed finger. "That's Benson the first!"

She stared, drinking in the unimpeded sight. The musician sat solitary at a booth, although burly bodyguards squatted on the booth at either side, Keplerians who wore black armor and black visors that gave them the look of surly robots.

The musician was drinking the same kind of drink that Pam had served Lucy. She was tall and angular and had long curls of silver that fell nearly to the table's polished surface. Her eyes were amethyst, and around her neck she wore a band of gems that seemed to match her eyes when Lucy first looked, but then cycled through a round of colors, *amethyst* to *turquoise* to *sapphire* and then dark flashes. Around her wrists were matching bands.

"You might not think it," someone else at the bar said, "but she's wearing as much on her body as this whole place is worth."

"That's a lot," the bartender said.

"Oh stars," Lucy breathed, looking at the gems again. "Is that a Forerunner artifact? It should be in a museum!"

"She likes this place because she can wear it without most people saying that sort of thing," the bartender said. "The rich are different. They don't think of the good of everyone the way we spacers do. They don't understand that an open airlock kills anyone, no matter how much money is in their pocket."

Her tone rang oddly against the happy backbeat of the music.

Lucy was frowning at the jewels. Something about their *blue blue white blaze* itched at her, something she'd heard or read, perhaps recently. "Hey," Pam said, watching her face. "I've got to go take care of a couple private parties, but I'll be back down here within the hour. Want to hang in the employees' lounge?"

That tickled her, the idea of being in the inner sanctum, but after Pam had installed her and given her a couple of gossip-buzzes to entertain her, she found it fairly boring. Everyone around her was intent on their work, or on their own conversations. She did find mention of the Bensons on one of the buzzes, and there were the jewels again. She studied them, then tapped into her own study net. Scholars have access to databases that ordinary folk don't, sometimes. Other times you can swap access, a question of favors. And she had some reason to go diving around in Forerunner artifact territory since it was believed (by most) that they had also created (and flown) the spacemoths.

She found the gems buried deep in a database, the account of the explorer who had found them initially. She read through the passages with growing horror, thinking this must be the set around the Benson's neck. Usually, such stories ended with "passed into the hands of a private collector," but this one indicated that the gems were destroyed in an accident, so this must not be the same.

She didn't wait for the bartender to come back, but went to

seek out the Benson, who surely didn't know the nature of the things she wore. It wasn't hard to do; the bartender had given her a visitor's chip that let her wander. She found the Benson she wanted in one of the lounges, a bubble of glass overlooking the side of the spacemoth, where lights had been installed to play in floral patterns, shifting one into another.

"I need to tell you something about the jewelry you're wearing," she said.

The Benson caressed the sparkle at her throat, tilted her hand to admire the way a bracelet fell slant across her skin. "I know they're very rare and special and expensive," she almost sang, her voice a velvet cadence, flecks of sweetness scattered in it like rhinestone burrs.

"They're intelligent," Lucy said. "They're intelligent beings."

The Benson held the other hand up as though loathe to afford one bracelet preference over the other. "Oh, I know," she sang, almost a lullaby, "I know, I know. I know."

She lowered the hand and smiled effulgently at Lucy, the doting smile of someone who finds a pet particularly sweet. "I can't wear them on any of the so-called civilized planets. They have low-level telepathy. Given enough time, they can establish a bond, influence someone's actions. I've had my mind augmented so they can't do it to me, so have the other Bensons and Robert. And most of the time, they're in a damper box. But here?" Her shrug traveled across her shoulders, culminated in the lift of another hand to present one of the bracelets. "The necklace is the main cluster, anyhow. They're fascinating things. The being that found them discovered them all together, a cluster. I had them mounted, in galactinum, the only substance precious enough to hold them."

"You are holding them captive," Lucy said with horror. Her gentle Adoran soul could not contemplate the sort of egotism it would take for someone to claim another being as adornment. "You are a monster!"

The Benson's eyes were placid. "I am an artist," she said. "It is difficult for me to find new sensations."

Her gaze held enough speculation that Lucy fled.

Pam found her in one of the silence gardens, in a secluded arbor, huddled. "What's wrong?" she asked.

The story tumbled out. The bartender seemed perhaps a touch less surprised than she should have, but Lucy, full of indignant fervor, paid no attention to that.

"It's wrong!" she finished, her anger stirred to a rare depth. "Someone needs to do something!"

"What if," said the bartender, "I said there was a way for you to do something?"

By the time the bartender had shown her the replicates of the jewels, had explained how she had happened to arrive at Scintilla Five in possession of them, it did occur to Lucy to wonder at the timing of things. But surely, she told herself, it was not possible for anyone to have anticipated these events, to have calculated her arrival or her knowledge of Forerunner artifacts. Or that the Benson would have looked at a gawky Adoran girl with speculation.

And more than that, the image of the jewels against the Benson's skin itched at her, their *sparkles of shattered light, white sapphire green moving and moving and moving*. She wanted to take them. She wanted to free them, to correct the great injustice of one being thinking it could hold another captive.

It turned out there was enough speculation in the Benson's gaze to bite on Lucy's lure. Clumsily thrown, surely, but perhaps that lack of sophistication was part of the draw. They went to bed together, and afterwards the Benson curled long arms around Lucy and sleepily invited her to go on an excursion in the morning, to look at the spacemoth from close up, and protested only a little when Lucy said she had other things to do.

Or who knows how much the Benson knew, or how much she cooperated, whether she lay still in her bed pretending to be asleep when her lover was swapping things in the drawer near the bed? Perhaps betrayal was just another sensation. Perhaps she had something else planned.

The spiced dumplings were good as an early lunch, and they ate them privately, in a secluded nook Pam said was out of the way of surveillance. She had been grumpy at Lucy's unexpectedly late arrival, but now nudged sauce over to Lucy, said, "Heard the news?"

Lucy's mind was full of the *scream shine of jewels white green blue.* She rubbed at the case under her palm and said, absently, "What?"

"The trip to see the moth's eye got smashed by something. They're not sure if it was things come out of the moth or something else."

Lucy's attention jerked out of the haze of speculation to focus on Pam. "What? Those are safe; they undergo all sorts of checks." She'd been aboard it that morning, earlier. What had she been doing? Perhaps that had been a dream. Surely it had been a dream. She wiped at her aching head.

"It's for the best," Pam said, licking a trace of sauce off her lips. "So much fuss and bother about the accident, particularly with all the fake clues I planted while arranging it. No one will think to look at the jewels for years and find them fake." She reached to touch the case. "Only a few more loose ends to clear up."

The gun glinted, pointing at Lucy. Her eyes widened. "What?" she said, feeling an acid rush of realization, the wretchedness of realizing pretended affection has paid false coin for true.

"I appreciate your help," Pam said. "If I were the sort of person who felt regret, I'm sure I would be very bothered by this, because you have been sweet. But I don't experience that.'

"Too bad," Robert Battle said from the doorway. "I think you might want to." He stepped aside to reveal the security officers behind him.

"No manager lets his clients wander around getting stolen from," he said patiently when everything was getting sorted. "I had an eye on this plot as soon as I knew we were coming here. This gang's been after her for a while and I figured I'd draw them out. I had the Benson's mechanical doubles shipped off in the shuttle, and it was flown remotely. All's well that ends well." He started to pick up the case where it had fallen, but a security bot nudged him aside, scooping it up and presenting him with a tag redeemable once all evidence had been processed. He sighed and tucked the tag away.

Lucy nodded, feeling numb. Something prickled at the back

of her mind but the lights were muted for the moment, lurking in a *crackle flare of white and sapphire and amethyst*.

It wasn't until a day later that she had a chance to use the drone to pick through the radioactive debris from the shuttle's explosion. She was looking for the package she had put there. Why hadn't she remembered doing so until now? It had been taped under a bulkhead, securely, and there was the tiny dot of supra-magnetic material she'd used to tag it, as she would have a specimen she was collecting, to let her find it.

She unwrapped it with trembling hands. The gems shone up at her *blue blue red green white*, light echoing inside her skull. They said thank you thank you and she breathed out a sigh of satisfaction, as though coming home.

Somewhere else, the Benson was looking down at the false jewels with a frown and then a shrug, throwing them aside.

Deep in the jewels, new life pulsed. To be born required the force of an explosion. So hard to engineer.

But not impossible, when you had time to spin a plan out of greed and fervor and vanity colliding, reaching deeper into anyone's head than the Benson had thought possible. Perhaps that misunderstanding had itself been engineered, over time. And there had been plenty of that, plenty of time to cast a glittering lure, its coruscating facets flashing blue blue white green, as they toured the Known Universe, looking for the impressionable mind of a child, watching someone on stage, not feeling the sparks of light sink into her mind and catch and snag and trap and draw her into this *inevitable white shot through with shards of light blaze*.

～

Nebula Award winner **Cat Rambo** has published over two hundred short stories, five collections, two novels, two books on writing, and a cookbook. Their space opera, *You Sexy Thing*, appears in 2021 from Tor Macmillan. Their school for speculative fiction writers, The Rambo Academy for Wayward Writers, has been in existence for over a decade. A longtime volunteer with the Science Fiction and Fantasy Writers of America, they served as its President from 2014-2019. Find out more about their fiction at their website: http://www.catrambo.com.

PUSH COMES TO SHOVE

PETER DAVID

There was nothing left.

Luk had never been to Rygor before, didn't know what to expect. It was a rather small colony, a couple of hundred residents who were mostly agrarian and largely young families. The terraforming of Rygor had taken about two years, according to OB1's research, and supposedly, they had done a good job. Initially, it had been a barren world, but now it was rather lush with forests and farming areas occupying thousands of acres.

The residents described themselves as misfits, largely feeling unappreciated on their home worlds and believing that they could accomplish much if they were just able to be left to themselves. Some had come from nearby, others from another section of the galaxy far, far away. So they had found backers and fashioned Rygor into their own personal paradise. Although they had voyaged to Rygor from different sections of the galaxy, they had come together and bonded as one new race. To the best of Luk's knowledge, everything had been going swimmingly.

Clearly, that was no longer the case.

Much of the city was gone. It had simply been obliterated, as if some sort of massive explosion had been set off within its perimeter. There were shards of buildings left, and the ground was blackened and scorched. There were no bodies; instead, there were piles of ashes. The poor bastards had been incinerated.

Luk tried to imagine what it had been like for them. Had there been any warning, any alarms sounding to inform them that danger was imminent and their lives were at risk? Or had they been simply going about their business, strolling, chatting, planning what they were going to be doing that evening for dinner or entertainment and then, bang, just getting blasted out of existence? He couldn't even begin to understand it.

He glanced to his companion, OB1. The cyborg was right behind him, taking in their environment, no doubt running a data scan to try and determine the reason for the destruction they were encountering. OB1 scratched at the beard that lined his aged face. "Do we know what the devil happened here, Luk?"

Luk shook his head. "No clue. All I know is that I got the distress call a few days ago..."

"A few *days* ago?" said a surprised OB1. "And we just got here now?"

"We were busy, OB1," said Luk with thinly disguised irritation. "If the Sentinels and I hadn't stopped Obscuro's plot, then the entire rebellion would have fallen apart. I got us here as quickly as I could. One has to prioritize."

"I am sure that will mean a lot to the Rygorians," said OB1, touching one of the piles of ash with a gleaming metal toe.

Luk sighed in irritation. OB1 could sometimes be somewhat hard to take. Granted, the cyborg remained the greatest living teacher of the sciences of the Push that anyone could have asked for. His tutoring had served to make Luk the Sentinel warrior he was today. But damnation, he could still be irritating from time to time.

Choosing to ignore OB1's comment, Luk studied his tracker. "The signal from the beacon is up ahead."

"It may well just be automatic. If everyone is dead, then obviously there's no one left to be sending it."

"That's true. But it won't harm anything for us to check. Just to make sure."

OB1 shrugged. "As you wish. You're the lead Sentinel; I am merely your humble teacher."

Humble. That's a laugh. But Luk kept his opinion to himself in that regard.

That was when he heard a high-pitched whine, a noise that was very unusual.

Immediately, he snapped out his Slayzer and activated it. The gleaming sword of light flared to life, and he brought it up defensively. OB1 swung his into view as well, and they both stood there, prepared for potential battle.

"Obscura?" asked OB1. Luk didn't know. But he was ready for anything.

The sound was coming from behind the shattered remains of one of the buildings. It continued for several moments and then stopped. Two figures emerged from behind it.

Luk's eyes narrowed, suspicious that the two newcomers might be there to start some trouble. They were both armed; they appeared to be holding module pistols, and they had them leveled and ready to be used. They were a man and a woman, dressed identically, wearing black slacks and what appeared to be uniform jackets of red and yellow. The man was the older, with a shock of brown hair and an array of lines on his forehead that indicated he was constantly concerned about something, though Luke had no idea what.

When the woman spotted Luk and OB1, she immediately stepped in front of the man in a protective manner, which indicated to Luk that she was some sort of guard or protector. The man studied Luk, and then something seemed to click.

"Where did you come from?" said Luk. "I don't see any ship. How did you just...show up here?"

"We used our MT," the man said.

Luk turned to OB1 for clarification. OB1's knowledge was encyclopedic. If there was something to know in the universe, it was safely lodged in OB1's memory.

"Molecular transmitter," OB1 immediately said. "A technology that enables travelers to have their bodies broken down to molecular essentials and then reintegrated in another place."

"That's...that's impossible. That doesn't exist," said Luk.

"Oh, it exists," the man said. "In our world, it's quite commonplace." He regarded Luk another moment and then said, "Luk Starkiller. Unless I miss my guess."

"Your guess is spot on," said Luk. "May I ask how you knew that?"

"Your reputation has preceded you, Master Starkiller. You're quite the talk of the Congress."

"The Congress. You mean the United Star Congress?"

The man nodded. "The very same. We've been monitoring your battle with the Reich. They're rather a formidable establishment; indeed, there are some in the USC who are worried that sooner or later, the Reich is going to turn its interests in our direction. So we've been monitoring your battle against them very carefully." He gestured toward Luk's weapon. "Your 'slayzer' swords are quite distinctive."

"As are your module pistols."

"We call them 'masers,'" said the man, and he holstered his. The woman did likewise. "Hope you didn't feel threatened. It's standard procedure to be armed when transporting down into an unknown situation."

"You have the advantage of me, sir. You know me, but I don't have any idea who you are."

"I am Captain James Hornblower of the space vessel *Venture*. This," and he indicated the woman standing next to him, "is my security officer, Lieutenant Kenee." Kenee then tossed off an offhand salute.

"This is OB1, my training borg," said Luke, indicating the cyborg standing next to him. "Now would you mind explaining why you're here?"

"We received a distress call," said Kenee. "We were somewhat busy with another matter, transporting an ambassador to a key peace conference, so we had to complete that undertaking first. But as soon as we did, we came here." She glanced around woefully. "Seems we got here too late."

"The same with us," said Luk. "We were just tracking the distress signal's source."

"As were we. I suggest we combine forces," said Hornblower.

Luk readily agreed. It was nice for him and OB1 to have backup for once.

The group made their way across the shattered terrain, trying to determine what in the world had happened that had demolished Rygor so comprehensively. Neither of them knew for certain. They kept comparing notes, trying to figure it out, coming up with a variety of theories, but none of them seemed to fit.

"Was it a war?" Luk said. "Is that it?"

"But who were they at war with? Each other? There weren't that many of them," said Hornblower. "Certainly, if they had issues, it wasn't anything so severe that they couldn't come to some sort of reasonable compromise."

"You believe in reasonable compromise?" said OB1. "How very quaint."

"Quaint," said Hornblower with a cocked eyebrow. "The USC is governed by the concept. We come together, we talk out our differences, we negotiate settlements. It's how the USC has kept peace for centuries."

"So there's no conflict in your section of space?" Luk was openly skeptical.

"Well, there are the Remusians," Kenee spoke up. "An outlying race, always trying to start trouble. We've run into them a few times, given them some bloody noses. One hopes that they will eventually learn their place in the galaxy. But other than them, yes, we get on fairly well."

"I envy you," said Luk. "I've been fighting every day of my life for as long as I can remember. Ever since the Reich came to my homeworld searching for some plans and slew my entire family because they thought they were hiding them."

"They weren't, I assume."

Luk shook his head. "I was. I was a part of the rebellion and my family knew nothing about it. They died for my sins."

"Fighting oppression is never a sin."

"Tell that to their corpses."

They arrived at the shattered remains of what appeared to be a group domicile. It was smaller than the other buildings, more residential. But there didn't appear to be much left of it, and certainly it seemed unlikely that anyone could be living there.

They exchanged puzzled looks, and Luk once more checked his guiding device that seemed to indicate this was definitely the source of the distress signal. "Where is it?" said Luk.

Suddenly, there was a noise from directly in front of them, the sound of a lock being unlatched. Luk and Hornblower immediately reached for their weapons, but OB1 stepped forward and said, "Wait. It's nothing to worry about."

As it turned out, he was correct. A small area of ground

shook in front of them and then a trap door was pushed upward, dirt and ash sliding off it. A man emerged from the square hole in the ground. He had brown hair, brown eyes. He stepped out of the enclosure and stood at his full height of nearly six feet. His face was scruffy, as if he were desperately in need of a shave.

"You came," he said icily. His voice sounded like something of a cross between incredulity and indifference. "You finally came."

"I am Captain James Hornblower of the USC." He stepped forward, curiosity in his face. "You sent the distress signal?"

The man nodded. He wasn't young; he appeared to be in his early 40s. "Yes. I did."

"Are there any other survivors?"

"No. Just me."

"And you are?"

"Jason Thees. I called you and you didn't come." His voice rose. "*You didn't come!*"

"We got here as quickly as we could," said Luk. "I'm Luk Starkiller and this is—"

"I know who you are. I know who all of you are."

"You're obviously upset, Mr. Thees," said Hornblower. He stepped forward and put a hand on Thees' shoulder. "Why don't you tell us what happened?"

Thees shook the hand off his shoulder and glared at him for a moment. But just as quickly, the anger seemed to dissipate. Instead, it was replaced with weary resignation. "They wouldn't shut up," he said finally.

"They? They who?"

"Everyone." He gestured around himself, taking in the entirety of the colony. "Everyone kept arguing."

"About what?"

"*About you!*" he shouted. "You had fans. Both of you."

"Fans?" Luk said, puzzled. He turned to OB1. "Fans?"

"Fanciers or fanatics," said OB1. "Enthusiasts who follow your adventures and comment on them."

"I have fans?"

"Oh yes," OB1 assured him. "Many of them, following your battles against the Reich."

"Well, yes, my other rebels who..."

OB1 shook his head. "No. These aren't participants. They are people who simply keep abreast of your undertakings and comment on them."

"Comment?"

"On computer systems or, in some more primitive cultures, magazines."

"But...what is there to comment on?"

"Speculation, mostly. Romantic involvements. What your next mission is going to be. Relationships. Some, for instance, believe Pater Obscura is your father."

"My *father*," said Luk incredulously. "He's my greatest enemy. He's tried to kill me innumerable times. Why in the world would they think he's my father?"

"No clue. Also, some don't believe you exist."

"That I *don't exist*? I'm standing right here!"

"They think you're wish fulfillment. Something that other rebels made up to be their ideal leader. Oh, and others think you and I are romantically involved."

"*What?*"

"Go argue with fans."

"Why didn't you ever tell me about any of this?"

"Why in the world should I? It's idiocy. It's a waste of your time."

Hornblower stepped forward. "And does the USC have fans as well?"

"Oh yes," said OB1. "They're just as idiotic as Master Starkiller's are. In fact, many of them argue over who is better."

"Better?" Hornblower exchanged confused looks with Luk. "Better than what?"

"Better than each other. They have names for both of your 'universes.' Yours, Captain Hornblower, is referred to as 'Galactic Journey,' and your environment, Master Starkiller, is referred to as 'Cosmic Combat.' Fans of Captain Hornblower refer to themselves as Journeymen. Your fans don't really have a name, Luk."

"I still don't understand what we're supposed to be better at," said Luk. "I mean, we each have our own missions, our own priorities. We each do our own thing. It seems somewhat ridiculous to compare us. It's like comparing apples and some other fruit."

"Kumquats?" suggested Hornblower.

"Yes, exactly, apples and kumquats. It's just a waste of time."

"You think I don't know that!" Thees suddenly exploded. He had been listening quietly the entire time, but now it seemed as if he had heard more than enough. "That's what I kept saying! And these...these idiots wouldn't shut up about it! Half of them thought Galactic Journey was better, the other half loved Cosmic Combat, and they would. Not. Shut. Up. About it! They would have gatherings where they would convene and espouse the merits of each group and act like the other was inferior. I kept saying to them, for God's sake, just get along with each other—but they never did! I couldn't stand it anymore! So I had to settle it!"

"Settle it how?" Hornblower said cautiously.

"How do you think? I built a bomb."

For a moment, silence descended on the group like a shroud.

"A bomb," Luk finally said.

"I called it the Rygor Mortis. Perfect name, don't you think?

I set it to go off and then sent out the distress signal so that you gentlemen would show up and disarm it. You were going to save the whole colony. It was a win-win situation. You, Luk, or you, Captain Hornblower, would take the initiative and save the day or—worst case scenario—you'd team up to do it. No matter what happened, that would settle the argument. Either the people who disarmed the bomb would be seen as the best, or you'd work together, which would prove that you could co-exist with each other.

"And then you *didn't show up! And the damned bomb went off!*"

"You could've turned it off!" said Luk. "Disarmed it yourself! Saved all the lives!"

"And what would that have proven? It wasn't about me! It was about you! But you couldn't be bothered to show up until it was too late! All these people are dead, and it's all your fault!"

Hornblower was bristling with fury. "You are a murderer," he said intensely, "and you're going to pay for your crimes."

"Yeah? Who's gonna make that happen?" said Thees contemptuously. "Rygor is outside of USC space. You have zero authority here. You can't arrest me."

"He's right, Captain," said Kenee. "We don't have the right to arrest him. If we do, the USC will order that he be released. There's nothing we can do."

Hornblower considered that a moment and then, with two quick strides, he approached Thees, cocked his fist, and delivered a roundhouse punch to his jaw. Thees was knocked off his feet and tumbled to the ground. He lay there for a moment, looking stunned.

The captain advanced, and then Luk put himself between Hornblower and his target. "What are you going to do? Beat him to death?"

"It's what he deserves."

"And is that what the USC stands for?" demanded Luk. "Making independent judgments as to what different people deserve and then allowing their representatives to act accordingly?"

"They..."

Kenee rested a hand gently on his arm. He looked at her and very softly she said, "You can't. You know you can't."

That was when a steady beeping noise began to sound.

And Thees laughed. He raised his hand and brought into view the source of the beeping: a silver bracelet around his wrist.

"As I suspected," he said. "You see, my instruments told me when you'd arrived. So I sent a summons to some people I suspected would be interested to know you were here. You may have taken days to arrive—days that cost the lives of everyone here—but their priorities were in order."

And suddenly, a small, W-shaped one-man craft descended from on high. Luk watched it grimly as it smoothly landed some yards away and the hatch spiralled open.

A figure clad in black leather emerged. Immediately, Luk swung his slayzer into view, activating it so that the glowing blade flared into existence.

"Obscura," he said with a snarl.

It was indeed Pater Obscura, his long black cape swirling about him, his gleaming skull-shaped black helmet on his head. His slayzer was already on, and he stared straight at Luk. "**At last**," he said, his raspy voice echoing in the still air.

Then, more whining filled the air—similar to the sound the beam had made that had brought Hornblower and Kenee to the planet's surface—and two individuals materialized. Obscura might well have been tall, but these new arrivals were the largest beings that Luk had ever seen. They were massively muscled, with pointed ears and wrinkled foreheads that made them look as if they were wearing crabs in their faces. They each had long black hair, and their skin was dark orange.

"Remusians!" shouted Kenee as she swung her weapon up, but she was too slow. The closer of them unleashed a blast from the force gun he had in his hand, and a perfect hole was blown through Kenee's chest. She fell without a word.

"Oh my God!" shouted Hornblower. "You killed Kenee! You bastards!"

"We're going to do more than that," said the larger of the two Remusians. "Captain Hornblower. It's been an age. Perhaps you don't remember me."

"I remember you all too well, Zadok," said Hornblower, and he aimed his maser and fired.

The beam coruscated off the armor that lined Zadok's chest, not even coming close to penetrating it.

"Is that the best you can do?" roared Zadok. "You think your toys will work on me? This has been a long time coming, Hornblower. You have caused great inconvenience for the Remusian empire. But now...now is the time to end it! Now is the time for you to join your pathetic security associate! Now is the time to—!"

At that moment, a somersaulting figure came hurtling through the air and landed squarely in front of Zadok. It was Luk, and he swung his slayzer around with practiced efficiency. It sliced through Zadok's neck, and his head tumbled off his body. He didn't even slow as he spun to face Zadok's associate. The associate fired a blast from his weapon, but it did no good; Luk deflected the blast off his slayzer and slammed forward with his weapon. The maser blasts might well have been deflected by the Remusian armor, but it did nothing to slow the gleaming light blade. Seconds later, the associate's head was rolling on the ground next to Zadok's.

"Sorry," Luk said to Hornblower. "They were just beginning to irritate me."

"No, no, that's fine," said Hornblower, perfectly happy for Starkiller to have interceded.

Pater Obscura then strode forward. "**Your skills haven't deserted you, Starkiller**." He stretched out his hand. "**Let us see if your mastery of the Push is still as strong as it was**."

Starkiller was immediately sent hurtling back, slamming directly into Hornblower. They both tumbled to the ground.

"**Ah. You seem lacking. Let us reeducate you**," he said.

That was when OB1 charged, bringing his slayzer around, ready to use it against Obscura in deadly combat.

He never had the chance.

Obscura caught him approaching out of the corner of his eye and thrust out his free hand. OB1 wasn't thrown back; instead, he was blasted apart. His body fragmented, arms flying in one direction, legs in another, his chest shattering, his head rolling away.

"You son of a--!" Luk started to say, but he never got the words out. Instead, he was shoved back once more, Hornblower catching him before he was flattened.

"How is he doing that?!" said Hornblower.

"The Push," Luk grated. "All things are bound together in one universal field. If you are a master of the Push, you can move anything with your mind."

"And you are, too?"

"Yes, but not on his level."

"**None are on my level**," Obscura said with a rumble. Slowly, he approached, keeping Luk at bay with a mere outstretched palm. "**This has been a long time**

**coming, Starkiller. Many times we have met
before, and many times, you have narrowly
escaped. But your luck is finally over. Now this
ends. Now this—"**

"Are you my father?"

Obscura stopped in his path, his hand still outstretched. He
actually seemed surprised. "**Your father.**"

"That's right," said Luk, getting to his feet, dusting himself
off. "Are you my father? I mean, you said it yourself: so many
narrow escapes. So many times you could have killed me, and
yet you didn't. Why am I still alive? I can't be that lucky. Do you
have a personal reason? Are you my father?"

"**So close,**" said Obscura.

And he reached up and removed his helmet.

Luk and Hornblower both gasped in surprise.

Luk's face was staring back at them. He was older, his hair
streaked with gray, but it was him.

"It took you long enough to figure out," said Obscura. "Or at
least as close as your limited imagination allowed you to get. You
are my clone, Starkiller."

"Your clone," echoed Starkiller.

"That's right. Long-lived I may be, but not immortal. Sooner
or later, my body will break down. On that day, I will transfer
my mind into your body and finalize the Reich's hold on our
section of the galaxy. And on that day, Hornblower," and he
shifted his attention to the Captain, "I'll be coming for your crew
next."

"My crew?" said Hornblower. "Not for me?"

"No. Because you will already be long dead."

He moved toward Hornblower, bringing his slayzer around,
and Luk got between them, ready to battle him to the death.

He never had the opportunity.

The air shimmered, and Pater Obscura dissolved into nothingness.

Slowly, a puzzled Luk lowered his blade. "Where did he go?"

"I had my ship beam him up," said Hornblower.

"Beam him up? So he's on your ship now? That wasn't wise, Hornblower. You have no idea of his power. The things he could do—"

"Oh, I know exactly what he can do. I didn't say I had beamed him *into* the ship."

"What? What're you...?" Then, Luk's voice trailed off, and he understood. He grinned widely. "You had him rematerialized in space."

"Not quite," said Hornblower. "Actually, I had his molecules dispersed throughout space. I doubt he's going to be able to inconvenience anyone ever again."

"That's very kind of you to have dispensed with him."

"Well, I felt I owed you, considering the way you jumped in and took care of the Remusian."

"He irritated me."

"That's understandable."

"*Oh my God!*" howled Thees. "Will the two of you just shut up! Both of you, just getting along so well! It's infuriating!"

Starkiller was surprised to hear that reaction. "I'd think you'd be pleased that we're getting along," he pointed out. "As I recall, you were the one who despised the notion of people arguing over which of us was 'better.' I would think that the two of us being cooperative and appreciating each other would bring you cheer, not frustration."

"But you stand for different things!" said an anagry Thees. "You, Starkiller...you're all about fighting. About solving things through force of arms and battling your enemy to a standstill. And you, Hornblower, you're all about exploration and everyone getting along. You're the antithesis of each other. You shouldn't be finding common ground. You should hate each other!"

Hornblower and Luk considered that for perhaps three seconds, and then Hornblower said, "Need help with your cyborg?"

"No thanks," said Luk. "He's already pulling himself together."

He was right. OB1's parts were reassembling themselves. His legs and arms had rejoined with his torso, his chest was largely repaired, and he was placing his head atop his body. His jaw clicked a few times, producing no sound for some moments, and then his voice reactivated. "Where is Obscura?"

"Terminated," said Luk.

"Really? That is excellent news. What about him?" He pointed at Thees.

Luk stared at him a moment and then, to Hornblower's surprise, he tossed him his slayzer. Thees stared at it uncomprehendingly. "What am I supposed to do with this?" he demanded.

"Sooner or later, you're going to get tired of living with what you've done. And you're going to want to end it. So I'm giving you that to make it easier for you."

"Gee, thanks," said Thees.

"You're being sarcastic. That's fine. But at some point, you're genuinely going to appreciate it. OB1—up for walking yet?"

"I believe I am."

"Captain Hornblower," Luk said to his new compatriot. "May the Push accompany you."

"Long Life and Great Fortune," replied Hornblower.

They walked in opposite directions, Hornblower carrying Kenee's body, and as they did, Thees stood there and screamed at them and taunted them, shouting challenges and derision and demanding to know why didn't they just kiss because they were both obviously so attracted to each other, and how they didn't really care about what they were doing anyway, and they would definitely be better if they were younger and looked completely different, and how stupid was it that Starkiller was a clone of Obscura, that was just proof that ideas had run out, and neither of them was really better than the other because both of them sucked, there were other people out there undertaking endeavors that were much better than they were, and how they were just recycling the kinds of adventures that they had already accomplished, and new people should really just take over for them and show everyone how it was really done...

And the slayzer was starting to look somewhat appealing...

Peter David created and wrote the *Star Trek: New Frontier* fiction series, plus many other classic *Star Trek* novels and comics. He has written a multitude of comics for major publishers and continues to do so. He has also scripted episodes of the *Babylon 5* and *Crusade* TV series and co-created the Nickelodeon scifi series *Space Cases* with actor/writer Bill Mumy.

CROWN OF THORNS

MIKE BARON

The United Earth Alliance deep space cruiser *Narwhal* was fifty days out from Ganymede when it detected the anomaly. Carrying two squeeze bottles of zero-G coffee, First Officer Garretson knocked softly on Captain Jefferson Nunn's door.

Nunn was napping after an eight-hour shift. He sat up in his bunk, the webbing preventing him from floating, and rubbed his eyes. A rugged-looking man with Andy Rooney eyebrows and a four-day stubble, he opened the door with a wave and accepted the coffee Garretson offered him. "What?"

"Captain, unidentified craft approaching. Range four thousand twenty-three kilometers."

"How do we know it's a craft and not some flotsam?"

"I bombarded it with theta beam particles, and it indicates the hull is made with ruthenium, osmium, and as yet unidentified elements. It is also transmitting a staccato code. The main computer is trying to translate."

Garretson, a talkative man whom the crew called Garrulous, kept his beard neatly trimmed, suctioning the clippings with the vacuum tube provided to every lavatory. He was a stocky Scot whose Alliance uniform was perpetually rumpled.

"Lopez' finger hovers over the torpedoes. You'd better come quick."

Nunn swung his legs out of bed and pulled on his blue Alliance one-piece uniform with the captain's bars on the shoulders. A zipper ran from his neck to his crotch. "Five minutes. Alert the crew."

"Done, Captain."

Nunn stood, one hand on the low ceiling, and patted Garretson on the shoulder. "Good man."

By the time Nunn reached the bridge, the crew was on full alert: Lopez at his station, eyes glued to the screen; Science Officer Chanticleer at the com console pressing keys; Ma at the Systems Board ready to lower the shields. It was 2089.

No one stood as Nunn glided to his seat, a meter above the floor, and strapped himself in. "Systems report."

"Ninety-five per cent capacity," Garretson sang from his seat, lower and to the right of the captain.

"Photon missiles armed and ready," Lopez said from his perch before the curving sweep of the main console.

"Clear beam to Ganymede," Ma reported. "Time to reception fifty-nine minutes, thirty seconds."

"What are they saying, Lieutenant Ma?"

"Don't know, Captain. We're running it through every algorithm. Lucille is heating up."

They called the computer—which occupied fifteen per cent of the *Narwhal's* volume—Lucille.

"Mr. Chanticleer, are you transmitting the standard greetings?"

"Eight hundred and twelve frequencies, Captain," the Nigerian replied, Bible in his lap.

"How long before it arrives?"

"Fifty-nine minutes, Captain," Garretson said.

"Ma, run diagnostics on the design. Put it up on the main screen. Perhaps the computer can cast some light on its purpose."

A bizarre craft appeared on every screen and in the holo box that hovered mid-cabin. The alien craft was a tapered cylinder with the stern, if it was the stern, surrounded by five spheres, each approximately twelve meters in diameter. A carrot-like appendage thrust out over the bow, like the figurehead on an ancient man-o'-war. Circles of lights gleamed at irregular intervals, front to back.

Ma made a slight adjustment, and the craft came into focus, floating in the hologram as if it were there in the ship with them, a three-meter-long invader. "Captain, the diagnostics tell us nothing. We are dealing with an alien technology. We have game-theoried its offensive capacities, and we just don't know what they might be. We know what *we* can do: lasers...particle beams...nukes. I do think it's safe to assume they will be armed with nukes...but we just don't know. Judging by the craft's advanced design, however, it is safe to say they are *highly* intelligent."

"Yes," Lopez said, "it looks advanced to us, because we don't know their history. However, perhaps this is an ancient race, and they have been using that design since before the dawn of human civilization?"

"Where's Immasch?" Nunn said.

"Here I am," the Eurasian beauty announced sleepily, floating languidly in through the crew hatch.

"Are you up to speed?"

"Aye aye, Captain," she announced sharply, as if a switch had been turned.

"You're our extraterrestrial expert. What is the protocol?"

"Mr. Chanticleer has followed the protocol exactly. Greetings and we come in peace in every known permutation. But as Lieutenant Lopez observes, this is our first real contact with an alien species. Their intelligence is obvious in their technology. Beyond that, we don't know. I would suggest beaming music."

"Music? What music?"

"I would start with classical. Something by Mozart or Brahms. Mozart's Number 40 in G Minor. Certainly, there are enough radio broadcasts to reach from here to Tau Ceti and back. If they are pulling in our transmissions, they must have heard it. There's nothing about it that's threatening or bellicose."

"Do we have that, Lopez?"

"Yes, Captain, as performed by the Berlin Philharmonic, Frances Edgar conducting. I also have versions from the New York Symphony and the Budapest Orchestra."

"Send it. Pipe it in here while you're at it. It can't hurt."

Seconds later, Mozart's violins danced through the ether and inside the cabin. Nunn noticed the subtle relaxation in posture, the all but imperceptible nodding of heads and tapping of feet. They often had music playing during the long hours. After fifty days in space, the crew sought diversion where they could. They listened to music. They watched old movies and television shows stored in the computer. They played cards.

And did other things, as well. The *Narwhal* carried a crew of twelve. They had all undergone rigorous psychological and physical testing, but they were, after all, human, and Nunn had resigned himself to the fact that some might pair off, and rivalries and animosities would manifest. The *Narwhal* stretched two hundred meters prow to stern, but there were no secrets aboard a star craft. Immasch and Lopez had been flirting for nearly two months...though if they'd hooked up, Nunn didn't know it.

He wished he could say the same for Ma and ship's doctor

Marybelle Marsten, a sleek redhead. Not even the shapeless coveralls could conceal her curves. She looked like a bagged Ferrari. Every now and then, he would catch Ma and Marsten silently mouthing to one another. Marsten dispensed prophylactics and birth control pills. He trusted she used them herself.

Personal entanglements aside, Nunn was proud of his crew, representing all races, creeds, and orientations. The giant Cray supercomputer at Los Alamos had selected them from over a million candidates on the basis of knowledge, proficiency, personality, compatibility, and physiology. They were the best of the best.

No one had expected them to encounter intelligent life. Earth had been screaming at the heavens since the dawn of radio, and no one had answered the call, conspiracy nuts notwithstanding. Nunn had been to the secret government lab at Dulce Base, inside Archuleta Mountain. There were no flying saucers, no mummified aliens. He had watched endless footage of countless UFO encounters. A few escaped explanation, but that was to be expected. They were only human. They could only do so much with the tools at hand. Some of the UFOs might be weather phenomena. Everyone associated with the base was familiar with the Sun Prairie Incident, in which a group of high school students had constructed an elaborate UFO out of balsa wood, clear plastic sheeting, and birthday candles. With an airtight pyramid protecting every side but the bottom, dozens of tiny birthday candles had created enough heat to send the craft skyward. Dozens of calls had flooded the Sun Prairie Police Department, the local news agencies, and the State Police.

Truax Field in Madison had dispatched two B-58s to intercept. Their turbulence had upended the pyramid, killing the candles, and sending it into Milton Thomas' back yard. Police had surrounded the device until they'd ascertained its nature.

The boys had turned themselves in the next morning and received a stern lecture on how they'd alarmed thousands of people and might have started a forest fire.

The ship faced by the *Narwhal*, however, was anything but a hoax—and its occupants were finally getting talkative.

"Incoming!" Ma said. "We are receiving a transmission on jade frequency 995. Shall I put it on the speakers?"

"Is it safe?" asked Nunn.

"It falls within the parameters of normal hearing and reveals mathematical order."

"Put it up."

The first four notes of Beethoven's Fifth Symphony sounded throughout the bridge. The crew listened in wonder as the great composer's most famous work filled every cubic centimeter of the room.

"Can you identify the version?"

Ma turned dials and tapped keys. "Nay, Captain. If this originated on Earth, it's not in our library, and I thought we had every version. Shall I transfer it to Ganymede?"

"Go ahead. It'll never get back to us in time, but at least they'll have a record."

The music stopped, leaving a pop of silence. Everyone looked at the hologram of the alien ship. Suddenly, a smooth baritone voice emanated from the speakers.

"Greetings, people of Earth. We are the Tremfya. That is the nearest approximation to a verbal representation of our world. We know almost everything there is to know about you, and you know nothing about us. You may refer to me as Rinvoq. I am a composite entity created for your understanding. We will be within transfer distance in forty-eight Earth minutes." The voice paused. "We anticipate this meeting with the keenest alacrity. We, too, have been searching for intelligent life for millennia. We do not broadcast through space, as do you, but we have been receiving your transmissions for many years, and enjoy and admire your culture. Who shall speak for you?"

"This is United Earth Alliance Captain Jefferson Nunn. Our mission: to seek out intelligent life. I must confess, we are dumbfounded. We never expected to fulfill our mission."

"Speak for yourself, Captain," Immasch coolly whispered, and winked at Lopez.

"We understand that you are apprehensive about first contact, as are we. Therefore, we propose an exchange of inner atmosphere prior to our actual meeting."

"Why don't we just meet over the hologram?"

"An excellent suggestion, Captain Nunn. We are prepared to do that. We are also prepared to stay as long as necessary to convince you of our good intentions. We have brought gifts, including food, gemstones, hand weapons, and seeds."

"We yearn to see your paintings and listen to your music," said Nunn.

A great silence filled the bridge. Rinvoq spoke in a low voice. "We don't *make* art." His voice swelled with enthusiasm and bonhomie. "That is why we so eagerly anticipate your arrival! I can't tell you how excited we all are. The whole planet! We have been listening to your music and watching your dramas for hundreds of your years! Before your broadcasts reached us, we were morose and emotionally exhausted. It had never occurred to us to tell tales and sing songs. Your culture saved our civilization. We are forever in your debt."

Nunn glanced at Ma, who gave him the thumbs up. She was recording everything. Nunn considered that it might be some elaborate practical joke, but the cross-cultural implications of that were too great. They hadn't come this far for slapstick.

"On Earth, we crave entertainment," said Nunn. "What you see is the result of commercial enterprise devoted to frivolity.

Oh, occasionally there's something worthwhile, like *Citizen Kane*..."

"Love *Citizen Kane*," Rinvoq said.

"But mostly, you get *My Three Sons*, *The Tonight Show*, *All In the Family*..."

"We were hoping you could explain that one to us."

"Had we known you were listening, we would have broadcast the great books. *Moby Dick*. *War and Peace*..."

"We admire you so much because we have no imagination."

"Nonsense," Nunn said. "It took imagination to build that spaceship."

"Your broadcasts have sustained us through times of trouble. They give us hope."

Garretson looked up. "Captain, ten minutes to rendezvous."

"Rinvoq, we are transmitting airlock specs. We are as excited as you for this historic encounter, but I must caution you, our history has been one of war and monstrous cruelty, as well as soaring hope and great artistic achievements. We will take precautions should this prove to be a deception."

"I understand. I propose an exchange. We invite five of your members to visit our ship at the same time that we visit yours."

"I can't spare five members, but I will send two volunteers."

Immediately, Ma and Immasch raised their hands.

"How many are aboard your craft?"

"Sixty-five, by your count. We have chosen six for this honor. We hope that you will accept them in the spirit in which they are offered, with respect and gratitude."

Nunn signaled the crew to arm themselves.

Garretson pointed toward the front of the ship, where a curving panel that resembled a windshield transmitted the images. The alien ship was visible to the naked eye, its concentric lights gleaming as it rotated slowly toward them, the peculiar horn circling. All watched in awe as it stopped one hundred meters in front of them.

A blue bubble emerged from an iris on the ship's nose.

"We are exchanging atmosphere samples," Rinvoq said.

At Nunn's command, Garretson released their own atmosphere sample in a gleaming cylinder. Propelled by air, the two samples passed within a meter of each other. The *Narwhal*'s robotic arm plucked the blue sphere from the ether and delivered it to analysis. Instantaneous results revealed air aboard the alien ship was 78% nitrogen and 21% oxygen. Perfectly calibrated to Earth's atmosphere.

"Captain Nunn, with your permission, we will send over our six representatives. We are prepared to welcome yours."

Nunn signaled for Ma and Immasch to suit up and use the shuttle. Every step was recorded. The crew was silent. The only sound was the clicking from the automatic ice maker.

Ma and Immasch entered the corridor to the shuttle. The door hissed shut behind them. Seconds later, the silver, cylindrical shuttle slid silently from its sideport. A flame erupted at its rear, and it beelined toward the strange vessel, passing the Tremfya shuttle at midpoint. The alien transport looked remarkably like their own.

"Docking," Chanticleer said. The ship clicked and whistled.

"Entering airlock."

All crew members save Garretson, who concentrated on the alien vessel, turned toward the inner airlock door. Hissing, it swung inward.

Out stepped Clint Eastwood, wearing a floor-length duster and his characteristic flat-brimmed hat, followed by Sally Field in a pleated skirt and a letter sweater, followed by Pam Grier as Coffy, followed by Johnny Carson, followed by Roger Moore as James Bond, and finally, Richard Pryor.

The crew stared, dumbstruck.

"'Bout time this town had a new sheriff," Clint said.

"You have a great profile," Sally Field said.

"Oh Meg," Coffy said. "You don't have any salad."

"If it weren't for Philo T. Farnsworth," Johnny Carson said, "we'd still be eating radio dinners."

"We all get our jollies one way or another," Roger Moore said.

"Everyone carries around his own monsters," Richard Pryor said.

For an instant, then, there was silence.

"How is this even possible?" Nunn said.

Clint Eastwood stepped forward, hands clasped behind his back. "Our true forms would be repulsive to you. We are highly malleable, however. Because of our great admiration for your culture, which has saved us from drudgery, we have adapted these forms that we believe will give both us and you great satisfaction." Clint tipped his hat. "It is a tribute to your culture, without which we would have no entertainment. We did not realize how empty our lives were until we began receiving your transmissions. On behalf of the entire Tremfya race, you have our utmost gratitude. We look forward to a long and mutually beneficial relationship. You have much to teach us, and we believe we have some modest discoveries that you will find useful in turn."

Chanticleer offered his hand. "It is our tradition..."

Clint Eastwood grabbed his hand and shook it. The Tremfyans went from crew member to crew member, shaking hands. Sally Field and Pam Grier hugged everyone. Pam began to cry.

"This is such a great moment," said Clint. "We have long yearned to discover another intelligent species..."

The crew's eyes filled with tears. This was the greatest moment in history.

"Break out the champagne!" Nunn sang.

Within minutes, everyone held a squeeze bottle of champagne. The newcomers expressed their delight.

"That'll put a kick in your pants," Clint said.

Pam Grier regarded her bottle with admiration. "Now this is more like it."

Johnny Carson held his in a toast. "Over your lips and down your throat, then back over your lips and down your coat."

Chanticleer put on Queen's "We Are The Champions," galvanizing the visitors into herky-jerky dance steps. Richard Pryor sang "Freddie's Dead." More champagne flowed. Clint danced with Sally Field. Soon, they were bumping into the fixed deck chairs and the control console. Crew members stood to protect their equipment. Chanticleer put on Little Richard.

One hour and five bottles later, Roger Moore tapped Clint on the shoulder. "I say, old chap, I'd like a turn with Miss Field if you don't mind."

Eastwood stepped back, putting his hand on the heretofore unseen revolver on his hip. "What if I *do* mind?"

"Then I'll have to convince you."

"Do your best, you limey fop."

Roger Moore slugged Eastwood on the jaw, causing him to stagger. Eastwood drew his revolver and plugged 007 three times in the chest. Moore fell to the deck, oozing green ichor. As the crew watched in horror, his shape drew within itself, spindling, atrophying, throwing out tendrils, becoming a loathsome, stinking thing. Nunn gasped as the creature's smell permeated the cabin, assaulting the eyes and skin, lacerating the lungs, urging every cell to rebel.

An invisible signal passed between Pryor and Grier as she drew a straight razor and he a pearl-handled revolver. Chanticleer burst back onto the bridge wearing a spacesuit, armed with a hand-held particle beam. He put beams through Pryor, puncturing the hull. The whistle of escaping air filled the cabin until the auto-seal took hold.

Sally Field reached into her mouth and pulled out a gleaming tentacle. Johnny Carson pulled a blaster out of his ass. Sally's first bolt incinerated Chanticleer. Another bolt grazed Garretson just as he drew his air gun and punctured the remaining Tremfyans.

"Captain," Garretson whispered. "What about Ma and Immasch?"

"Get them back here."

"Sir, what if they were transmitting?"

A blue bolt appeared between the two craft, causing the *Narwhal* to vibrate as electric current ripped through the crew's bodies.

"Shields up!" shouted Nunn.

Garretson was barely able to activate the shields before he collapsed from the pain of his injury. Suddenly, James Earl Jones' voice boomed through the ship.

"Traitorous scum! We came to you in good faith, and this is how you repay us? Watch now as we eviscerate your diplomats!"

The holo viewer flickered, revealing Ma and Immasch jerking spastically in a barrage of energy beams fired from the Tremfyan vessel.

"Mr. Garretson, hit them with the photon torpedoes," snapped Nunn.

"Sir, do you really..."

"Do it now before they suffer!"

Rival beams met at midpoint, creating a fusion that drew on every piece of matter within a thousand parsecs. The storm of debris obliterated their view of the enemy ship.

"Mr. Garretson, get us out of here!"

"Aye aye, captain, but with all this interference, there's no telling where we'll end up!"

"Just do it! All hands, strap in!"

Toxic smoke obscured their vision. The remaining crew members slapped on their helmets, sealing them to their uniforms, and strapped themselves in their seats, which doubled as crash pads.

Garretson sat at the controls, entering their destination via touch pad. He had to expose his finger, which peeled and began to bleed.

"Ten...nine...eight..." the ship recited in a monotone.

There was an instant of vertigo followed by a whipping sensation. The cockpit elongated to infinity, stretching forward and behind, then snapped back into place with a bone-rattling report. The *Narwhal* hurled through space like a shuriken throwing star.

It seemed to go on forever, but it only lasted two minutes. The ship automatically deployed its maneuvering jets, bringing it to a standstill.

"Mr. Garretson." Nunn coughed. "Lower the shields."

The shields came down. The crew looked out on a space unlike any they had ever seen, with brightly colored spheres dancing in the distance, worlds ringed like Saturn.

"Captain, the navcom is fried. I don't know where we are."

Nunn, Marsten, Garretson, and Lopez fell silent, realizing they might never see Earth again.

Their long-term prospects looked bleak. They would only survive aboard the *Narwhal* as long as life support functioned and they had enough food. Their only hope was that in this strange new universe, they might find a planet that could sustain life.

"Mr. Garretson, see if you can find us an Earthlike atmosphere," said Nunn.

"Captain, if you don't mind," said Garretson, "I'd like to say a few words first about Ma, Chanticleer, and Immasch."

"Go ahead. It's not like we're in any rush."

Garretson removed his helmet; the scrubbers had restored the atmosphere, making it breathable again.

He picked up Chanticleer's Bible and spoke solemnly as he held it. "'The Lord is nigh unto all them that call upon Him, to all that call upon Him in truth. May the good Lord bless our dear friends Chanticleer, Ma and Immasch, and conduct them unto the Kingdom of Heaven."

Just then, Lopez gasped and pointed. "Look! Something comes!"

On the holo viewer, they saw an alien vessel approach, a gleaming sliver surrounded by a helix of rings.

"Should I play them some music?" Lopez asked.

Nunn held up his hand. "Wait."

A wooden prow protruded from the alien craft through a swirl of what looked like white linen.

"Magnify it, Mr. Garretson," said Nunn.

As Garretson increased the magnification factor, the view of the alien craft filled the screen. It was surrounded by something frighteningly familiar—something suggesting that human influences other than entertainment had penetrated this far-flung sector of reality.

And the alien interpretations of those influences might be just as unwelcome as the movie star impersonations of the Tremfya had been.

The frighteningly familiar structure around the vessel looked just like a crown of thorns.

Nunn did not hesitate to give his next order. "Get us out of here, Mr. Garretson."

And Garretson did not hesitate to follow it.

❧

Mike Baron is the creator of *Nexus* (with artist Steve Rude) and *Badger,* two of the longest lasting independent superhero comics. *Nexus* is about a cosmic avenger 500 years in the future; *Badger* features a man with multiple personalities, one of whom is a costumed crimefighter. Mike has won two Eisners and an Inkpot award and written *The Punisher, Flash, Deadman* and *Star Wars,* among many other comics. He has published many novels, including *Banshees, Domain, Helmet Head, Whack Job, Biker,* and *Florida Man.* He lives in Colorado with his wife Ann and some dogs.

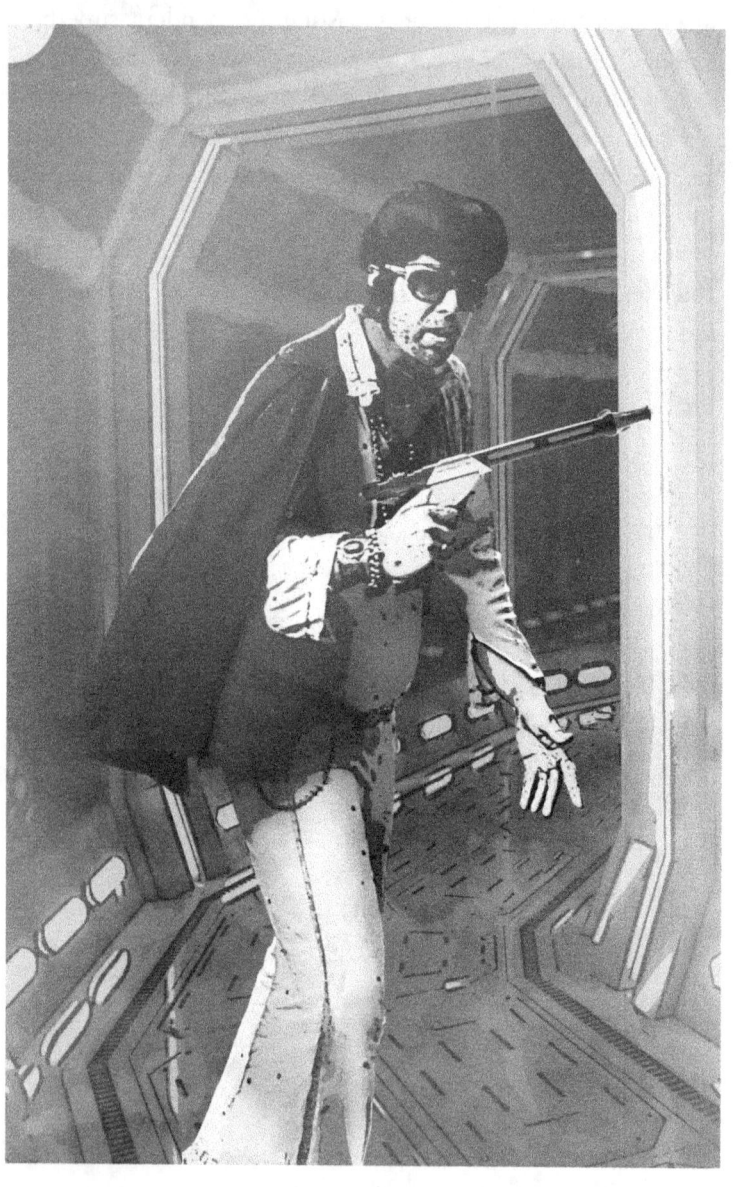

DEATH BY DISCO VACUUM IN SPACE REALLY SUCKS

MARK LESLIE

Isolation Station Alpha. Mars Orbit. 1999-05-25. [21:12:03]

One of the Bee Gees' most recognizable songs was pumping over the com system at a volume that made the metal walls of the corridor vibrate while Barry tried desperately to catch his breath and stay hidden behind the large janitorial cart.

Not that there were many places to hide on this relatively small space station.

But he needed to think, to keep his wits about him, and figure out a way to fight back. Or at least buy some time.

If only the music wasn't so damn loud, making it difficult to have a coherent thought.

It didn't help that he was high as balls.

"Stayin' alive, indeed," he whispered.

If only *he* could stay alive by staying hidden from the rampaging lunatic who was after him. He estimated he had another fifty, maybe sixty minutes tops, before help arrived.

"Come out, come out, wherever you are!" Dyson Harper yelled as he walked past the caddy, laser gun waving back and forth in sync with the sing-song way he delivered the line.

It was fortunate that he, too, was hopped up on ludes and blow, and thus didn't have the presence of mind to look behind the large caddy where Barry was crouched.

The man pranced by in his white Elvis-style jumpsuit with the glittering rhinestones and waist-length red and white cape, the blaster waving to and fro, sashaying to the beat of the music like John Travolta in the opening sequence of *Saturday Night Fever*. His thick black Elvis wig now shifted askew, making him look that much more twisted.

Not that he needed the look.

His actions were straight bat-out-of-hell.

Dyson Harper had gone crazy; had already killed the three other inhabitants of the space station. He was beyond reasoning with. That had already become startlingly clear, even with the drugs coursing through Barry's veins.

And now Dyson was intent on taking out Barry.

Thankfully, he had just walked past without even looking.

Barry figured he could slip out from behind the cart and duck back into the large rumpus room that had been temporarily converted into a 1970's style discotheque. The disco—which had since become a murder scene—had been set up for a planned celebratory evening before the shuttle from Mars was scheduled to meet up with them.

That shuttle was supposed to take the five inhabitants of Isolation Station Alpha to the planet's surface and an entry spot called Isolation Dome Beta. There, they were scheduled to undergo an additional fourteen days of quarantine before being integrated into the main network of connected domes and stations, officially claiming Martian citizenship and joining the growing population on the red planet.

But becoming a Martian citizen wasn't Barry's main concern anymore. He just needed a good place to hide.

And the rumpus room/discotheque might just be that hiding place. Going back to the room where the other murders had happened made sense. Barry could hide there and bide his time waiting for the shuttle to arrive while Dyson searched the rest of the space station. That hiding spot would likely buy him the most time, he thought.

His course of action chosen, Barry came out of his crouch. He rose at a bad angle, though, and his shoulder connected with the handle of the janitorial cart, sending it toppling on its side.

The crash was loud enough that it could be heard over the throbbing of the music.

Dyson turned, his beady eyes spotting Barry.

"I'm going to terminate you with extreme prejudice," he said, pointing the laser directly at Barry's head.

∾

[21:08:05 – About 4 Minutes Earlier]

Michael W. Lucas was dancing with the vacuum when he was killed in the most bizarre manner that Barry had ever seen.

The portly bald man had always been a little odd, so when he grabbed the stick vacuum cleaner, flipped it upside down and started slow dancing with it, with the side of his face pressed up against the power head of the vacuum, nobody really batted an eye.

They were all laughing, in fact, as Lucas caressed the vacuum cleaner wand while singing along to the Johnny Rivers tune "Swayin' to the Music (Slow Dancin')."

It was when he pretended to French kiss the vacuum that things got weird.

No, not just weird. Things had already been weird, with the odd "leaving this stage of the migration" 70s theme party Lucas had been adamant about hosting. The man had been obsessed with two things: the 70s and J.R.R. Tolkien. But not just Tolkien; specifically, the brutish species of orcs the author had made popular.

The man, who, come to think of it, looked a little bit like an orc himself (a hairstyle he likely adopted because it was more orc-like) surprised them, on that last day, with an entire wardrobe and set of trunks dedicated to 70s clothing and props.

Each of the five Martian migrants had been allotted two large, portable, upright wardrobe closets about six feet high, five feet across, and three feet deep, along with four trunks. Those containers were all they could take with them on their permanent migration to Mars. And Lucas had wasted more than half of his space with kitschy 70s costumes and paraphernalia.

"C'mon," he'd said to the other four that morning as they finished off what would be their last breakfast on the space station. "We have about twelve hours left in this tin can. We're one step closer to becoming citizens of another planet. Maybe only a thousand people so far have done this. We are freakin' pioneers, man. Let's party. But let's do it 70s style."

The 70s were an appropriate era to celebrate because that's when the space program had really taken off. The summer 1969 moon landing had heralded a proper space age, with NASA accepting capital funding from multiple international businesses and individual investors, also collaborating with foreign superpowers so they could effectively double down on their continued exploratory missions. By the time the Apollo program had reached its twenty-fifth mission in 1975, people had been able to live on the surface of the moon for a full month. From that perch, one step deeper into the cosmos, humankind's thirst for pushing further had continued, leading to the current Mars colonization project that Barry, Lucas, and the others were preparing to join.

But first, there would be a party.

To get ready for it, Lucas had spent the rest of the day decorating and programming the rumpus room into a 70s-style disco and passed out era-appropriate clothing, costumes, and wigs.

The drugs he had hidden in the trunk didn't come out until their costumes were on, the regular lights went down, the disco ball was engaged, and the music started up.

"What do orcs want more than anything else?" Lucas had asked the group, prior to revealing the drugs.

The four colonists had looked at each other, recognizing the setup for yet another of his groan-inducing jokes.

"I don't know," Warren had said. "But I'll bite. What do orcs want more than anything else?"

"More doors."

"Huh?"

"Moor doors. *Mordor*. Get it?"

"It's a Tolkien reference," Henry had said, rolling his eyes. "Should have known."

Lucas let out a laugh. "And what do four men on a multi-month mission to another planet want more than anything else?"

Warren had shrugged his shoulders. "I don't know."

"A day at the beach?" Barry had asked.

Dyson shook his head. "An escape from your puns?"

"A hot woman?" Henry had smiled.

"No," Lucas had told them. "More drugs."

That's when Lucas had shown them his stash.

There had been a mixture of hallucinogens, nitrates, stimulants, and psychoactive drugs, more than enough for all of them.

"Let's get down! Let's boogie!" Lucas had said. "Time to

party like it's 1999...'cause it *is*. Let's *get* down before we *go* down to Mars!"

Though Henry and Warren hadn't been into the 70s theme, only donning their assigned wardrobes begrudgingly, Barry had noticed that most of them didn't hesitate to participate when the drugs were handed out. Only Dyson had seemed reluctant to claim his share.

"I-I don't know," Dyson had said. "I've never had anything stronger than aspirin."

At the time, Barry had thought it was funny that the man in the Vegas-years Elvis getup was the one most resistant to consuming the drugs. He hadn't thought more of it.

And none of them had considered possible side effects. Not until the incident on the disco floor, at least.

Lucas had been mouthing the words to the Johnny Rivers song, his face pressed up against the power head of the vaccum cleaner like he was dancing cheek to cheek with his lover, making them all laugh.

"Stop it," Warren yelled. "You're killing me! I'm going to pee my pants!"

That had made everyone laugh even harder.

It had been such a bizarre moment. Five men from Earth in orbit around Mars on a space station, laughing like hyenas as they watched another man on the dance floor swaying along to the music with a stick vacuum, against the backdrop of an over-sized digital monitor that Lucas had programmed to look exactly like kitschy wood paneling from a 1970s basement. The multi-colored lights of the disco ball had been swirling around the floor, ceiling, and walls, a parallel to the way the space station was rotating as it revolved around the planet below.

That's when Dyson, who hadn't been laughing, strode over to Lucas like he was about to ask to cut in. It had sent the others into a more intense round of laughter.

Everything had happened so quickly after that, yet it had also seemed to Barry as if it were in slow motion.

The Johnny Rivers song had ended, and another ballad, this one from the Commodores, had started playing.

Dyson had reached forward and tapped Lucas on the shoulder as Lionel Ritchie crooned on, thanking the woman he was singing to for the times and memories she had given him.

Lucas had made another goofy grin and twisted around and away from Dyson, refusing to give up his partner. Wanting to keep her for another song.

Dyson had tried to tap his shoulder again, but Lucas had twirled around one more time, shaking his head adamantly.

Then, Lucas had spun the vacuum stick around and appeared to be pretending to make out with the "mouth" of the device.

Only he hadn't been pretending at all. His lips were actually *connected* to it.

"Leave her alone!" Dyson had yelled. "She's my sister!"

It hadn't been clear that Lucas's tongue was actually thrusting into the beater bar until Dyson reached down and switched the vacuum on.

Lucas had let out a wail as his tongue and lips were pulled by the suction and turning beater bar head. He'd managed to wrench most of his face free, but blood and hunks of flesh had been left behind.

With his left hand, Dyson had grabbed Lucas by the throat and squeezed tight. The portly, bald man had reached up, trying to pry his fingers away, but it was no use. Dyson stood six foot three, was made of solid muscle, and likely had a good fifty pounds on the shorter man. Lucas' eyes were bugging out as he struggled to force oxygen into his lungs.

With his right hand, Dyson had grasped the handle of the vacuum cleaner, pulled it back, and then slammed it three times into Lucas' head. Ironically, the blows were done in time to the chorus of "Three Times a Lady" that was playing in the background.

Once.

Twice.

Three times.

Lucas' eyes had bugged out further as his head recoiled with each blow. Dyson had turned his own head to look at the other three crewmates who were watching in complete disbelief. Dyson had let out a maniacal laugh, as if seeing them standing there, slack-jawed, was one of the funniest things in the world. He'd waited a moment for Lionel Ritchie to repeat the words of the chorus, then had run out of patience.

"Ah, screw it!" Dyson had let out another peal of laughter.

That's when he'd started to viciously and repeatedly beat Lucas with the vacuum head. Over and over and over.

Barry, Warren, and Henry had just stood there watching.

Eventually, Lucas' body had gone completely limp, and Dyson had let it collapse to the floor. He'd stood there then, his eyes going wide, flitting back and forth between the dead man on the floor and the half-destroyed stick vacuum in his right hand.

"What have I done?" He'd kicked the dead body. "Look what you've made me do!" Cradling the broken vacuum in his hands, he'd collapsed to his knees. "Damn you all to hell!"

Henry had been the first to overcome the shock and walked up to him. "Listen, Dyson..."

That's when Dyson had reached into a pocket on his jumpsuit, pulled out a laser gun, and aimed it at Henry.

Henry had stepped back, thrusting his hands in the air.

Dyson had let the vacuum go and gotten to his feet, keeping the weapon trained on the man.

Henry had taken a step back.

Dyson had taken a step forward.

"Listen, Dyson," Henry repeated. "This was an accident. We're all high. Let's just put down the laser and talk this over."

"No, I'm *not* going to listen," Dyson had snapped. "I'm not going to talk this over, either. I'm sick to death of *everything*. I'm tired of being a *good boy*. I'm tired of following the *rules*. *I'm as mad as hell, and I'm not going to take this anymore!*"

With that, he'd fired the laser, catching Henry directly in the chest.

The discharge had functioned the way it was designed, burning through human flesh and bone. Henry had fallen on his back, a perfectly sculpted crater, six inches in diameter, carved into his chest.

The smell of cauterized flesh had filled the dance hall as Lionel Ritchie continued wailing, one last time as the song finished, that he loved his woman.

"I love the smell of burnt flesh in the morning," Dyson had muttered.

Just as the opening bass beats to *Stayin' Alive* had started up, Warren had leaped forward. Dyson had been quick, though, sweeping the weapon in his direction and firing again. The energy blast had caught the upper left side of the man's face and burned off almost half of his head.

As Warren's body fell to the floor, Barry had turned and bolted for the door.

He'd heard the laser gun fire another blast and felt the whoosh of the beam as it flashed by the left side of his head.

That's three shots, Barry had thought, making it to the doorway before another shot was fired.

Laser guns, he knew, only held enough of a charge for *four* shots.

That meant there was only a single shot left...so maybe, Barry still had a chance to survive Dyson's rampage.

~

Or maybe not. Knocking over the janitorial cart he'd been hiding behind may have put the kibosh on his survival.

As soon as the cart hit the floor, Dyson turned, raising the laser pistol. "I'm going to terminate you with extreme prejudice," he said, pointing the laser directly at Barry's head.

"No, please!"

"I know what you're thinking," Dyson said, his beady, drug-glazed eyes fixed on Barry. "Did he fire four times, or only three? Well, to tell you the truth, in all the excitement of what's been going down, I kind of lost track of it myself.

"But being that this is a Maxum 4, the most powerful laser ever made, you've got to ask yourself one question: Do I feel lucky? Well, do ya, *punk?*"

Barry recognized the line that Dyson had almost quoted verbatim. It was from a scene in the movie *Dirty Harry*, starring Clint Eastwood.

It was then, recalling other things that Dyson had said and done during his rampage, that Barry realized Dyson had fallen into some sort of trippy 1970s pattern. He was quoting and acting out things from the 70s.

"Wait!" Barry thrust out a hand as a pivotal scene from the *Star Wars* franchise rushed into his mind. Perhaps, he could twist what was happening into that scene, see if the drug-addled mind of his shipmate would follow along.

"Dyson, help me," said Barry. "You're our only hope!"

Dyson stopped, the expression on his face immediately softening. "What? What did you just say?"

Barry reached for other quotes from *Star Wars*. "Dyson, these are not the answers you're looking for."

Dyson shook his head. "No, you're right, they're not."

"Dyson, I've got a bad feeling about this."

Dyson lowered the weapon. "What have I done?"

"Dyson, you killed him. You killed Lucas. You killed Warren. You killed Henry. But not me." He let out a long, rasping breath. "Because, Dyson, *I am your father*."

"No!" Dyson yelled, immediately falling into the role of Luke Skywalker from the film.

"Dyson, you do not yet realize your importance," said Barry. "You have only begun to discover your power. Join me, and I will complete your training. With our combined strength, we can end this destructive conflict and bring order to the galaxy."

Dyson was shaking his head. "No, no, it's not true. It's impossible. You're not my father."

"Search your feelings, you *know* it to be true."

"Noooooo!" howled Dyson.

"It is your destiny. Join me, and together we can rule the galaxy as father and son."

Shaking his head, Dyson picked up the laser and considered it.

"Come with me, Dyson. It is the only way!"

"Noooo!" Dyson fired the laser at his right hand. The blast took his hand off at the wrist.

Barry took the opportunity to rush him, tackling him to the floor. Grabbing a metal dustpan from the overturned cart, he used it to club Dyson's head repeatedly.

Eventually, Dyson fell still, his face beaten to a bloody pulp. Barry took a deep breath, then slowly got to his feet and surveyed the mess in the corridor.

It was nasty, to say the least, and even nastier in the rumpus room.

He took another step back, then righted the janitorial cart and decided to keep himself busy. He had maybe an hour before the shuttle would arrive.

He might as well tidy up as much as he could. Mop the floor, vacuum up the mess, soak up some of the blood stains. Make it a bit nicer for the next set of interstellar travelers to come through. Besides, it would keep him busy and not having to think about what had just gone down, that he had just killed a man after watching three other men get murdered.

He started up the vacuum that was attached to the janitorial cart. It echoed through the corridor.

As long as he finished the cleanup before the shuttle docked and opened the airlock, no one would be the wiser that anything terrible had happened on the station. No one in the arriving shuttle would be able to hear it from outside the facility, any more than they would have heard the sounds of the murders that had just happened. Real life wasn't much like the movies in that regard; the noise of spaceship dogfights and explosions in certain 70s scifi films had not been true to the laws of physics.

Though now that Barry thought about it, he realized one 70s SF flick had gotten it right, at least when it came to the tagline. Smiling, he kept vacuuming the floor, recalling that line —which was perfect, with his own special twist, for the moment at hand.

In space, no one can hear you clean.

Mark Leslie is the author of more than twenty books and close to one hundred short stories. His speculative fiction has earned him nomination for an Aurora Award and Honorable Mention in *The Year's Best Fantasy and Horror*. Mark is the editor of the science fiction anthologies *North of Infinity II* and

Tesseracts Sixteen and is a recurring series editor for *Fiction River*. He grew up on a diet of John Wyndham, Larry Niven, Joe Haldeman, and Piers Anthony in terms of books, as well as *Star Wars, Battlestar Galactica* (the original TV series), *Star Trek: The Next Generation,* and *Space: 1999.* Most of Mark's elementary school photos show him to be a definite child of the 70s. You can find Mark online at www.markleslie.ca.

THE FLOATING HEADS OF ANTIOCH
BOW BEFORE THEM!

CRAIG MARTELLE

"Bow before your gods!" The black-robed curator shook his staff at the subjects. A carved wooden head floated above the ground, its visage forever scowling at the craven knaves prostrated in the dirt. The landscape rolled to the horizons, and planted fields and wildflowers rioted for dominance.

The massive head floated along behind a woman wearing a shiny black bodysuit. She did not seem to be of the same world as the curator and the subjects.

"All manner fair, Gort," she called. "Sweetness of the air, nectar provided by our god Draezul." She gestured broadly to take in the floating head nearby.

The curator bowed deeply to the visitors. When he rose, his mouth stayed neutral, not a smile, not a frown. Guarded. "Your Grace."

She stroked the image's sullen brow. It bounced serenely in disdain.

The subjects kept their foreheads pressed to the ground as she passed. One dirty farmhand turned to gaze upon her taut form. Gort tapped the man on the back and shook his head, and the hand looked away. The curator took the opportunity to do what the minions could not—admire her shape. He was a curator, one of seven. She was the priestess.

"What brings you around here, Your Grace?"

She slowed. Draezul floated past and kept moving up the road. "Feeling guilty, Gort? Are you ashamed of your area's weak production?" She glanced over her shoulder at him. He stopped in his tracks, bowing his head to her.

"Production is up. You'll see that if you visit the transloading facility."

"Why are your people working without equipment?" she wondered, looking down upon the unkempt and dirty souls on their knees beside the road. Even though she was eye to eye with Gort, she looked down on him, too.

"Priestess, repairs have not come from the city. They have not come!" He stepped back and said a short prayer. "Forgive my insolence, Your Grace."

The priestess turned to face him. "Only the gods can forgive, Gort." The floating head rose into the air. Lightning flashed, scarring a long section of the road to the city. Draezul rotated and floated back to where the priestess and Gort stood. It hovered over the curator. The seconds stretched to a minute.

Sweat started to roll down Gort's face. He bowed, and when the burden of bowing became too great yet not enough, he dropped to his knees and rested his forehead on the ground.

The priestess strolled away, taking in the sights as a casual traveler might. The head followed.

She spoke over her shoulder indifferently but commandingly. "Come, curator."

He jumped to his feet, but his head started to swim, and his knees threatened to fail him. He leaned heavily on his staff. After a few breaths, the feeling passed. He took a measured step forward, then another. With his recovered balance, he kicked dirt at those still cowering by the side of the road.

"Get back to work," he implored them. He glared at the woman before him. She remained an enigma.

The curators should be priests of the floating gods, he thought. *I'm little more than a field hand.*

The priestess walked along without a care in the world, while the very weight she seemed to have thrown off landed squarely on Gort's shoulders. He struggled, wondering if the carved god was punishing him.

I serve you, Master, not her, he prayed as he hurried to catch up.

They traveled the road for two hours before speaking again.

"Are you not curious, Gort?"

"It's not my place to question, Your Grace." Gort bowed his head even though she was in front of him and not watching.

She stopped and motioned for him to walk beside her as she led Draezul toward Antioch, the capital city.

In the distance, trains cruised, going and coming from the city. The lumbering giants squealed on the tracks, coming from the outlying regions, bringing raw materials, bringing foodstuffs.

Bringing life, while the priestess walked because the gods demanded it. Leave the equipment for the basics of life. Manpower was cheap. Keeping the equipment running was expensive.

"No vehicles for personal use." Gort repeated the standing orders. "Surely, our gods deserve to ride."

"Surely," the priestess parroted, but she didn't hesitate or look forlornly at the trains running along the twin lines of tracks. She scanned the fields on both sides of the road. Farmhands worked them, scattered like clouds across the sky and moving just as slowly and with as much purpose.

"I appreciate the opportunity to join you today," Gort tried. He wasn't sure if he was being led to his death, given a mission, or being punished by having to walk three hours out of his region and three hours back. He'd do as commanded. It didn't mean he had to like it.

He didn't press the priestess when she continued walking without speaking. The closer they came to the city, the more he expected to be thanked for joining her and turned loose to walk back home.

He had no business in Antioch, no reason to stay.

One always needed a reason to be in Antioch. The people there were different. Even curators were not free to roam like the citizens of Antioch. The approaches to the city remained mostly empty. People did not move about freely.

The priestess walked down the middle of the road, with Draezul following. Gort moved to the side in deference to the floating head's triumphant return. There were three floating heads, and never more than one was absent from the city at any point in time. They ruled from there, but occasionally, they graced the minions with their presence. The lone priestess escorted them every time. Three gods, but only one priestess.

Ours is not to question why, Gort told himself.

The main gates opened as they approached. The priestess slowed, and Gort matched her. She stopped and faced him. He bowed. "It has been a pleasure to accompany you, Your Grace. I shall return to my region and redouble my efforts to get our equipment repaired to increase production. Your guidance has not fallen on deaf ears."

"No." Her face didn't change. Her posture remained the same as it always was. No aggression. She had delivered the short answer to the unasked question, *"May I go?"*

Gort's heart started to race. It was time for her to put him out of her misery. He waited. The next move was not his to make. He served at the pleasure of the gods.

Draezul floated between the two massive gates standing between stout walls rising ten times the height of a tall man. His thunderous voice boomed.

"I am Antioch, and Antioch is me!"

Gort fell to his knees, ears ringing from the sound. He had not heard a floating god speak before. It had always been the priestess.

What about the other two gods? Are each of them Antioch, too? The uncomfortable questions grated on the curator's soul. He fought his blasphemy, tamping it into the farthest recess of his mind.

He fervently whispered a prayer to Draezul. "May the gods cast their light upon the unworthy for another day of joy and good fortune." The curator waited until he was given the order to rise.

The priestess stood tall, reveling in the praise given to the floating head. Draezul moved away from her, casting off the invisible tether between the two when they were outside the city. The citizens were within, most dressed like the priestess in shining body suits revealing every curve of their lithe bodies. The curator pulled his robe closer around him.

"Come with me," she said and walked away without waiting to see if Gort followed. She and he both knew he had no choice. The power of the floating heads compelled him, even if it was only within his mind.

He hurried after her, staying one step to the left and one behind. An array of shaped stone buildings gave way to the power and beauty of others crafted of steel and glass. They stood like beacons on the coast, reflecting the midday sun and increasing the intensity of the heat.

The priestess lifted her face toward the sun and spread her arms. "Does the wonder ever cease to amaze, Gort?"

Under his heavy robe, the curator was sweating. He hadn't had a drink in hours. Was she to deny him until his demise? Was he supposed to ask?

"Your Grace," he started, "may we stop for a drink of water?"

"No." Her answer confirmed what Gort had been thinking. He was on his way to shackles and torture. His time had come. If only he had held his tongue. He could go without food, but water? He was already parched. "We will drink when we reach the hall, water as sweet as nectar squeezed from the freshest peaches, and eat sweetmeats like you've never tasted before."

"I am not worthy, Your Grace." Gort's reply was strangled and forced, while the priestess' words rolled from her tongue, as light as the breath upon which they were carried.

"None of us are worthy, but the feast is served nonetheless because the gods provide."

At the next magnificent, terraced structure, the doors opened as the priestess approached. She stepped through. Gort stayed close, not sure if the doors would remain open for him. They swished closed once he had passed through.

The floor of polished marble continued across the brightly lit entryway. Gort could not see the sky, but the light of the sun was inside.

He had heard of these marvels in rumors whispered in the darkest shadows of family homes, stories made up to wow the unsophisticated like him. He had never believed them, but here he was. And here was a world completely foreign to him. A curator!

Gort squinted against the wash of light. Sweat streamed down his body. Only a little farther to walk. Their destination had to be close. His head started to swim. His legs felt weak and acted on their own. He staggered, stumbled, and fell heavily into a nearby wall.

"I apologize, Your Grace, for my weakness." He thought he spoke aloud but could not be sure as the world slipped away from him. Darkness consumed his final thoughts of abject failure.

∼

When he next opened his eyes, it was to the welcome embrace of the dusky twilight and a soft bed.

"You're awake," a young man's voice said. "I'm Dewey, the official physician for the central hall."

"Official...physician?" Gort croaked. He tried to sit up, but tubes were taped to his arms. When he attempted to pull one off, Dewey stopped him.

"You need a little more fluid. Give it until this bag is drained, and I'll turn you loose."

"What happened?"

"Dehydrated. You didn't drink sufficiently before or during your journey here. The high priestess feels bad about not seeing your distress until it was too late. She hopes she'll be able to make it up to you somehow."

Gort tried to clear his eyes, but he couldn't rub them. He settled for pressing his face against each shoulder in turn. "The priestess feels bad for me? I was weak. I must apologize! Please let me go."

"Not until you're ready. Don't make me restrain you." The young man with short brown hair and aquamarine eyes loomed over the curator.

"Shackles!" Gort knew it. He had deluded himself into thinking he wouldn't be tortured, but his fears were coming true.

"We don't use shackles. This is the health and well-being directorate. I don't usually get patients because we're healthy in Antioch. You were a fun distraction from my daily duties. I should thank you for that."

"Distraction? I don't understand."

"Genetic manipulation to improve muscle resilience isn't the most exciting work, but it ensures our continued existence. The rewards are exceptional," the doctor said softly, smiling. He didn't seem to be a threat. Gort calmed himself.

"I don't understand your words, but if you say it's important, then it must be. People must believe in the work they do."

"*People.* Yes. I like how you put that."

He hummed as he ran through a series of examinations using equipment that never touched Gort's skin. He checked a device next to him, a screen that showed whatever the instruments measured. The numbers and lines meant nothing to Gort. He considered himself advanced, but he had only been in Antioch one time before, and he hadn't been inside any of the buildings then.

Never had he seen anything like this. In his region, they used herbs and unguents to treat injuries. There were no instruments such as those used by the physician.

"Can we get something like this for the wheat region?" Gort asked, feeling much like his old self.

"Of course not. This equipment is sensitive and in limited supply. It is for the exclusive use of the citizens."

"Aren't we?"

"Antioch? You are not, but Priestess Regina wanted you taken care of, so you are taken care of."

The priestess has a name? Gort wanted to know all that had been denied him.

Dewey removed a needle from one arm and a second from

the other. After putting a small bandage on each, he invited Gort to stand.

"How do you feel?"

"I am clear of mind and strong of body. I thank you for your tender ministrations to restore my health when I showed only weakness. Praise be to the gods for their mercy."

"Yes. The gods. Of course. Follow me, please." Dewey walked into a corridor, and the light shocked Gort's senses. "Reduce brightness by fifty percent."

At the doctor's words, the lights dimmed to a tolerable level.

Gort resisted the urge to articulate his wonder at the experience of an indoor sun. In his region, some of the buildings related to the transloading facility had indoor lighting. They were both mechanical and magical. They worked by an arrangement of wires and switches, but how? That was the magic.

The will of the gods? Gort had that opinion, as had everyone else. It was easy to substantiate and perpetuate.

It begged the question. Why was the priestess showing him things that would shake his faith?

Might he become a citizen of Antioch? He hoped so. He watched the man before him, the bodysuit leaving little to the imagination. Nearly everyone in Antioch wore them, but in this building, he had seen nothing else. Would he get one? He didn't look like the citizens. He was soft in the midsection and narrow through the shoulders, but strong of leg from walking. His hair had thinned, while those from Antioch sported heavy manes, thick and vibrant.

Dewey turned down a side corridor and faced the third door down. It opened for him without a word or motion. He gestured for Gort to go inside.

He nodded to the physician. "Thank you for your help. Peace."

Inside, Gort found a small room decorated all in white, with a table set near the far wall and a single chair centered before it.

"Sit. Someone will be along shortly."

The walls were pristine, without a hint of brush strokes or color variation. Gort could discern no seam between the wall and the floor. Pristine. *Antiseptic.* The door had disappeared, blended into the wall. If he hadn't just walked through it, he would not have known where it had been.

Gort waited and waited. Finally, the call of nature became too strong to resist. He stood and walked around the room, looking for a way to contact someone. He knocked on the wall where he knew the door to be. There was no reply. He had been locked in, left on his own to perish in the sterile world of Antioch's greatest building.

"I must have need of an outhouse, or a commode if that's what is available."

Gort jumped when the wall bulged and a commode slid out of it. He studied it only briefly, the need to go overwhelming reason. He relieved himself, and the commode disappeared.

Next, a sink slid from the wall. Two nozzles were positioned above it. He twisted and turned them, unsure of what to do. He waved his hands under one and then the other. The first gave him nothing. The second spurted soap onto his hands. He sniffed it...and realized there must be a reason the first nozzle hadn't dispensed anything yet.

With the realization came understanding. He soaped his hands, then held them under the first nozzle. Water ran freely to wash the residue away.

With his hands still in the sink, fresh air blew heartily from the front. He held his hands in the breeze until they dried.

"A test?" he said aloud. He looked to see if someone was watching; despite the lack of windows and peepholes, he didn't discount the possibility. "A drink of water, please."

The sink returned with the nozzle facing upright, and a jet of water arced upward. He dipped his face into it and drank.

Water as sweet as nectar, the priestess had said. *Shouldn't all water taste the same? Surely our water has never tasted like that. It is warm, with bits floating. If it looks too bad, we filter it through a sleeve. Otherwise, we drink it as is. It quenches all the same.* He drank more and agreed. This water *was* different. *It was better.*

When he stepped back, the water stopped, and the sink disappeared into the wall.

"I am hungry," he said and watched for a section of the wall to move and deliver an apple or even a sandwich of sausage and hard cheese, delectables from the neighboring region, held between slices of the wheat region's bread.

A small alcove appeared within the wall. A plate with four squares of bread sat on a small table. Gort took one of the squares and examined it—heavy, more like a cookie bar than bread. He took a bite. Sweet, but not. He continued eating and consumed all four. In the end, he felt full.

The far wall opened, and three chairs with occupants slid forward to fill the space behind the table. The high priestess was in the middle. At her sides were a man and a woman who both looked strikingly like the priestess. *Siblings?*

They didn't speak. Gort saw them staring and realized he was standing. He hurried to the empty chair, to find that it was lower than theirs. He was forced to look up at them.

"My apologies, Your Grace." He bowed his head and waited.

"Gort. Curator. Wheat region," the young man said.

The curator waited. The man hadn't made it a question. Gort was used to speaking when talking to his people, but not when it came to the priestess and her folk. The bodysuits set them apart. The priestess wore black. The man wore fire-red.

The other woman wore a white so bright it blended with the wall behind her.

Gort cleared his throat as he tried to continue smiling pleasantly at the three watching him. He started to sweat under their relentless stares.

Finally, Gort had to say something. He was withering. "What have I done wrong, Your Grace?"

"What you have done is shown a different understanding than the others. You knew that your shipments had increased. Others would not have been so bold with their claim. Can you guess the difference between this year and last?"

"I would estimate that we've added one train car in ten."

"Ten percent." She looked at her colleagues and nodded. "The exact number is nine point six. Very good, Gort. I thought there was something different about you, but there's also much of the same, isn't there?"

"I don't understand, Your Grace." Gort wasn't playing coy. He was confused.

"He figured out the system in the room despite how unnatural it was for him," the other woman said. "It is not intuitive for the outsiders."

"Estimated IQ?" the priestess asked the man.

"Roughly ninety-seven, but the number is not based on cognitive studies. Rather, it is an estimate of where his perception ranks against other humans'. Let me have him for a day, and I'll get you a real number."

None of it meant anything to Gort. They were discussing him in a detached way as if he weren't there, or it was irrelevant that he heard their deliberations.

"I think not, Belzan. We have what we need from him." She turned to face the curator. "Gort, we have chosen you as our liaison with the outside world."

"I saw a number of people like me." He gestured at his robes. "Are they also liaisons?"

"No. They are on their way outside the city to work in biomass fulfillment. I mean, they'll return to the fields and the pastures to work in production. While your region was up nearly ten percent, the others are static, identical to the prior years. We need you to encourage all the regions as you have done your own."

"But the gods..." The priestess raised an eyebrow, but Gort didn't stop. "The gods have clearly smiled on the wheat because of our piety and worship."

The three looked at each other. The woman to Gort's right spoke. "I'm sure that answer is meant in all humility." She waved a hand dismissively at the look she received from Belzan. She talked to Gort. "It came because of your personal engagement and sharing a vision with your people. Your efforts that delivered, not the gods. We want more of that while we withdraw to more intellectual pursuits."

Regina, the high priestess, took over. "You see, it is only now that we feel we have someone to represent our interests fairly and ensure that those within the city have the food and raw materials they need. The regions surrounding Antioch will continue to provide, but we don't have to be out there. You will take care of it for us."

"The floating heads, our gods..." Gort said softly.

"Indeed," the priestess said. "Your job is to raise production. You have our leave to start immediately."

Gort remained seated. The door appeared in the wall and opened.

The priestess stood and spoke. "The gods shall reward you in ways you cannot imagine."

"Will the floating heads continue to visit us?" Gort asked, but he already knew. The priestess opted for a non-answer.

"The gods will do as the gods do." She gestured at the open doorway.

"Your Grace," Gort said, bowing his head as he stood. He strode from the room, happy to be out of there.

Soaked in sweat, he felt as if he squished when he walked, but the hallway offered a cool breeze. He let the air flow through his robe to comfort him. Yet another woman, a younger version of the priestess, waited to escort him out. "What do you call this place?"

She looked at him oddly before answering. "It is called the Ziggurat."

"The Ziggurat of Antioch. A fine place to pass a few hours. Your hospitality is exceptional, and I thank you for it. I would implore you to be so kind as to pass on my appreciation to the Priestess Regina since I did not before departing the white room."

"Of course. Is there anything else you need before you leave?"

"Your name, please, and water as sweet as nectar?" Gort ventured. He wasn't ready to go. He expected that he would never be back. They were closing the city to outsiders like him. Good enough to provide the food, but not to eat it with them. "I would like my staff back. I'm not sure what happened to it."

"I am known as Axaendara, and your staff will be near the exit." She pointed at a doorway near them. "We can stop in there for water." She guided the curator into the room. It seemed small when they entered but expanded into more than a single space. It was white in the way of the others Gort had seen.

"Thank you, Axaendara. You look familiar, like Regina. Are you a sister?" Gort chanced.

"Sister? We are all sisters and brothers here ever since the crash, but we are back to thriving again, thanks to the local population. To people like you."

"I love to help but can't take credit. There are a lot of people out there working for the greater good." Gort watched Axaendara closely.

She shrugged indifferently. "Your water." She stepped away from the fountain. A glass was there so he could take his fill from a running stream. He indulged himself, but only sipped it. Axaendara watched him, cocking her head slightly in surprise when he didn't simply drain the glass.

"Antioch, a city of wonders. None of these advances are outside the city besides those that help bring materiel in," Gort said casually. He walked slowly with one hand behind his back, pacing and looking at the floor while watching his escort from the corner of his eye.

"Of course," she replied. He turned and stared at her, using the technique they had used on him. He remained that way. A little sip here and there, never taking his eyes from hers. She tried to match him but finally caved. "We don't have enough to supply all, not if we wish to live in the manner to which we were accustomed. Only recently have we returned to it. Eventually, we will expand, but that will take generations for the outsiders, who have annoyingly short lifespans."

"Annoyingly short. Indeed." Gort nodded knowingly, but his mind reeled from the revelation. "Outsiders have always been as they are, but Antioch? From where have you come, dear lady?"

Gort refilled his glass. Her resistance had broken. He had no need to continue staring her down.

"The stars, a place called Antioch. We have been here for a millennium, and we will be here for millennia more before we can return. In between, we will make do."

"Of course. It is beautiful, is it not?" Gort asked to perpetuate the conversation, but Axaendara inched toward the door. His time was drawing to a close.

"It is the best we can do with the lack of resources we are forced to deal with."

"And that is my task, Axaendara! I am to go out and expedite the increase in production to better supply what you need. I live to serve."

"Although you need not understand to serve, you are an exception. You have been chosen."

"How so?" Gort put the glass down and acceded to her body language that it was time to go.

She talked while they walked. "Every generation produces a leader who is able to get more. You are at the forefront of the current human generation."

"I don't know what to say," Gort replied. He questioned why she was sharing with him, but the physician had been forthcoming, too. Only the priestess had been elusive. And the gods... Gort sucked air between his teeth and clenched his jaw shut when the reality dawned on him. *The floating heads of Antioch are a lie!*

She took Gort to a storage area, where his staff had been tossed in with a variety of items from the mundane to the fantastic. He took his staff along with two other items, both made of metal, shining, with buttons, and secured them under his robe. He tapped his staff on the floor with every other step, leaning as he walked.

Axaendara stood before the door, holding it open for him.

"I trust you can find your way out of the city."

"I shall head for the gates straightaway. Thank you for your time and kind words." Gort bowed deeply and walked outside. The door slid shut the instant he was through. He turned to face them, but the doors did not open for him.

Not for an outsider.

Gort strolled through the streets. It was bright, and the sun was rising in the morning sky. *How long was I in there?* he wondered, but there was no one to answer him. The streets were nearly empty. One person was walking briskly between buildings, another standing outside a door watching, both in shining bodysuits. No outsiders.

They had been sincere. Gort would be the last. When the front gates came into view, one stood open while a carved floating head waited in front of it. The curator's legs stiffened, and he struggled to maintain an even pace.

Not real! Thoughts battled for primacy in his mind. *Blasphemy!*

Gort finally reached the floating head and stopped. "My god Draezul. I live to serve."

"Leave them," the booming voice commanded.

"I am leaving," Gort countered, but that wasn't what the head demanded. It remained in front of the gate, blocking his way. "I see."

The curator took the items from within his robe and set them on the ground.

"My curiosity got the best of me." He bowed his head. "I beg your forgiveness."

The head floated to the side. Gort didn't want to be forever cut off from the city, but that was his fate—to work for the rest of his days for a city of masters using the people like herd animals.

He decided that would not be his lot in life.

"I know you are not a god, and I also know that changes nothing. I ask to return here once a year to refresh my soul within the Ziggurat."

The head bobbed closer, but Gort held his ground, something he would not have dared do before coming to Antioch.

He continued talking. "The people will rebel if they never see those who they are supposed to support."

"Stop them," the head called Draezul replied.

"No one will be able to stop them. Your trains will cease to run because there will be nothing to put in them. How long will that go on before Antioch is forced to respond?"

"Stop them."

"I'll be dead and won't be able to stop them because they'll rebel against me, too. Come with me, Draezul, and teach me about the stars. Teach me about your home, and together, we'll keep the trains full and running on time."

The head's lifeless wooden eyes gave the curator no hints.

"It's time to go, Draezul. If you want supplies for Antioch, it'll take both of us. How much are you willing to invest in the city and its people? My guess is that you're not real." Gort had become an upstart. He pushed the head with his staff, and it drifted away before floating back. "Kill me with your lightning or join me, whoever you are."

The volume decreased. "I am Draezul, but not a living being as you understand them."

Footsteps alerted Gort. The high priestess ran toward him, her feet barely touching the ground in her rush.

"What are you doing?" she demanded.

"Well, Regina, I'm making sure that Antioch is supplied for more than today. My goal is to make sure the trains keep running for the foreseeable future, but that will take far more than just me. I've asked Draezul to accompany me."

"Bow before your gods!"

Gort looked at her calmly while she fumed.

"You give no orders here," she added.

"Not an order," Gort replied. "A request that makes sense. What will happen to the people of Antioch after the war?"

"What war?" she spat.

"The inevitable war when the people rebel against the ungrateful overseers."

"You would lead a rebellion against Antioch?"

"No. I'll be dead because they'll rebel against me first, and then there will be no one to stop them. With Draezul, we'll keep them focused on a higher ideal. Isn't that what you've been selling all these years? Something greater than yourself? The gods will provide..."

"What are these?" The priestess pointed at the devices on the ground.

"I took them. I wanted to learn more about where the people of Antioch came from. I hoped I could learn something from those, but there is no need because Draezul is considering teaching me. There is power in knowledge."

She rolled her head to loosen her neck, and her fists clenched and unclenched. Her lips turned white.

"For the citizens of Antioch, Regina," the floating head said softly, "I will go. I am intrigued by the curator's understanding of his people. I will go with him. I will learn. And we will return. There might be a better way."

"Shall we?" Gort motioned for Draezul to precede him out the gate. The carved wooden head floated through. The curator never bothered to look at the priestess. Draezul might not have been a god, but he held a higher place than the so-called high-priestess. His word was final. Gort spoke over his shoulder as he walked out. "Regina, please make sure the equipment in the wheat region is repaired."

Once they were outside the city, the gate closed, snapping shut with a harsh click and clunk.

Gort walked beside the floating head, equal in seeking knowledge from the other.

"Let us talk about the family structure of the humans," Draezul said.

"This is how it's going to be?" Gort asked.

"Yes. It is a long road to where we're going, and I suspect we might forever be on this journey."

"The floating heads of Antioch. Bow before them!" Gort said

with a chuckle. "I'll answer your questions, but I need to know why you created such a thing. I've lived my whole life under a lie."

"A lie with a purpose. The humans were barbaric and combative when we arrived. A few lightning strikes and we had their attention, but more than that, they prostrated themselves and prayed for us to stop. We did, with conditions. That was ten generations ago. All humans since our arrival have been raised to believe that we are gods because it keeps them doing what we need them to do. But evolution has been friendly to you humans. Regina is in denial, but I suspected.

"If you as a curator were comfortable challenging us, others would, too. You are correct that war would be inevitable. Your ability to figure out the technology within the Ziggurat suggests a different relationship is necessary, not parasitic but symbiotic. Because you will not be the only one who figures things out. That is why we must close the city."

"But you would have been happy to let me walk out, even though you suspected."

"I would not have let you go alone. It was a test."

Gort collected his thoughts. "If I hadn't figured out the room, none of this would have happened?" He pounded his staff on the ground.

"Eventually, someone else would have been the catalyst. It was inevitable, although your rise came earlier than any of our projections indicated."

Gort relaxed. *Inevitable.* "We humans are pretty good people when you get to know us. As a benevolent god, you'll learn that. Thanks, Draezul. Let's see, where were we? Family structure..."

In addition to being the cofounder of the 20BooksTo50K indie author movement, **Craig Martelle** is a fiction-writing machine with a long list of publications to his credit. His science fiction work includes novels in the *Free Trader* and *Kurtherian Gambit* universes and the *Darklanding* and *Judge, Jury, and Executioner* series. Visit his web page, craigmartelle.com, for the latest posts and updates or find him on Facebook as Author Craig Martelle.

INTRODUCTION TO "GRIZZLED SPACE JOCKEY"

MARC SCOTT ZICREE

A few words about this story. A couple of years back, I had the idea to shoot the two-hour pilot of *Space Command*, a hopeful vision of the future that I hoped would inspire a new generation in the way *Star Trek* had inspired me when I was a kid. Via Kickstarter and selling investment shares, my fans gave me enough money to open my own studio and shoot the pilot (to date, we've actually shot five hours of the show, and have begun shooting hour six). I reached out to my friends, many of whom I'd worked with previously, and Doug Jones, Mira Furlan, Robert Picardo, Bill Mumy, Armin Shimerman, Francois Chau, Christina Moses, Barbara Bain, Bruce Boxleitner, Michael Harney, James Hong, John Hennigan and Faran Tahir came aboard, among others.

In the tradition of Alfred Hitchcock, who appeared in all of his films, I decided to shoot a cameo in the pilot. When I was twelve, Western Costume, the company that provided costumes to all the Hollywood studios, had a one-day sale that was open to the public, and for $25 my Mom bought me a real honest-to-gosh spacesuit!

In reality, it was a Navy high-altitude suit, but it had been used in the *Twilight Zone* episode "The Parallel," and God knows how many other productions.

So when I was planning the *Space Command* pilot, I knew I would be wearing that spacesuit. I wrote a scene set at the Red Sands landing field on Mars, in which I witness the spectacular crash landing at the beginning of the show, when Lt. Jack Kemmer (Ethan McDowell) saves Dr. Vonn Odara (Mira Furlan) and her daughter. I gave myself just one line: "Wow."

The only problem was that, in the intervening years, the zippers on the suit had rusted and no longer worked — we couldn't get it off the mannequin! So we shot the suit on the mannequin for the body, then put the helmet on my head and, through the magic of VFX, my head on the suit. *Et voila!*

When my team asked me the name of the character to include in the credits, I came up with "Grizzled Space Jockey," which amused me (and everyone else).

I intended that to be my only appearance in the pilot. But sometime later, we were shooting the Battle on Titan between Synthetic mercenaries and a ragtag group of human freedom fighters wearing cobbled-together spacesuits (by now, I had acquired additional spacesuits used in *The Outer Limits, Outland, Aliens, Jane the Virgin* and *Cloverfield Paradox,* as well as ones worn by Benedict Cumberbatch, Carol Burnett, Bob Hope and Lucille Ball). One of the actors playing a freedom fighter didn't show up, so I said, "I can wear a spacesuit," and threw together some bits and pieces.

So now, in the first hour of *Space Command,* you can see me say, "Wow," in the beginning and get vaporized by a beam from a blaster at the end. To top it off, a scene at the end of hour two features a sculpture garden on Mars boasting not only a statue of Jack Kemmer, but in the background, one of me too!

Given these three cameos, I started thinking it might be fun to link them together as all being about the same character.

When I was approached to provide a story for *Space: 1975*, it seemed the perfect opportunity.

I hope you enjoy the story. And if it leaves you hungry for more, you can catch my glorious thespian turns as the Grizzled Space Jockey at https://youtu.be/lEKdrVeUTAE

GRIZZLED SPACE JOCKEY
A SPACE COMMAND STORY

MARC SCOTT ZICREE

There are any number of ways you can say something that completely screws your life.

It might be, "I'm just not feeling it anymore, Harold."

Or, "I'm sure that's not loaded."

Or, "'Don't feed the lions' certainly doesn't apply to *me*."

Or just in general, "What's the worst that can happen?"

With me it was, "Wow."

And let me be clear about this. It didn't exactly *screw* everything, but it sure turned it topsy-turvy, ass over teakettle.

And so on.

But I'm getting ahead of myself. I'm leaving behind this narrative of how I got in and out of the fight, then back into it, as sort of a will and testament if things don't work out too well.

Not that I have anything to leave anybody particularly, except maybe a word picture for someone who comes after me with a nagging curiosity about how things went down on Titan during the uprising. And if that happens to be a clone of me, hey buddy, don't believe what everyone says about you, you look just fine.

So, where to start? With Anson Kemmer, or his kid Jack?

Captains both, and heroes both too, I suppose. But at least Jack had manners.

See, that's the problem when you get old. The past is all a jumble. Something that seems only months ago is forty years. And other things fade into the past like they're swallowed up in fog.

Not to say there aren't good things about getting old. Which reminds me of the joke about the old guy who took so long answering that question they thought his mind had wandered, until he said, "I'm just trying to think of one!"

Here's the good thing: When you're young, it's like your life is a big white canvas, and you think you can paint anything you like on it. But pretty soon, you find they're out of the cerulean blue you want, or the chartreuse doesn't look anything like you envisioned. And before you know it, the painting is a total mess, different from anything you imagined, and now what the hell do you do with it?

But when you're old, you can look at that canvas, most of which is filled in now, and see what the picture really looks like. You can't erase any of it, but you can decide what you want to add to complete it, to bring it balance, and meaning, and light.

And it's all yours.

So what the hell. Let's start with Anson, that maniac. Back when Space Command was part of the American military, and I was part of Space Command.

So anyway, I'm at Vandenberg minding my own business in my off hours, when there's a knock at the door.

"Unless you're a blonde with a bottle, go away!" I yell at it.

"Open this before I kick it in, God dammit," says Captain Anson Kemmer.

Like I said, no manners.

But Christ, we'd met in kindergarten and been pretty much joined at the hip all the way up through OTS and beyond. So against my better judgement, I hoist myself up out of my Appalachian rocker, cross the room, and slide back the bolt.

In he saunters, cocky like always, with those blue eyes like a pilot light that never goes out, just simmers.

He settles into the rocker, knowing full well it's *my* seat. "Make yourself at home," I say, plopping onto the sofa.

He looks around the place. "You got any chow here? I'm famished."

"Knowing you, raw meat should fit the bill."

He just glowers. "Help yourself," I say. This is my place, and I'm certainly not taking orders—at least, not as a fry cook.

Grumbling, he levers himself out of the chair and stalks heavily into the kitchen, starts rooting about in the fridge with all the delicacy of a grizzly bear that's emerged from hibernation and kicked down my door to break its fast.

He pulls out the leftover lasagna I'd been planning to have for dinner, sniffs it, shoves it into the microwave and punches two minutes. Then, he turns to face me.

"Griz, are you as fed up with this shit as I am?"

First, a word about Griz. At the time, it stood for Grizzled Jet Jockey, a moniker he'd coined for me at Officer's Training that had stuck.

"Which shit specifically?" I ask.

He waves a broad hand. "All of it. Fires, floods, wars, military bullshit. The works."

Now I know he's just come back from our War in Sri Lanka, where he got his ass blasted out of the sky by one drone and laid out flat in the foliage by another. Listed as MIA, and then two months later up he pops, on the mend and spouting a wild story about some messianic peace activist dame who tended his wounds and rendered aid and comfort... if you know what I mean.

"It's Sheena of the Jungle," I say, knowing full well what an antiquated reference it is. "That dame. She poured all sorts of crazy in your head."

"There's crazy and there's crazy," he says. "And her name's Anoka."

The microwave beeps and he pulls out the lasagna, starts shoveling it into his mouth.

"There a point to this?" I ask.

"How do you feel about throwing your career away, ending up in Leavenworth or worse?" he says.

I'm just young enough and dumb enough to say, "Go on."

"I'm thinking of getting the band back together. You, me, Charlie, one or two others."

By Charlie, he means Chilton. We all served together in Sri Lanka, and none of us felt all that good about what went down there. What was continuing to go down.

"To do what?"

He's finished the lasagna, tosses the plate in the sink (he'd never think of washing it). Pops open a cerveza.

"Steal a ship. Put together an international flotilla on the sly. Lasso an ice comet, haul it back to Earth to get the Gulf Stream going again."

I blow out a breath like someone's just punched me in the gut. "Christ," I say. "You must really love that girl."

He lets out a grunt (his version of a laugh), then says, "So... are you in or out?"

"I could call the brass right now and tell them what you're up to."

"You could, but what fun would that be?"

Aw, geez. He's got my number.

And yes, I know when you're in the service, the worst thing you can do is disobey orders and violate your oath and spit on the sidewalk and not help old ladies across the street. But Christ, if you were around then you know that the whole damn world had gone shit-ass sidewise and all the rules were off the table and nothing made any sense anymore. It was just bad and getting worse and no one seemed to be doing anything about it.

And if you weren't around then, take my word for it.

Now if this were the kind of story that's all adventure and just out to give you some jollies, I'd walk you step by step through how we managed to pull the spaceship heist, get the word out to astronauts and cosmonauts and taikonauts and whatever other nauts, snare the comet, tether it to the Pole and blah blah blah.

But you've read the history books and know all that. How they wanted to hand Anson his ass on a platter, but the thing worked so well and he was such a hero—hell, we all were—that High Command couldn't do shit but pat us all on the back, give us promotions and file it under Fuck-Ups That Miraculously Turned Out Okay.

Oh, and how after that Grand Mission to the Cosmos, I was still called Griz, but now it stood for Grizzled *Space* Jockey.

But that's not what I'm getting at here. The point I'm trying to make is that I was *young* then, and with just enough fire in the belly and foolhardiness and desire to make the world a better place that I'd stick my neck out, put everything on the line, just so my life would *mean* something.

But just because you win the day doesn't mean you win the fight, because the fight just keeps going on, one way or another. But hey, you figure you've done your part, so you step back and let other people take their ticket and have their number called.

Which is exactly what Yours Truly did. The years rolled by, and thanks to our efforts with the Big Ball of Ice, the whole world saw we could all work together and United Planet was formed and Space Command became part of that, and as we ventured out into space and started colonizing the planets,

United Planet became United Planets, and I got to wear a spiffy new uniform that wowed the girls.

Well actually, the uniform was okay. The girls... not so impressed.

And oh yeah, Anson married Anoka, and things being what they usually are, little Jack came along. I put in my twenty-five, claimed my pension and hung up my spurs. *Adios*, Space Command.

Which is how I ended up on Mars, tending Terraforming Plant Number Eight, just to keep my hand in.

Why Mars, you ask? Well, Earth had just gotten too damn boring, and I got the itch to go off-world, like your Great Aunt wanting to see Machu Picchu before she drops dead any minute now.

Now me, I always prefer at least one-third g. I don't tend to do too well below that, with my guts floating up to where my esophagus should be. So when I got the wanderlust to travel off-world, it was Mars for me. And as for muscle and bone atrophy, well, if you just wear weighted suits that take you up to something approximating Earth normal, you're okay in the long run. It's a pain in the butt most times—literally!—but worth it when your lazy-ass drinking buddies end up gelatinous messes by age fifty, while you can still piss standing up.

Here's the thing about living on an alien planet, or moon, or whatever. It's essentially the same as living underwater back on Earth. I mean, H_2O, vacuum or methane, the rules are much the same. You can't go outside without a suit *ever*, can't stay *al fresco* longer than your air supply, and other than that you're okay so long as you're inside an environment that keeps all the good stuff in and the bad stuff out.

It's like humans are a protected species in an enclosed sanctuary. Just like we do with those Martian fish-things we found deep in the caves. Only mine is a condo in Muskopolis.

Back to me and Terraforming Plant Eight. I'm there in the pressure suit my Mom bought me when I was twelve ("What the hell am I supposed to do with *this*?" I whined. "You'll grow into it," she said—and she was right). I'm adjusting the O2 output when I hear this rumbling in the sky that vibrates up through the deck plating and into my suit and eye sockets. This is when the air was thicker than when we first got there, although not yet thick enough to breathe—but it still conducts sound pretty well.

I look up at the near horizon and my jaw drops. There's this big gray Space Command patrol ship, and clamped on top of it is this scorched red piece of crap planet hopper with flame belching out of the back of it.

It doesn't take Einstein to piece together what's going on there. That patrol ship got an SOS from POC (Piece of Crap) and the only way it could figure to save the morons inside was by grabbing hold of the craft and muscling the two of them in tandem down onto the tarmac.

Now me, I like my suicide a good deal less public and dramatic. But whoever the officer on the SC ship is, he's clearly got *cojones* of steel and two ears with nothing between them. Because it's a sure bet when all is said and done that the only thing that'll be left in the next minute or so is a mile-long scorch mark on the runway and enough salvageable parts to put in a shot glass.

I can't look...but I do anyway. The joined ships scream past Phobos and Deimos, the two moons hazy in the mid-sol sky, then descend short and steep toward the Red Sands emergency field, trailing all the flames of Hell (where they'll no doubt be shortly).

The big patrol ship—which I now see bears the name *Thomas Paine*—extends its landing gear and touches down. But the added weight of the piggyback hopper causes the skids to buckle and collapse, sending the linked vessels careening out of control down the runway, throwing sparks off the underside of the *Thomas Paine*'s hull.

But miracle of miracles, somehow the pilot has touched down just right, and the *Paine* slows to a stop and settles with a hiss of metal and a *pharumph* of steam.

I bolt my jaw back in place and say the only thing I can think of.

"Wow."

~

Soon as my shift is over, I head over to this Marsport dive I know called the Marinarus Club, where VIPs have skyboxes and the rest of us Great Unwashed are lucky if we can get a stool at the bar and a cocktail napkin with bridge mix (which tastes worse than the iron oxide grit mashed into the soles of my space boots at end of day). Party girls human, Synth and virtual hang out there, so naturally your standard-issue red-blooded Space Command *hombres* will be drifting in as the night draws on apace. But there's only one guy I want to meet—the wild man commanding the *Thomas Paine*.

I spy a dashing young Lieutenant with black hair and a goatee nursing a Cherry Coke at the bar and introduce myself.

"Jorge Borges," he says of himself.

"Like the writer?" I ask.

He looks perplexed. "There's a writer?"

"Forget it," I say. "You know anything about that lunatic brave crash landing that happened with the *Paine?*"

"Indeed I do," says Borges. "I was inside it."

"Well, Lieutenant, I would very much like to meet your Captain and shake his hand."

Borges slowly shakes his head. "Captain had nothing to do

with it. It was entirely the pilot who took the initiative to save the two women in that ship."

"Know where I might run into that fella?" I ask.

Borges smiles. "Try turning around."

I do, and spy a tall Space Command officer walking up to join us.

I haven't seen him since he was a kid, but with that blond hair and lanky frame I recognize him right off the bat.

"You're Jack Kemmer," I say, extending a hand. "I served with your Dad."

He takes my hand, and his grip is firm and solid.

I order drinks all round and we adjourn to a corner booth with Jack and his pal Jorge.

"I saw what you did with the *Paine* today," I tell him as we settle in. "Pretty fancy flying there."

"Just a mix of adrenaline and stupidity," he says.

I smile. "Now you're starting to sound like me."

He returns the grin, but a thought crosses his mind like a dark cloud and it fades.

"Something on your mind, son?" I ask.

So he tells me all about how his Captain answered the distress call from Dr. Vonn Odara and her daughter Jelena, trailed them to the upper Martian atmosphere—then decided it was too risky to try to save them, so he'd just let them burn.

Parkhill, that prick. I remember him from the bad old days. He was the one who had the hard-on to fricassee me and Charlie Chilton and Anson when we saved the Earth with that comet. Thank Zeus and all the other dead gods that he didn't get the chance then—and didn't get this one, either.

Young Jack Me Lad here decided to develop Sudden Deafness Syndrome and ignore Parkhill's orders. Just add water and his instant mutiny saves both women's lives and leaves two ships ready for the scrap yard.

I put my hand on the kid's shoulder. "Good for you, Jack. You did the right thing."

His look is sardonic. "Remember that when I come round begging for a janitor job, or whatever table scraps are available."

I don't have to ask what that means. Recall what I said a while back about disobeying orders? Jack Kemmer has every expectation that come the dawn he won't be wearing that snazzy uniform or those lieutenant bars anymore.

But I've gotta say, he's a chip off the old block. He doesn't excuse his behavior or ask any favors. He just knows what's right and does it, come hell or high water. Then takes his licks, even if it's a fucking shame, not to say a downright injustice.

I pay the bill and stand. "It's been a pleasure meeting you, Jack," I say. "Don't sweat a thing."

He lifts his drink in salute. "Words to live by."

When I return to my digs that night, I get busy on the vidphone. I still have friends in Space Command, some full-bird colonels and even more with stars on their shoulders. By the time I'm done, the sun is rising outside my window, and the brass have their ears ringing so hard from hearing a piece of my mind that it's a wonder I have any mind left.

But the upshot is the boy will do just fine. Sometimes the good guys win.

At the same time, as I look out at the dawn, the Martian sky blue at sunrise, I realize something else has been roiling in my gut, and it's not the day-old enchilada I scarfed down sometime around three A.M.

Every now and then, someone's actions are like an alarm clock going off, and you wake up and look around and think, *Where have I been all this time?*

Jack Kemmer's act of lunacy has started me thinking. Maybe I need to take on that kind of courage again, not just sit on the sidelines like some bum waiting for the Reaper.

What gets me fired up? Where if I was twenty again, I'd say, "Count me in." Then ask yourself—why not do it now?

Everybody says you're as old as you feel. Me, I say you're as old as you think. And most people think like rusty dinosaurs.

So I start ruminating on the hotspots throughout the system, those David vs. Goliath situations, or Sisyphus trying to push that damn rock up the hill.

Plus it's got to have some half-decent gravity. Remember what I said about my guts and esophagus?

There's those Children of Job nut cases on Mercury, the cloud cities of Venus—little more than a shopping destination, really—and the mining squabbles on Ganymede. None of them really my cup of tea.

But then the light bulb goes off: *Titan*. Atmospheric pressure four times that of Earth, gravity better than the Moon. Plus there's these rag-tag guerrillas that seem pretty decent and are getting their asses kicked by the forces of the United Kingdom's Outer System Export Company.

Bingo. Just the sort of Lost Cause I like. Not to mention, where else in this Century would you have a chance to go up against the British Empire?

So I put out the word through the grapevine that I'd like to join the freedom fighters; you know, a friend of a friend sort of thing. And like a horse showing its teeth, I mention I've got certain attractive features—former military, knows his way around guns and munitions, can dress himself, works for little or nothing, not to mention I've got my own spacesuit (thanks, Mom).

And what do you know? In no time I hear back: "Welcome aboard."

So I ship out to the Saturnian moons on my own dime, they give me my very own decoder badge, and I'm in. The Grizzled Space Jockey is a grunt again!

And I've got to say, the ethanol lakes they've got here are pretty as hell under the nitrogen methane clouds.

Have to tie a bow on this now. We've just been alerted there's a contingent of Combat Synth contractors headed our way, with some Limey human commander in a walking machine. The way we're outfitted, I'd say our odds are about as good as the Messiah dropping in.

Now going out in a blaze of glory, I can take it or leave it. But just to be safe, I've downloaded all my thoughts and memories on a drive up in orbit—they used to call it the cloud, now it's the nebula. I guess you call that progress.

And of course when I say "safe," I'm being ironic. First off, although they can *save* your mind (even yours truly's, who no doubt lost his ages ago), they currently have no way to reconstitute a body or implant it into same. You just put down a deposit and hope for the best.

Hope. That's about as reliable as what I said I'm leaving in my will.

And anyway, even if they someday can cook up a body that looks a whole lot like me, it won't be *me* they'll be depositing that so-called consciousness into. It'll be a copy.

Point being, if there is some Space Jockey part *deux* running around at some time yet to be determined, he can thank me for being his *raison d'etre* – and everything else.

Or just pay it the fuck forward. I really don't care much one way or the other, expecting that in a few minutes I'll likely be flash-fried by some Mazzey/Patillo plastic soldier, or whatever the hell they make those Synthetics out of nowadays. Bouillon cubes, for all I know.

And if I *do* buy the farm, at least my fellow *quixotes* on the battlefield might get the warm fuzzies knowing that *someone* gave his last laughable measure so maybe they could have a say over what happens to this godforsaken rock. Here's hoping I don't soil my space drawers when I look down that row of Tin Soldiers aiming their blast rifles at me.

And who knows? Maybe someday someone will put up a statue of me.

But I wouldn't count on it.

~

Dr. Vonn Odara and her wife Lynn strolled through the parkland under the night stars and Martian moons. After all these decades, the air was finally breathable if a bit thin, like staying at a mountain resort.

They drew near a statue, gleaming bronze under the starlight. Vonn recognized the face. She had known him well in his day; in fact, he had saved her life many times over.

At the base, a simple inscription: *JACK KEMMER, A bonae spae, visionem de future.*

"A hopeful vision of the future," said Dr. Odara, translating. "You got that right, Captain."

"So hard to fathom you knew him," said Lynn.

"It seems a breath ago," Vonn murmured.

"This came for you." Lynn touched her wrist, and a holographic email popped up.

Vonn quickly read it, reacted in surprise. "The excavation on Altair. They approved it."

Lynn smiled. "So another adventure for the two of us."

Vonn nodded. "Into the unknown..."

They continued on through the sculpture garden, came to another statue and considered it. Had Jack Kemmer been there, he would have known the man, a friend of his father's whom he had last seen at a major turning point of his life. But the two women did not.

"*Titan's Guiding Star,*" Vonn said, reading the inscription.

Checking the plaque's date, she tilted her head quizzically. "That was the year of their resistance. Whatever do you suppose... he did for them?"

Marc Scott Zicree is the author of *The Twilight Zone Companion, Guillermo del Toro's Cabinet of Curiosities*, and the *Magic Time* trilogy of novels, as well as a writer for *Star Trek – The Next Generation, Sliders, Babylon Five* and *Deep Space Nine*, among many other shows. To watch more of the *Space Command* saga, check out his Mr. Sci-Fi YouTube Channel.

DISCO DANI AND THE BAD PENNY

ANNIE REED

A white-hot blast of fire from a laser pistol split the air over Dani's head as she dove behind the remnants of a blasted permacrete wall.

She tucked her shoulder right before she hit the debris-strewn dirt, turning her dive into a roll, and came up with her own laser pistol in her hand. Not that she intended to use it unless she absolutely had to.

More laser fire erupted from behind her. Return fire hummed from a building in front of her and off to her right. Shouts and screams and the pounding, scrabbling sound of shooters running for cover filled the dusty, smoky air, and somewhere in the distance came the booming report of something with a hell of a lot more firepower than a hand pistol.

And to think, less than an hour ago, this sector of the crumbling old settlement had looked completely deserted.

"Another wonderful day on the job," she muttered, her voice amplified as it bounced off the clear protective helmet of her environmental suit.

Planet Tongusta's atmosphere supported human life—including the lives of the idiots who'd decided to wage a private little war while she was underground crawling around the basement of the settlement's old municipal building—but who knew what kind of nasty bugs (viruses and the creepy crawly kind) had taken up residence down there. She'd donned the suit as a safety precaution, and now she was happy she had.

Dani had been hired to retrieve an object secreted in a safe room in the basement. In the centuries since the building had been abandoned, sections of the main floor had collapsed into the basement.

Just finding the safe room, which was remarkably intact, had taken her longer than she planned. The safe room itself insulated her from everything going on in the world around her, which she supposed was its purpose, so to say she'd been surprised by the battle when she emerged onto the surface was the understatement of the century.

She didn't like the feel of the suit on her skin, and the clear bubble helmet, as vital as it was to her health and welfare, made her feel mildly claustrophobic. She especially hated the sound of her breathing echoing loud in her ears. She'd planned to take the suit off and collapse it back into a pocket on her belt, right next to the hidden pouch that currently held the little stasis box she'd retrieved from the safe room; then she'd heard the hum of laser fire, and the sensors in the suit informed her the air was rapidly becoming toxic thanks to fires burning through the abandoned buildings.

She kept her pistol at the ready, even though she had no plans to blast her way out of here. She could count on the fingers of one hand the number of times she'd fired the thing, and half of those shots were learning how to use it. With any luck, she could stay out of sight long enough for the fight to burn itself out or move to a different sector; then, she could hotfoot it back to her ship and get the hell off this planet.

While she waited, she rehearsed exactly what she'd say the

next time she talked to Tom Leap, the customer who'd hired her to go to Tongusta and retrieve the little stasis box in the first place. Tom was a collector extraordinaire who focused on memorabilia from old Earth of the Twentieth Century, as the years had been counted back then. No matter what he paid her to retrieve, he always told her exactly where to go.

How *he* knew, Dani had no idea. But if he knew enough about the planet to tell her where this little stasis box was located, why the hell hadn't he told her to be on the lookout for roving bands of idiots with laser pistols and heavy artillery?

"Simple job," Tom had told her. "You'll be in and out without a hitch."

Not exactly.

She should have known something was up when Tom had agreed to pay her "a pretty penny" for the job. She'd thought it was just because he'd pinged her about the job during her vacation. He'd always dealt fair and square with her, and he'd never ever called her "Disco Dani," so it never even entered her mind that he'd been withholding information.

She should have known better. Collectors were notoriously single-minded when it came to getting their hands on whatever they absolutely *had* to have for themselves.

She'd done her own research on Tongusta, of course, but there wasn't a lot of recent information available. Homeland Alliance still considered this sector of space the frontier, and like a lot of frontier worlds, the original colonists who settled here hated any kind of government telling them what they could and could not do. "Remarkably independent" was what liberal-leaning historians called them. "Ferociously rebellious," more authoritarian sources insisted.

From what she could see, "remarkably independent" and "ferociously rebellious" had merged into "unbelievably belligerent" over the centuries since the last historians had visited the place. No wonder the Alliance had withdrawn its presence from the planet. Tongusta wasn't exactly strategically located and probably not worth the Alliance's time or attention.

It wouldn't have been worth hers except for Tom.

Who was going to get an earful the next time she talked to him.

She risked a quick peek around the corner of the wall. Another laser shot hummed over her head. Damn.

Her suit wasn't laser-proof. If someone tagged her with a direct hit, or even a glancing blow from a high-powered pistol, the suit—and Dani—would be in a world of hurt.

She patted the hidden pocket on her belt to reassure herself the little stasis box was still there. The thing weighed next to nothing. If she had to risk her life for a job, she damn well better deliver the goods—whatever they were—so she'd get paid.

That was the thing that irked her the most. She had no idea what was in the box, and Tom had given her strict instructions not to open it.

How stupid would it be to die and not know what you were dying for?

Too bad her ship wasn't closer. She'd stashed it next to a rockfall at the base of a scrub-brush covered hill at the far end of the old settlement. Her ship was sleek and fast, the hull a dull black that made it difficult to see in space unless someone directly pinged it. On the ground, given the right surroundings, it might look like a deep shadow. If she'd left it closer to the municipal building, say on the rooftop of a nearby structure, she might have been able to make a run for it. The ship had shields that would protect it—and her—from ground fire as it took off.

Of course, if either side in this battle had eyes in the sky, they'd just blast her ship to pieces. The ship's shields wouldn't protect it from a direct hit from the heavy artillery blasts she'd just heard.

Did the fighters have eyes in the sky? She hadn't seen any drones overhead, but that didn't mean no one was looking. She scooted back away from the corner of the building and craned her neck to peer upward.

And that's when she stepped on something that wasn't just debris.

"Son of a bitch," she muttered as she heard a distinctive metallic click.

The ground opened up beneath her, and she fell into absolute darkness.

Dani had been born on a planet not that much smaller than Tongusta, but she'd spent a good portion of her life in her sleek little ship, going from job to job, with occasional vacations spent on stations scattered throughout Alliance-controlled space. She liked exploring old places, and she worked well alone, which made her perfectly suited to a life procuring all sorts of abandoned oddities, curiosities, and memorabilia—wherever those things might be located, either planetside or in deep space—for the collectors who hired her.

Including an ancient mirror-covered sphere she'd retrieved from the bowels of an abandoned generation ship.

She'd managed to retrieve the sphere without breaking any of the little mirrors, which were exceedingly fragile. The customer had insisted on celebrating her success by not only sharing a drink with her—she always had a drink at the end of a successful job—but also dancing with her. Apparently, the mirrored sphere came from an era on old Earth when people danced beneath the things.

She should have given him his money back, but she'd been

fairly broke at the time, so she'd agreed to one drink and one dance. That had been one dance too many.

The customer had made a vid of Dani's awkward, alcohol-fueled attempt to dance. Without her permission. Then he'd uploaded it to the net. Also without her permission.

She'd used some of the money she'd earned on that job to hire a lawyer, and her lawyer had sued the pants off the customer. The customer had settled out of court for an exorbitant sum, which had set Dani up in business. It had also earned Dani a nickname she couldn't quite shake, no matter how hard she tried: Disco Dani.

She hated her nickname with a passion. The only good thing about it was that some customers only heard of her because she was "Disco" Dani.

Not that any of that would matter if she never got off this planet.

The further she fell down the long, slick chute of an emergency escape hatch, getting off this planet in one piece seemed less and less likely.

Old colonies used escape hatches to ferry the colony's administrative staff away in a hurry from whatever had decided to attack them on the surface. It made sense that the municipal building would have an escape hatch outside. If staff couldn't get to the safe room in the basement, the hatch would provide a secondary escape route.

What didn't make sense was that the hatch was still in working order. Government officials had abandoned this settlement centuries before Dani had even been born.

The chute had no illumination. Dani thought about turning on her suit's built-in lights, but that might make her more disoriented than she already was. The chute felt slick and metallic beneath her body. She didn't dare try to stop her fall with either her legs or her hands. Her bones would break before she could stop herself, so she tucked herself into as much of a ball as she could and concentrated on keeping a grip on her laser pistol.

Just in case she needed it wherever the chute was sending her.

When she finally came to a stop, the abrupt cessation of movement disoriented her so much it took her a full minute to realize she hadn't broken anything when she finally hit bottom. In fact, it appeared the chute had deposited her in a surprisingly comfortable chair, apparently designed to absorb the force of the impact while molding itself to the contours of her body.

"Okay," she muttered to the absolute darkness surrounding her. "That was fun."

She triggered the forward-facing lights attached to the shoulders of her environmental suit. The chair responded by sliding her to the right, away from the bottom of the chute, before it began to move her forward.

She'd never been in an emergency escape system like this one before. The room she was in had been constructed with gray metal-plated walls studded with rivets and marred by old-style welded seams. Her chair was attached to a track on the floor, but other than the chair, the track, and the chute, the room was empty.

The track was guiding her chair toward a set of double doors which were currently shut.

Dani tried to get out of the chair, but the thing held her firmly in place.

Wherever the chair was going, she was apparently along for the ride.

She held the laser pistol in her lap, not exactly at the ready, but close enough if she needed it.

Whatever Tom had gotten her into, he wasn't paying her nearly enough.

In fact, not only was she going to give him a piece of her

mind, she was going to demand hazard pay before she turned the stasis box over to him.

Provided she got out of here alive.

~

The job had started out like any other job, except she'd been on vacation.

A fact she'd mentioned to Tom when he'd pinged her.

"Where the heck are you?" he asked. "I can barely see you."

Dani smiled at him as his pleasantly bespectacled face fuzzed in and out of focus on the holo that floated above the control console on her ship. She didn't tell anyone exactly where she was at any given time, not even Tom, who happened to be her best customer. She just turned the gain down on her communications equipment whenever a ping came through from a customer. It made her location harder for any competitors to trace.

"What can I do for you?" she asked.

"Got a line on something," he said, pushing his glasses up his nose.

Fussing with his glasses was a sign Tom was really excited about something. The wire-framed glasses were part of his main collection—old Earth memorabilia. He'd worn them ever since Dani had known him, even though he could have gotten enhancements to correct his failing eyesight.

If he was this excited about his find, she might be able to negotiate a higher fee.

"Gonna cost you," she said.

He sputtered, which was part of his standard negotiation tactics. "I haven't even told you what the job is yet!"

She leaned back in her chair. "I'm on vacation. If you can wait until I get back..."

She let the implication lie there. If he couldn't wait, that would tell her how much extra he was willing to pay.

He hadn't come out and said the job was time sensitive. Instead, he'd rubbed his nose, raked his fingers through his graying hair (something else he could have fixed with enhancements but didn't), and finally agreed with a rueful smile to pay not only a higher than normal fee, but also a "vacation surcharge" once the job was done.

"It's a good thing I like you, Dani," he said after he'd transferred the non-refundable portion of her fee into her business holding account.

"I like you too, Tom." She'd acknowledged receipt of the funds, and then he'd sent her the coded instructions on where and how to acquire a stasis box he said would fit in the palm of her hand. "You sure these instructions are accurate?"

"As sure as I can be," he said. "Remember, don't disengage the stasis field. It would ruin what's inside."

She smiled at him. "And you're not going to tell me what's inside, are you?"

He'd pushed his glasses up on his nose. "As always, I'm paying you a pretty penny for something that's worth a pretty penny." Then he'd smiled at her, tilted his head, and waggled his eyebrows, an expression that came through clear enough even with the static.

She'd chuckled, which was the response he'd expected. Just like his glasses and his graying hair, Tom always talked to her about money in antiquated terms of dollars and cents.

Well, whatever was in the stasis box better be worth more than a pretty penny. So far, she'd been caught in the middle of a battle and shot down an escape chute that was now taking her who knew where, and all for something so small it weighed next to nothing.

If she got out of this job in one piece, she might think about making that vacation permanent.

~

Right about the time she thought the chair might crash her into the double doors at the end of the track, the doors slid open with a rusty-hinged squeal (the first sign that the emergency escape system might not be all that well maintained). A bright blast of light hit her in the face, and she thanked her lucky stars again that she still had on her environmental suit.

Her suit automatically dimmed the light, which had the unfortunate side effect of plunging the rest of the room into darkness.

"Just who the hell are you?" came a male voice from out of that darkness.

Dani raised one hand to block the light. "Want to turn those things down a notch?" she asked, trying to keep her voice as calm as possible even while her heart was hammering hard in her chest.

She hadn't really expected anyone to be on the other side of the double doors. In fact, she'd been wracking her brain trying to remember everything she'd ever read about escape systems like this one. She figured she'd have to boot up ancient tech to find out how to get back to the surface.

If the system would even allow her to get back to the surface. Some systems were designed to keep administrators alive for months—even years—until it was safe enough for them to leave.

"I'll turn down the lights if you let go of that pistol," he said.

She didn't want to do that—who knew if this guy was armed —but if he was, he could have shot her the second the doors opened. She didn't really have a choice.

She took her hand away from the pistol, leaving it in her lap. "I'd put it away, but it's normally attached it to my belt, and your chair won't let me stand up."

"Oh, yeah. Sorry. I forgot about that."

She heard something click, and then the chair relaxed beneath her. She leaned forward far enough to confirm she could get out of the chair if she wanted to, which was good enough for now.

The lights dimmed, and the sensors in her face shield adjusted accordingly.

She was in a control room approximately twice the size of the cockpit on her ship. Instead of viewscreens, a series of holoscreens hovered over control panels that might have been state-of-the-art a few centuries ago.

The holoscreens all displayed various overhead views of the battle raging on the surface.

The man who'd asked her to put away her laser pistol was the only other person in the room. He was about Dani's height, dark haired, dark eyed, and scruffy faced.

And he was dressed only in a pair of sleek exercise pants that left nothing to the imagination.

Apparently, he hadn't been born in space either. No one born in space had muscles like that.

Dani felt heat rush to her face.

At least he didn't appear to be armed. He wouldn't be able to conceal a weapon in those pants.

She suddenly felt more than a little overdressed in her environmental suit, but she wasn't ready to take it off just yet.

"Who are you?" she asked.

He crossed his arms over his chest. "I think I asked first." He nodded toward the nearest holoscreen. "You're not one of them."

"Guess the suit gave it away," she said.

"That and your ship. And the fact that you knew exactly where to go to get what you came here for."

Clearly, she'd been right to worry about someone spotting her from overhead. Whatever he was doing here, the surveillance equipment he had outside was way more sophisticated than the equipment in this room appeared to be.

"You were spying on me," she said.

"Not intentionally. I'm spying on them. You just happened to show up about the same time they did."

Okay, so he'd seen her going into the basement of the abandoned municipal building. There was no way he could have seen what she did inside the safe room, and therefore he couldn't know she'd taken anything that didn't technically belong to her.

Could he?

"Are you Alliance?" she asked. If the Alliance was thinking about reasserting their authority over Tongusta, they'd probably send scouts in advance. If that's what this guy was.

If he was Alliance, and the Alliance was planning to take over Tongusta again, the Alliance might claim that everything in the old municipal building was Alliance property. In that case, if she was caught taking property from the safe room, and if that property was worth a pretty penny, as Tom claimed, she could be in some serious trouble.

"Are you?" she asked again when he didn't say anything.

He sighed and cocked his head to one side. "If I'm Alliance, I'm seriously getting busted for being out of uniform."

It took her a second to realize that he was joking.

"That's not really funny," she said, although she found herself smiling anyway out of relief.

"Not used to having company." He extended a hand. "Michael Trumby, historian."

She looked at his hand for a moment before she decided to

shake it. "Dani," she said. "Just Dani. Procurer of oddities, collectibles, and rare memorabilia."

He grinned at her, what looked like a genuine smile. "Dani? Really? I think I've heard of you."

She steeled herself for the dreaded nickname, but he didn't say it, and she let herself relax. "How would a historian who's spying on"—she waved a hand at the battle on the viewscreen—"whoever they are have heard of me?"

"Well, we're kind of in the same business, really. I study history. You go and find things that are a part of history."

She supposed that sort of made sense.

"So, Michael Trumby," she said, finally getting up from the chair to go stand in front of the holoscreens. "What is a person who studies history doing hiding away down here?"

"Recording what will be history tomorrow," he said. "Tongusta's factions are constantly waging war against each other. History—accurate history—gets lost when there's no one official to record it."

He gave her a sideways glance.

"In fact, I'm sure none of the people trying to kill each other up there have any idea that you just found the most valuable artifact left behind by their ancestors."

She'd made a serious mistake. She'd told him her name and her profession. He'd seen her go into the old municipal building, and he probably knew about the safe room. He was probably also good at connecting various pieces of information to form a whole picture. Wasn't that what historians did? When they weren't recording history, anyway.

"How do you know I found anything?" she asked.

"It's your job. You wouldn't have left until you found what you were after."

"How do you know I'm not on vacation?"

He snorted. "No one comes to Tongusta for vacation."

So much for that bluff. "So, smart guy, tell me what I was after." Hell, she didn't even know that.

"A legend," he said. "The silver penny."

~

Every belief system has an ultimate, unobtainable object. The Holy Grail, as one mostly forgotten old Earth religion called it.

For some in the Alliance, the unobtainable object wasn't an object at all—it was peace and prosperity for all member worlds. For others, it was wealth beyond measure. For the customer who'd captured Dani on vid trying to dance to the music of a long-forgotten era, it was a mirror-covered sphere.

For an ancient Earth memorabilia fiend like Tom who still thought of money in terms of dollars and cents, it was the silver penny.

Dani knew about silver pennies. She'd researched the coins of ancient Earth after her second job for Tom just because she was curious about the meaning of "a pretty penny."

Silver pennies weren't pretty, and they weren't made of silver—they were aluminum coins produced on old Earth in 1974 as the years were measured in those days. The coins—bad pennies, every one of them—were recalled for some reason Dani couldn't remember now and were destroyed by the government that minted them. Rumor had it that a few remained intact, but since they were government property—Earth was part of the Alliance, after all—it was illegal for anyone to own a silver penny. Their existence was, as Michael had put it, just legend.

Or not. Somehow one of those coins had found its way to a safe room on Tongusta and was now housed inside the tiny stasis box in the pocket of Dani's environmental suit.

An intact silver penny was worth a fortune.

"Son of a *bitch*," she said under her breath. "I'm in a lot of trouble here."

"I don't think so," Michael said. "The administrator who brought the coin here, he might have been in trouble. From what I've learned, a lot of the collectibles he brought to Tongusta when he was assigned here were stolen from other collectors. One of the reasons he took an assignment way out in the frontier. I take it you don't do that."

"No." She never had. She made it clear to her customers she only retrieved property that had been long abandoned. "As far as I know, my customer doesn't, either."

At least she hoped Tom didn't.

"I'm pretty sure I know who your customer is," Michael said. "But I won't tell. I kind of like the guy."

Dani narrowed her eyes. Tom had to get his information from somewhere, and what better source of information on the past, and where to find things from the past, than a historian?

"So you're his source?" she asked.

"Me? No, not on your life. I only know him by reputation. Collectors of his stature and particularly his era of interest are pretty rare. So are historians who study that era, like my brother. And before you ask, he's not the source, either."

Michael had a glint in his eye that might have been amusement, but might have been something a little more avaricious.

"You're not going to ask me to look at it, are you?" she asked. "I'm not supposed to open the stasis box."

"Degrades the quality," he said, nodding his head. "And no, I wouldn't ask that. Not even to make sure the penny's still inside. I'm pretty sure I couldn't afford to reimburse your buyer for any damage to his merchandise."

The conversation lapsed into a not-quite-comfortable silence in which Dani was very aware Michael wasn't wearing much of anything and she still had on her entire environmental suit.

"So," she said, "I guess the only thing left is for me to ask you where the back door to this place is so that I can get on my way."

"You won't make it back to your ship."

He messed with some dials—actual dials!—on the control panel, and the picture on the holoscreen closest to Dani zoomed out to give her a view of her ship. The booming sounds she'd heard earlier turned out to be small explosions erupting in the area between where she'd left the ship and the central battleground near the municipal building.

"The 'back door' to this place lets out in the basement of that building."

One of the buildings on the holoscreen glowed red. From the amount of smoke billowing into the air above the building, she guessed it was on fire.

"How do I get out?" There had to be a secondary exit that didn't involve climbing up the chute that brought her here.

"Give it a day or two," he said. "The fighting will move on to a new sector, or they'll tire themselves out, or they'll call a temporary truce to tend to their wounded. Then it'll be safe for you to go."

A couple of days. She didn't have a timetable with Tom—jobs took as long as they took—but that meant she'd be stuck here with a virtual stranger.

Then again, he was pretty easy on the eyes. So far they'd gotten along pretty well, even considering she'd dropped in on him fairly unexpectedly.

Or had she?

He admitted he'd been watching her, and he knew exactly where her ship was. Had he triggered the old escape system?

"Did you bring me here on purpose?" she asked. She'd stepped on the trigger, yes, but nine times out of ten abandoned mechanical things didn't work the way they were designed to work, and definitely not that well.

He gave her a sheepish grin. "They were about to shoot you. I saw a couple of guys sneaking up on you, and you were practically right on top of the hatch..."

"So you saved my life?"

He shrugged.

Huh. Out in the middle of an abandoned settlement, a good-looking, lone historian in an underground bunker had kept her from getting toasted by the locals. Life, especially her life, was really weird at times.

She'd been on vacation. Spending a few extra days here might not be much of a vacation, but things could be worse.

The good-looking historian could have called her Disco Dani.

She released the seal on her environmental suit and removed her helmet. "I always celebrate a successful job with a drink," she said. "You have anything down here we can celebrate with?"

He grinned at her. "I think I've got a little something around here you might like."

"An historian who drinks? I'm shocked." She grinned back to let him know she was teasing.

"I don't dance, though," he said. "Never got the hang of it."

He must not have seen her vid after all, or he wouldn't have brought the subject up. This unexpected vacation was looking better and better.

"Don't worry," she said. "Neither do I."

A frequent contributor to both *Fiction River* and *Pulphouse Fiction Magazine,* **Annie Reed**'s recent work includes the near-future science fiction short novel *In Dreams,* the gritty urban fantasy novel *Iris & Ivy,* and the superhero novel *Faster.* Annie's short fiction appears regularly on Tangent Online's recommended reading lists, and "The Color of Guilt," originally published in *Fiction River: Hidden in Crime,* was selected as one of *The Best Crime and Mystery Stories 2016.* Annie also writes sweet romance under the name Liz McKnight. A founding member and contributor to the innovative Uncollected Anthology, Annie can be found on the web at www.annie-reed.com.

PLAYERS

A CORNELIUS LANGA CASE

BLAZE WARD

Cornelius studied the event around him with something of an academic disconnection...but as an Academic (that was his job title as an investigator for the EuroWest Science Authority), the play on words was acceptable.

His new partner, Analyst Osbert Gerstenberger—Oz—was also around somewhere, but Cornelius had lost him in the swirl of lights and music playing loudly over everything.

It was a cocktail party, though very few people actually drank alcohol these days, especially aboard an orbital station like this one. Atmospheric pressure and spin-induced gravity tended to make even a little alcohol have an outsized impact on most people.

This afternoon, Cornelius was surrounded by nearly three hundred people. Most were EuroWest politicians, along with a few merchants and local businessfolk from the station, but several folks had either come from other stations for this mixer or had actually undergone the rigors of launch to come up from the surface of Earth. There was even a fairly large trade delega-tion from the Anglo-American Alliance, though he hadn't bothered with the details beyond noting the faces and names of all the men involved.

Cornelius had gotten his own invite from a friend of a friend whom he had met after a recent investigation of criminal wrongdoing. The fellow had been cleared when Cornelius solved the case and saved his livelihood, so he had felt a debt and practically thrown the invitation at Cornelius.

It didn't help his humor that everyone seemed to be glowing. At least he had no crimes here that he needed to solve.

If fashion were a crime, however, he himself would be guilty of committing it in the first degree.

Cornelius was not required to wear the sort of uniform that other branches of the EuroWest Science Authority did, but he tended to think of his favorite suit as something for official occasions. He wore canary yellow bell bottom pants with only a modest flair at the cuff, high-waisted with a built-in cummerbund and seams done in a spruce green that matched his jacket.

The jacket was faced and trimmed in a matching canary, with lapels perhaps a shade wider than even the mods at the cocktail party might attempt, but their stylishness was always a hint conservative. He had even settled for two buttons on the front, flap pockets, and two vents with a tailored waist, just to convey seriousness, even as he remained around the fashionable edge of current. His shirt was the same canary as his pants, with lapels that hung out over the jacket like wings. Both set off his dark bronze skin that seemed to turn walnut in the current lights reflecting madly off the mirrored ball spinning over the center of the room.

At one hundred and eighty-five centimeters and eighty-two kilograms, he was tall and lean, a former footballer, unlike his young partner. But Oz had done rugby in college.

Cornelius caught a reflection of a polished surface as he stood in line for a drink and checked his look. His Afro was big and poofy today; he'd spent half an hour picking it just right. Might need to get it cut soon, assuming he didn't decide to go with braids for the winter. His long sideburns and heavy mustache were still black, but he knew there would be gray coming in on the chin one of these days, which was why he always kept it shaved clean.

If Cornelius retired and became a professor, *then* he would grow the beard in. Maybe.

But for today, he was *current*, which was good. Of course, current was a misnomer. More than a generation ago, the *Stodgies* had finally been dislodged from their death grip on men's fashion that had proscribed severe blue or gray suits done in the mid-Twentieth Century style, heavy on wool and occasionally even herringbone tweeds in brown.

Cornelius shuddered as he made his way closer to the bar serving boba and other liquid delicacies. His father still believed in *neckties*, of all things, while Cornelius had an open collar that let a man breathe.

With the Stodgies deposed, fashion had taken a bizarre, chronological cue—only a single step forward as it were—and gone all in on the Disco Era of the 1970s in the old United States, before the place turned into the Anglo-American Alliance and more or less collapsed inward socially under the weight of its racist past.

But the fashion they had given posterity suited his generation, so he was willing to give them that much due.

Cornelius was close enough to the bar now to study the menu of exotic beverage options with part of his mind, using the rest to appreciate the delicate neck of the young woman standing in line in front of him. She was white, like his partner and about a third of the EuroWest population, combining old Western Europe with most of Africa as a political and social entity responsible for the solar system.

She exuded an exquisite cloud of perfume that he had walked into, and long, brown hair was pulled up into a pile on top of her head like a coiled snake. She was well-dressed, at least from the back, in a long, brocaded gown of maroon felt that shouldn't have worked but did. A heavy gold chain hung from her neck, presumably holding up something he couldn't see without impolitely leaning over her shoulder to look. As her breasts appeared to be covered by the outfit, perhaps she wasn't necessarily intending to show them off.

Like the Anglo-Americans, some folks still had hang-ups about nudity and would consider uncovered breasts a great moral outrage when it might just be a Thursday in Bonn.

Covered breasts or no, the visual details of the woman were enticing, the evidence quickly obtained at a glance by a trained investigator used to solving crimes. It was her voice that best captured his attention, though, asking questions of the man behind the bar tasked with concocting liquid alchemy for the guests.

"I'll have the one with brown sugar and milk," she said. "But could you put a shot of cinnamon in and only do half the boba?"

Not a bad combination, thought Cornelius, but her voice didn't sound right. The tone was wrong. The accent. The pacing of her words, even.

Then he realized why it didn't sound correct to his ear.

The woman was American, and her German had slipped into an accent he had automatically classified as American Southern Seaboard. It was only for a sentence, though, before she regained her German pacing and accent.

She got her drink and turned to go, flashing him something of a warm, come-hither smile as she turned and looked at him. Cornelius returned it automatically and nodded, as though he might look her up in a bit.

Then, she disappeared into the crowd, leaving him with questions.

The woman hadn't been on the roster of faces he'd reviewed before attending, all of which were male. Why was there an American woman at a EuroWest political event pretending to be German?

Or was she an imposter?

Still a little rattled, Cornelius stepped to the bar to order and got his second surprise. He knew the man tending, although never expected to see him here. Not after that one case where...

Best not go there.

Sturm, that was the fellow's name. Thomas Sturm. Older male, perhaps in his mid-fifties, with short grey hair going bald in the front and neatly trimmed elsewhere.

The man's green eyes lit up when he spied Cornelius.

"Investigator," he said with a warm smile. "What can I get for you today?"

"Actually, it's Academic these days," Cornelius replied.

"Oh? Well congratulations on the promotion," Thomas said. "And thank you again for your help with...that other business."

"It was my pleasure," Cornelius replied, gesturing over his shoulder. "That woman, by any chance did you happen to know her?"

Cornelius had his boba, identical to the one the woman had, just to help get inside her head. He found Oz nearby and explained his instincts and reactions to him as he scanned the crowd for where she had vanished.

"That is odd," Oz replied, using his greater height to look as well. "Why would there be an American here? Is she a spy?"

Oz was wearing his crushed velvet pants in gold today, and

his favorite maroon smoking jacket, the one with the floppy patch pockets on the front, as well as a button-down Archer shirt, just to rebel against the sense of fashion of everyone in the room.

"I do not know, Oz," Cornelius said. "The scene just plays wrong, which was why my professional instincts took over. We need to find her and solve this."

Oz looked at his own glass for a moment, then nodded.

"Directly ahead of you and perhaps twenty degrees to the right," he said. "I think. About eighteen meters away, turned sideways and talking to three businessmen about something. Is that her?"

"I see her," Cornelius noted. "Businessmen, Oz?"

Oz was secretly the second child of one of the richest families in Old Germany. Business was in his blood, but he was still an Analyst with the EuroWest Science Authority, apparently to the appalled disgust of his parents.

Rebel.

"They dress better than politicians, Cornelius," the broad man replied with a broader grin. "And they tend to shy away from blue or gray. Brown suits are a tool they bring out for official meetings to get zoning regulations changed."

Cornelius laughed at what a useful font of obscure information his young partner could be.

"You circle her then, but do not engage directly," Cornelius instructed. "I need your ears and eyes."

Rather than answer, Oz turned inward and stepped away, as though he had forgotten something behind them.

Cornelius began to stalk the woman. Not directly, but letting the swirling crowd move him as they all listened to the heavy, funky bass line of the music that seemed to be piped in via speakers under the floor. He felt it more in his ribs than his ears, but that might be the solid sole, black leather shoes he was wearing. They were polished like mirrors, but without more than a three-centimeter lift, in an era where the truly ambitious might add go for more than ten.

You had to wear special bell bottom pants at that point, not to look like a complete wanker in action. Cornelius didn't even try.

The woman was indeed entertaining three men with a story about a recent dinner she'd attended, but Cornelius ignored the words. The men were Americans, chattering mostly in English and then using fairly-accented German. Cornelius listened to her vocal characteristics instead, absorbing her intonation. Her pacing was slow though the song playing in the background had a much faster beat that would cause most people to unconsciously speed up as they spoke.

She spoke in a clean, accentless German that sounded more Berlin than Bonn, and her head was tilted perfectly to convey innocence and invitation. Her laugh tinkled like a bell, high and clear as though she'd had formal musical training as a singer. And an actress, from the way she kept her tone pitched low enough that the three men had to lean forward to hear her words.

From the front, she appeared to be of average height, but if she was Anglo-American, then one hundred and sixty-seven centimeters (not counting those twelve-centimeter heels) would mean tall, as such people didn't have the healthcare of EuroWest. Her dress was cut low and rounded in front so as to show off the curved tops of her breasts and a great depth of cleavage. Her breasts even appeared to be real.

The men she was entertaining certainly seemed entranced by them.

She touched one of the men on the arm with just the perfect gesture, and his face lit up as though he'd been knighted (or whatever the Anglo-Americans did these days, hiding from the

Twenty-Third Century by reverting almost to Nineteenth Century moral and social codes).

One eye caught Cornelius standing close, and she gave him a private smile as she finished her story with the three men. There was much laughter and *bonhomie* all around.

Business cards were exchanged, but in that formal, quaint manner that EuroWest had adopted from the ancient Japanese, before demographics had turned them inward into a second Tokugawa Shogunate of a culture. Both hands on the card, holding it forward formally with a slight bow, for the other to take it the same way, as though it were some holy relic changing hands.

Archaic, but modern culture still had strange leftovers baked in.

"If you gentlemen will please excuse me?" she was saying to the three businessmen.

"Please, do not let us detain you," the tallest one—in the middle—replied, speaking German with a harsh accent. American. Almost one of the New York sub-dialects, or perhaps Boston. An Academic like Cornelius needed to be familiar with all of them, even though Anglo-American citizens were rare in EuroWest space. Perhaps *because* of that fact.

The three men withdrew like they had just lost a battle and the enemy cavalry was on their heels, leaving the woman alone. Cornelius took a moment to drink her in.

Gorgeous. Simply exquisite bones in her face. Pale skin, even lighter than he had initially thought, looking closely at her neck for cues. Lean, although she did have a chest well-framed by the top of her dress and the gold chain that held a ruby.

She studied him as well, eyes roving and a wry, knowing smile on her face, although what she might know was left unsaid. They had matching drinks in hand, and she positively glowed when she realized that. Cornelius took that as an entry point.

"It sounded tasty," he offered, noting that the gap between them had gone from three meters to less than two without either of them seeming to move. Invisible tides. Cornelius toasted her with the glass and she returned the toast, slipping even closer.

"You are a man of refined tastes," she said warmly, nodding to his glass. "As well as one obviously not stuck in his ways. Willing to experiment, perhaps?"

Cornelius smiled at the play of her words. Anglo-Americans had hang-ups about sex as a rule, but EuroWest handled those sorts of things in a more adult manner. He wondered if she was planning on taking him to bed at some point in the evening.

He took the last little step toward her, the one that left them dancing without touching.

"Kordula Abel," she introduced herself.

"Cornelius Langa," he replied.

Up close, she was older than he had initially thought. Thirty, plus or minus, though she had been playing the ingénue with the businessmen. Chameleon, then?

"Experimenting can be exciting." Cornelius continued to fence with her, returning to her comment. "If things stay on safe ground."

"And what do you do, Cornelius?" she purred, even with the music loud and funky around them.

"A little of this, a little of that," he replied ambiguously. "It involves a lot of travel."

Absolutely true. An Academic with the EuroWest Science Authority might be called in to solve crimes anywhere in the solar system. And he had been.

"So, you like seeing new things?" she asked, biting her bottom lip slightly in that perfect way intended to carbonate a man's hormones. "Exploring?"

Truly impressive performance, but he wasn't buying it. Or perhaps he knew it was all a mask and wanted to know what he might find beneath. And not just by getting her nude first.

"It has its rewards," he offered, playing her games with words. "And what do you do, Kordula?"

"I'm in sales," she replied with a quick flip of the head that would have tossed her hair perfectly if it was down.

"Oh?" he played. "What are you selling?"

"What are you buying?"

"Still studying my options," Cornelius offered, smiling at the woman. Her heels put her face at his level if they wanted to kiss.

"But you like what you see?"

"Indeed," he said. "But I chased off your other beaus. What were you in the process of selling them?"

Cornelius noted the quick flicker of agitation that crossed her face, as if perhaps he was slipping off her hook.

"Who knows what Anglo-Americans might want?" She changed tack now.

Cornelius shrugged eloquently.

"As a German of Scottish and prior to that, Kenyan, ancestry, I concur," he nodded. "But I was more interested in you, Ms. Abel."

"Oh?" She smiled an invitation now. It suggested a dark hallway or a cloak room, sweat, and loud pleasures.

Cornelius wasn't fooled.

"Earlier, your German accent vanished," he said with a bright smile. "If I had to guess, I'd say you were born in Georgia, in the Americas, or possibly the Carolinas."

Her face fell, went cold, turned angry, and she went from pale to white to red in a hurry.

"How dare you?" The woman started to turn away from him. Cornelius caught her upper arm in a hard hand, holding her in place. She started to say something more, and suddenly

Oz was looming close on her other side—big, white, and intimidating.

"I am also a criminal investigator with the EuroWest Science Authority, Ms. Abel," Cornelius said in a harder, implacable voice. "And I have some questions for you."

Cornelius followed Oz out of the main event and into a conference room nearby, possibly made ready for whatever deals or assignations might evolve out of the cocktail party behind them. Abel had not resisted, once he'd given her arm a hard squeeze... hard enough, perhaps, to leave a bruise the next day. He didn't like playing the role of the big, scary, black man, but Anglo-American culture still had some strange resonances there, so he would use them.

"Sit," he ordered, putting the woman on the far side of the large conference table with Oz lurking over her left shoulder. Cornelius, for his part, sat across from her, between her and the only door.

They had relieved her of her small purse, and Cornelius had her identcard in hand. Kordula Abel. Age twenty-nine. Born in Bremen, according to the paperwork.

Cornelius wondered if any of it was real, were he to truly put resources onto uncovering her secrets.

Kordula glowered from her side of the table. Cornelius was immune.

"I'll call you Kordula, for now," he said, putting her card flat on the table. "Why are you here, Kordula?"

He matched her glower with one of his own. At first, in spite of his badge and authority, she said nothing.

"Fine," he said. "I'm sure if I ask Bonn to start digging, they will find the truth for me quickly enough. They might even find the real Kordula Abel so they can ask her how her identity got stolen."

The woman stirred uncomfortably. Cornelius smiled at her.

"Yes?" he inquired politely.

"She died when she was two," the imposter replied quietly.

"And you assumed her identity?" Cornelius pressed.

"I needed something, and even computerized records still glitch," the woman said, her German accent melting as she spoke. It rang of coastal Georgia, rather than inland around Atlanta. Savannah, perhaps? "I had to escape."

"From?" Cornelius probed.

She wasn't broken. He wouldn't believe that for a moment, as she was too much of a chameleon...a player, as Shakespeare might have called her.

Playing for sympathy now? Likely.

"Do you have any idea how hard it is to escape the United States, detective?" she asked in a tone midway between plaintive and angry.

"Actually, yes," he said with a cruel smile. "My partner specializes in Anglo-American History and has taught me a great many things. You can walk into any embassy and fill out paperwork asking for refugee status. It is generally granted."

"Only for men." Her voice dropped to a growl now. "A four-teen-year-old female must have the approval of her father or husband in an American court to even be allowed to file."

"Husband, Kordula?" Cornelius asked, a bit surprised.

"Women are expected to get married by sixteen at the abso-lute latest, officer," she sneered. "And even that makes one some-thing of an old maid these days. Better to catch her on her thirteenth birthday and make it a wedding celebration as well."

Oz stirred uncomfortably behind her but remained silent. Cornelius glanced up, and the man nodded, pain etched on his face.

"I see." Cornelius leaned back in his chair and breathed in a little to reduce the electric tension that had built up. "So, you are something of an undocumented immigrant to EuroWest? Perhaps a wanted criminal back home if we were to transmit your identifying information to an Anglo-American authority?"

She flinched under his words, pulling in on herself to the point that Cornelius could see that thirteen-year-old suddenly thrust into a wedding dress. It would have been white and lacy, with a veil and a long train. That was how they did it in those parts.

Or she was a world-class actress. There was always that.

"And what might mitigate my findings, Kordula?" he asked.

"They have it coming," she hissed.

"Beg your pardon?"

"Those three you chased off," she explained. "Anglo-Americans. Brokers looking to import things from EuroWest or the Southern Bloc."

"And what are you doing to them, Kordula Abel?" he pressed, noting that the anger in her eyes seemed real.

"Conning them, copper," she snapped. "If you hadn't wandered along, I'd have had them on the hook for ten percent upfront as earnest money for a shipment that would have never arrived in Boston."

"Pig in a poke?" Oz spoke up now, causing the imposter to turn back to look up at him in surprise before she nodded.

"They're amateurs," she agreed. "Think they can pull a fast one and smuggle all sorts of machine parts in disguised as fish from a British export company."

"There are no machine parts?" Cornelius asked.

She turned back and smiled at him like a cat spying a mouse.

"There aren't even fish," she exulted. Then her whole

demeanor changed. "Or wouldn't have been. How did you find me?"

"I was standing behind you in line for boba," Cornelius answered.

"I know," she nodded, smiling. "I could smell you standing there."

Her eyes were back to dancing with him now. Or looking for a dark corner to grapple and grope.

"When you spoke to the bartender, your accent vanished at one point," he continued. "Other things did not add up. I am an officer of the law, and this is a EuroWest station, so I had to investigate. That brought us here."

She muttered something under her breath that he didn't catch.

"What was that?" he asked.

"I said it's not fair," she repeated louder. "They're the criminals, looking to smuggle things in without paying taxes or declaring them. I was just going to rob them. You should be giving me a medal."

"Two wrongs do not make a right, madame," Cornelius said, unwilling to call her by a false name at this point in the game.

She grumbled and subsided. Cornelius looked up at Oz and caught the shadow of something cross the man's face. Then Cornelius understood. Oz had indeed identified this as one of those odd spots where legality and ethics diverged. They had spoken of such places before.

To arrest this woman would be to condemn her to deportation back to the Americans, where she no doubt had an outstanding warrant for her arrest as a fugitive wife. Would a husband have waited for fifteen years, or however long it had been? Or would he have moved on to a next wife? Some subcultures even practiced an open polygamy, allowing one man many wives as a status symbol, especially in the south and west of the old country.

What fate would she face, if he sent her back?

"Oz, could you pardon us for a moment?" Cornelius asked his partner.

Oz blinked in surprise and then nodded, moving silently around the table to the door and exiting.

Kordula Abel, or whatever her real name was, had become perfectly still, like he was the cat now and she the surprised mouse, hunched forward and looking up at him from under hooded brows.

"I would make you a deal," Cornelius said carefully, watching pain flit across those lively, blue eyes.

He could see her expectation of the physical demands he might be about to place on the woman, perhaps right there on the conference room table. Rape, under the badge of authority, as it were, without any witnesses but a criminal about to be thrown to the wolves if she chose to contest things.

Cornelius kept the sourness off his face.

"If I send you home, you'll go to prison or to your husband's home, which might be worse, wouldn't it?" he asked.

She nodded, warily, bad expectations setting in.

"Whereas here, you're a petty criminal swindling other petty criminals in the shadows, mayhap as a sort of payback for what they've done to you, and perhaps all women?"

Again the nod. Slow. Angry, perhaps. Certainly put upon and expecting that his badge would let him do anything he wanted to her, whether she liked it or not.

"Say the word, Kordula," he instructed her.

"Yes," she snarled quietly. "I am fucked, any way you look at it."

He nodded and rose, stepping away from the table and putting a hand on the doorknob.

"Then don't get caught again," he said, opening the door and stepping midway out.

He paused to enjoy the look of utter surprise on the woman's face with a smile of his own.

"Will I ever see you again, detective?" she asked in a hopeful tone.

"Let us hope not," he replied, pulling the door shut and turning to Oz.

"Now what?" the big man asked, equally surprised.

"I think I have had enough of people for now," Cornelius said. "Let's find someplace quiet where we can perhaps enjoy some tea and dialogue on the nature of evil."

"I know just the place," Oz said brightly, gesturing to the right.

Behind them, Cornelius heard the door open. As he turned a corner down the hall, a timid face peeked out and turned his way.

He thought of Shakespeare and the claim that we are all of us players on a stage.

Cornelius winked at her and went on his way.

Blaze Ward writes science fiction in the *Alexandria Station* universe (*Jessica Keller, The Science Officer, The Story Road*, etc.) as well as several other science fiction universes, such as *Star Dragon*, the *Dominion*, and more. In addition, he is the founder, editor, and publisher of *Boundary Shock Quarterly Magazine*.

LET'S DANCE

AN EARTH PROTECTION LEAGUE STORY

DEAN WESLEY SMITH

CHAPTER ONE

For two months now, Friday Franks had admired Emma from a distance at Bryant Hills Nursing Home. Usually across the clattering dishes and smell of boiling chicken noodle soup that filled the lunchroom as an attendant fed him the green and brown goo they laughingly called his lunch.

Since he would choke on anything solid, it was the best he could do. Besides, his taste buds had vanished with his ability to move since his stroke three years ago, so it really made no difference at all. He just wished the food looked better.

For a woman two years younger than his ripe old age of sixty-eight, Emma had a real glow about her. She kept her long gray hair pulled back into a ponytail, which made her look younger, and she had fairly smooth skin and a smile that could light up the entire sad lunchroom.

Her laugh often drifted over the sound of dishes and light talking like a breath of fresh air over a death scene in a play, almost as if it didn't belong in such a serious event as feeding lunch to the near dead.

She always wore a blue dress that looked more from the

eighties than anything else, yet was festive and bright against the white aides' outfits and the older clothes of the residents. She always wore just a touch of makeup that accented her blue eyes.

He, on the other hand, wore the same gray tee-shirt, old jeans, and a stained bib to catch the food that didn't get dripped into his mouth. Yup, they were a pair.

She just didn't know it yet.

She wasn't a resident here like he was. She was a volunteer. The *Earth Protection League* had researched her on his request and found she was widowed now for fifteen years, lived alone in a small ground-floor apartment, and was allergic to pets. She had no real family, and her best friend had just died a year ago, so no real connections.

She was also one impressive person. A former pilot in the Air Force, she had spent twenty years as an airline pilot in a time when not that many women held that position. He knew she still had her own Cessna that she called "Freedom" and managed to get some flight time almost every weekend.

He knew for a fact she would be a great recruit for the *Earth Protection League*. She had the drive and intelligence that it took and skills the *League* needed. And the *League* had agreed with him.

So now it was up to him to talk her into joining up. The first trip out into space was always the hardest.

So the *League* had pulled some strings and got her assigned to feed him at lunch and dinner, and today was the first day. He couldn't swallow or move his arms or legs much at all, but thankfully he could still talk, still had his deep, rich voice.

And even at his age, he still had most of his long black hair from his youth. It had thinned some, but the aide that dressed him kept it combed back like he used to wear it in the 1970s, his disco days.

The attendant pushed him into position at the stained lunch

table and another put his plate of green and brown goo in front of him. He watched Emma as she worked her way through the tables toward him, smiling, a smile he could come to really enjoy being around. She had the ease of movement of a dancer, just like he used to have.

Just like he still had out on the frontier.

Damn, she actually made his heart race some. Not even in the heat of battle against the damn alien dogs, both blasters spouting fire, did his heart race like this.

"Mr. Franks?" she said, pulling up a chair beside him. "I'm Emma."

"Wonderful to finally meet you, Emma," he said, giving her a smile as best he could. "Call me Friday."

She smiled and sat down. "Friday Franks? I love that."

"Thanks," he said, wishing he could smile a little more. "Actually, a lot of my friends called me 'Disco' back in the day, so I go by Friday 'Disco' Franks."

He didn't add that actually, he was Captain Friday "Disco" Franks of the *Earth Protection League*. With luck, she would know that soon enough.

"Now that's fun," she said, the wonderful smile really reaching her eyes. "I loved disco when I was younger. Those were wonderful years."

"That they were," he said.

He looked her right in the eyes, and they held that gaze for a long moment.

A surprisingly long moment, where even the clatter of the lunchroom around them faded into the background.

There really was a connection.

An intense one.

Wow, just wow.

And after a moment, she actually blushed, then looked

down and picked up the spoon and said without looking up at him, "You ready for some lunch?"

"As long as you're buying," he said.

That broke the tension. She laughed, and they started into the humiliating routine of her easing green or brown mush into his mouth and then, with a napkin, gently wiping away the excess.

What a meet-cute if he had ever seen one.

CHAPTER TWO

Emma Dakota sat at her small glass kitchen table, sipping her second cup of morning coffee and nibbling on the remains of her second Eggo waffle. Around her, a soft jazz station played as she studied the screen of her iPad.

After a week of wonderful conversation with Friday Franks, she had decided to actually look him up. She had found after a week that she just couldn't get him off her mind. He was smart, funny as all get out, and seemed to have layers of secrets that made his eyes twinkle. On top of that, he seemed to have a zest for life that was amazing considering what the stroke had done to him.

It had been a long time since she had been so attracted to a man. And, of course, she had to pick a man who couldn't move much at all. She supposed that was a safe pick on her part. But who could blame her? That deep voice of his could charm a raging bull, and the intelligence in those green eyes made her want to spend time with him.

He clearly liked spending time with her as well. Many meals over the last week since she had started feeding him, they had been the last ones in the lunchroom, sitting and laughing and talking about everything from disco in the 1970s to friends having great grandkids, even though neither of them felt old enough to even have grandkids.

In one short week, she had come to treasure those hours with him, actually look forward to them all day.

Like her, he said he had no real family. So this morning, to kill some time while she waited to go in and spend lunch with him, she decided to see what she could find out about him in his previous life before his stroke.

She supposed she should not have been surprised, but it turned out he was one of the most respected businessmen in the state. He still owned six nightclubs around town, and from what she could find, he was still on the boards of five major corporations.

He had been married once, his wife died of cancer twenty years ago, and before his stroke, he was considered one of the most eligible bachelors in the city.

All news coverage and articles about him stopped after his stroke.

Pictures of him before the stroke with his long black hair combed back and a wide smile were everywhere, and even into his sixties, he was clearly one of the most handsome men she had ever seen.

He was also an avid pilot, which got her attention because they had never talked about that. He had not one, but two planes before his stroke and had sold both, but he still had access to his own private jet, although it was now in a rental pool.

She kept digging and found that he also supported a ton of different charity work around the state, mostly focusing on education for those who couldn't afford it. He actually had a master's degree in engineering as well.

After a time, she just sat back from the computer, shaking her head. He was amazing, just amazing.

One hour later, she was sitting next to Friday in the lunch-room helping him eat and laughing at one of his comments when a man, clearly military, but not wearing a uniform, approached them.

He stopped almost at attention facing Friday and said, "Sir, tonight at the normal time."

"Thank you, Lieutenant," Friday said, and the young man spun and walked away through the busy and noisy lunchroom.

Emma felt confused, to say the least. And a long silence sort of stretched out in front of her between them.

Finally, she said, "May I ask?"

"Can't tell you much," he said, his eyes full of life, even more so than normal. "And you wouldn't believe me if I tried. But I would love to have you come along. It's sort of an adventure. Trust me, it will make you feel young again. Disco dancing young."

"Oh, wouldn't I love that," she said, laughing. And she would. She had grown to accept the restrictions of her age, but climbing into Freedom every weekend still gave her a fleeting sense of the feeling, even for just a few hours of flight time.

"Great," he said. "Two young women will knock on your door at 9 pm. Just trust me and do as they say and they will bring me along shortly."

"Trust you?" she asked, smiling. "I don't even know you."

He laughed, that wonderful laugh she had some to enjoy over lunch and dinner. "Sure you do. How many boards of direc-tors do I sit on?"

She blushed, then said, "Five."

"Missed two," he said, again laughing. "How many planes did I used to own?"

"Two plus a private jet," she said, staring into his eyes.

"On the money," he said. "Still got control of the jet but

haven't used it since this stroke. So, Captain Dakota, retired, you up for an adventure?"

She sat back. She had never said anything about her military career or even her airline career. But he clearly knew. And that both excited her and scared her to death.

"So what really is going on?" she asked.

"Again," he said, his eyes twinkling, "you wouldn't believe me if I told you. But I can promise that you will thank me. And all I ask in return is the first dance."

She laughed. "Okay, you got a deal."

And that evening, over dinner, she kept trying in different ways to get more information from him, without luck. But his zest for life was even more pronounced, his joy, his humor. And she had to admit, that was contagious.

CHAPTER THREE

Friday waited in his bed in his small, private room, staring at the ceiling, just willing the time to pass. He hated this waiting time the most before every mission. And this time was worse, since he had no idea if Emma would be on the other side or not.

He had done everything he could do, including having a young lieutenant come up to their table to tell him the mission, even though he had already been informed.

And both the young women officers who would show up at Emma's house were not threatening, and both were smart. But still, with all recruits like Emma, the first time was the hardest because it was the most frightening.

Finally, Benjamin Smith appeared through Friday's patio door like a ghost appearing in the room. Benjamin snapped to attention and saluted.

Benjamin was a very large guy, former football player,

strong as anyone Friday had ever known. He had on jeans and a dress shirt and had his head almost shaved.

"At ease," Friday said.

"How are you feeling tonight, sir?" Benjamin asked as he stepped to the bed and uncovered Friday. Friday had on his nightshirt and adult diaper that he always had on in bed. Nurses changed it twice a night, even if he didn't need to be changed.

"Feeling excited for the mission," Friday said.

"Sure wish I could go along," Benjamin said, picking up Friday, holding his arms in place so they wouldn't just flop around, then turning and stepping to the patio door.

"You're still too young," Friday said. "But given time, you'll be out there."

"Hope so, sir," Benjamin said.

Benjamin took Friday out into the cool evening air of the nursing home's interior patio and used his heel to slide the door gently closed. Then, two steps later, the transport beam caught them, and they were in the transport ship.

Benjamin strode quickly down a corridor to a cabin on the left and went in, laying Friday gently in a coffin-like box that filled the center of the room. The interior of the box had brown tones and deep padding.

Then, Benjamin stepped back and snapped off a salute.

"Have a good mission, sir," Benjamin said.

"Oh, I will," Friday said, feeling the intense excitement as to what was to come as the lid of the coffin box closed over him, and the faint, orange-smelling gas took him from his stoke-ravaged life.

CHAPTER FOUR

By nine pm, Emma had completely decided that she wasn't

going anywhere. Nothing good could come of this at all, and who knew what strange plans those who worked for Friday had.

Granted, she liked the guy, more than she wanted to admit. But trusting him on some late-night adventure was just fool-hardy. She had taken her share of chances in her life, but always calculated chances. And he was rich enough, he could hire people to do his bidding.

So when the two young women knocked on her door at nine, she was ready to turn them away.

But as she opened the door, both of them snapped to atten-tion and saluted her.

By reflex, she returned the salute, now even more puzzled.

"Captain," the young woman on the left said, "I am Lieu-tenant Davis, this is Lieutenant Craig. We are here to escort you."

Both wore jeans, white blouses, and had their hair cut and styled short. Both were the same height at about Emma's five-six. Davis was a light blonde, Craig had dark black hair. Both wore no makeup and yet were strikingly pretty.

"And we can't begin to say how much we envy you," Lieu-tenant Craig said.

"Envy?" Emma asked, still trying to gain her footing from the salute.

Both young lieutenants nodded. "We are too young. You will understand shortly."

"Are you ready?"

Emma nodded slowly. Her resolve at not going had faded some.

"Good," Lieutenant Davis said.

And the next moment, Emma's house disappeared from around her, and she found herself standing in a large room with both lieutenants still facing her. No sensation at all of movement.

"We thought this would be a good place to start," Lieutenant Davis said.

She indicated that Emma should turn around. It was clear to Emma almost at once that she was on a large ship of some sort, but as she turned to face a viewport, all she could see was the planet Earth below her.

"We're in space?" she said, gasping slightly.

"On an *Earth Protection League* transport ship that is cloaked," Lieutenant Davis said, moving over closer to Emma and touching her back gently for support.

"The *League's* mission is to protect Earth and other member planets from any threats," Lieutenant Craig said.

Emma just stood there staring. No way she could be in space. More than likely, she was in some sort of holo program, still in her living room.

"Pretty amazing, isn't it?" Davis said. "The *League* has been protecting Earth since before the time of Atlantis. We are honored to be able to serve in-system, at least for now."

"So what really is going on and why me?" Emma asked, turning away from the image of Earth and facing the two young women, fighting to get her senses about her.

"The *League* is recruiting you as a pilot," Davis said. "Something we both hope to be, at least in near-Earth areas until we get older."

"I think I am a little old to be a pilot in some military organization," Emma said. "You have the wrong woman."

"It is your age and your skills the *League* needs," Davis said. "Let us try to explain as we take you to your cabin."

She didn't like the sound of the word "cabin" at all.

The two lieutenants turned her and headed for a door that slid open as they approached, showing a long, empty corridor beyond.

"This is an autopiloted transport ship to what is called the

Frontier," Davis said, "the area along the borders between *League* space and some enemies of the *League*."

"Imagine a large sphere with Earth as the center," Craig said. "That is a vast amount of space to patrol, and very few permanent patrol ships and crews cover it. Out along the edges, almost everything is automated."

"But when more crew and ships are needed in an emergency or due to an invasion into *League* space, they recruit quickly from Earth."

At that point, they reached a room on the right side of the long hallway. The door slid open to reveal a coffin-like container in the middle of the room.

And nothing else.

Emma just about bolted at that point, but the calmness of the two lieutenants held her.

"That's where the problem comes in," Davis said, "It seems that faster-than-light travel must anchor to a point in time. So when humans go out at top faster-than-light speeds, their bodies regress. When you get to the area of the frontier where you are headed, your body will be 26 years old, though your mind will remain the same."

"It's why Lieutenant Davis and I can't go out beyond the Earth system very far very fast," Craig said. "We're just too young."

"This is one of the largest transport ships," Davis said. "When it launches, it will carry over one thousand officers your age and older from all over the planet. And for whatever is happening now on the border, we know five more transports are headed out as well. Something big must be happening. But they never tell us back in-system what is happening."

"This is your sleep chamber," Craig pointed to the coffin. "You will be asleep for six days, both going out and coming back, all without dreaming. And even if you are out on the frontier for months, we will return you to your home within fifteen minutes or so of you leaving."

Davis laughed and shook her head. "It is really hard to get used to the strangeness of the fixed nature of space and time and matter mixed with faster-than-light travel."

Emma didn't know what to think. Or what kind of elaborate game this all was. Or even why she was a part of it.

She walked over to the coffin and leaned in, and as she did, she smelled a light orange smell and felt faint.

"Let us help you," Davis said as both women easily picked her up and laid her into the sleep chamber on very soft padding.

The last thing she remembered was both young women snapping off salutes as the lid of the coffin closed over her.

CHAPTER FIVE

Captain "Disco" Friday Franks jumped from his transport chamber with an easy bound, landing on both feet, enjoying that wonderful feeling of having a functioning and young body again.

He felt home again, on his trusted fighter, the *Disco Dancer*. Damn, he loved this ship and everyone on board it.

As always, his sleep chamber had been moved from the transport ship to his cabin on *Dancer*, so all his personal clothes were here.

In one simple move, he swept off the adult diaper and night-shirt and tossed them in a drawer that extended from the wall.

Then he quickly showered, combed into place his thick, rich head of black hair, and quickly worked to get dressed. He loved the feeling of being able to once again dress himself, a feeling he had never fully appreciated until it was suddenly taken from him.

First, his black leather pants, then his white silk shirt tucked into the leather pants. Then, he slipped on his tall, almost knee-high back boots and tucked his pants into the tops of them, securing them in place.

Then, his leather vest with the letters EPL on the front. After strapping on the wide belt that held his two Proton Stunners, he looked in the mirror. Damn, this would have killed back in the disco days. He loved the way it looked right now.

Suddenly, he remembered Emma. It took him only a moment on his link to find out that she had made it. Somehow, the two young women had managed to get her on board. He had assigned another one of his crew here, Bettie Daniels, to help Emma when she woke up if she did make it. Bettie was his communications officer and maybe one of the smartest and nicest humans he had ever met.

With one last look in the mirror, he headed out into the main corridor that split the ship. He had no doubt it would take Emma a little longer than it took him to get dressed, and for Bettie to explain a ton of things to her, so he had time to grab a coffee and Danish before going to see how Emma was doing.

He would take both her and Bettie their own Danishes and coffee as a peace offering. He had no doubt Emma was going to be angry, really angry, if he knew her as well as he thought he did. You didn't mess with Emma Dakota's reality without paying some price or another. He had learned that in only a week of conversations. Now he was so looking forward to seeing her in her prime, at 26 years of age.

He laughed and headed toward the mess hall, greeting and saluting his crew as he went. This was going to be so much fun, no matter what mission they were here for.

Five minutes later, sipping on a coffee and finishing off a strawberry Danish, something that more than likely would have killed him in the nursing home, the door to one of the officers' cabins slid open, and Bettie Daniels stepped out, followed by Emma.

Emma at the age of 26 was a strikingly beautiful woman with the same intense eyes he had come to know back on Earth. And he was right, she didn't look confused, she looked angry.

Her beauty just stopped him cold. Bettie came up and took one of the coffees from him as he stood there with his mouth open, staring.

Emma was wearing the same basic clothes he was—black leather pants tucked into high leather boots, silk shirt, and a single photon blaster strapped to one hip. Why did he have no doubt she could use that weapon if needed?

When Emma saw him, it took a moment before her eyebrows went up, and she shook her head as she recognized him.

"Friday," she said, stepping toward him. "How can this be real?"

"I tried to ask a *League* scientist to explain it to me once," he said, smiling and offering her a cup of coffee and a Danish. "Hurt my head after a few minutes."

Bettie laughed. "I didn't understand a word of the explanation I tried to get, but I learned not to question a chance to be young again."

Emma nodded to that.

"Welcome aboard the *Disco Dancer*," Friday said, "one of the best fighting ships in the *League*."

Then he nodded to Bettie. "Thank you. Better get to the bridge and find out what we are up against this time. Captain Dakota and I will be along shortly."

"Understood, Captain," Bettie said, tipping up the coffee cup as a way of saying thanks.

"Thank you, Bettie," Emma said.

"You did better than I did," Bettie said, smiling.

"Took me a week to clear up the black eye from you punching me on your first trip," Friday said, laughing.

"Didn't know that was an option," Emma said, winking at Bettie, who laughed and turned away.

Friday took a deep breath. So far, so good.

"So," Emma said, "during the trip out here, wherever 'here' is, somehow in my sleep I was given all the history of the *League*, its mission, and I assume instructions on how to fly a ship like this. Right?"

"Thankfully, yes," Friday said, not being able to take his eyes from the amazingly beautiful and powerful woman standing in front of him. "My copilot, Dan Lyman, died two missions ago."

"Something out here killed him?"

Friday shook his head. "Unexpected heart attack in his home before they could get him out and into space to save him. He was a good guy, a friend for a lot of missions."

"Sorry," Emma said, and it was clear she meant it. "So, I am to take his place?"

"You are," Friday said. "But at this point, now that you know what is happening, you can always turn the job down."

Emma laughed and indicated the incredible young bodies they each had. "You gave me a chance to be young again and fly in combat, something I was never allowed to do when I was younger. So what the hell in this dream is there to turn down?"

He laughed, feeling very relieved and even more attracted to his new copilot. "I had a hunch you would say that, Captain. Welcome aboard. Let me show you where all the magic happens."

"A little early for dancing, isn't it?"

"There is a reason this ship is named the *Disco Dancer*."

She laughed as they walked side-by-side to the bridge. Now the key was to survive the mission so they could do some dancing when it was all over.

. . .

CHAPTER SIX

The bridge of the *Disco Dancer* looked more like a blown-up cockpit on an airliner. There were four stations, all with screens, and almost no room to move around. But at first glance, Emma was impressed.

Bettie sat with her back to the captain's chair and was already bent over what looked to be a digital display, headphones on.

Beside her at a station behind the copilot chair was a guy who looked to be about twenty, if that, with a face-full of freckles and an unruly thatch of bright red hair.

"Commander Mason, this is Captain Dakota," Friday said.

"Friends call me Red when not on duty," he said, smiling at her and shaking her hand. "Fresh out of a retirement home south of Phoenix."

"Pleasure, Commander," Emma said.

"And you know Commander Daniels," Friday said.

Bettie just sort of waved but didn't look up.

Friday indicated the copilot chair for Emma to sit. Then, he dropped into his pilot's chair, and it seemed to almost mold around him as he turned to face the boards and screens in front of him.

She was amazed at how at home he looked in that chair, still stunned that he was the same man she had been feeding for the past week.

He put on his headset, and she did the same. Information about the boards and everything in front of her came into her mind as if she had known them all along. It felt very weird, but she didn't question it.

Just as she hadn't really questioned that she was back in her

26-year-old body, feeling no aches, no pains, and with so much energy she didn't really know how to direct it.

"Okay, Commander Daniels," Friday said. "How bad is it this time?"

"Bad," Bettie said. "On your screens."

In front of Emma, a screen showing stars appeared, more like a three-D map. A line across the map, Emma knew, represented the edge of League space.

There looked to be at least a thousand green dots in formations on the *League* side, each one a *League* fighter like theirs.

"Wow, they got five times the number of fighters we usually need," Friday said.

"Something bad is happening," Red said.

Emma knew from the information fed to her while she slept that this fighter not only held the four of them, but over sixty other old souls, now all young, all imported and recruited in their old age to serve in various departments like engineering, weapons, and even food service.

She knew that they were all from various parts of the country back home. If this ship were destroyed, fake bodies would be put in their places at home, and it would be announced they had died in their sleep. (The *League* didn't want too many deaths from the same place, though. In fact, she and Friday were the only ones on the entire ship from the same part of the country.)

It added up to a lot of older folks made young, manning a lot of high-tech fighter craft. Every green dot on that screen was another ship just like theirs.

"Not seeing the problem," Friday said, his voice full of command. "Where exactly are we?"

"We are in quadrant 335, the side of *League* space that faces the edge of the galaxy," Bettie said.

"None of our enemies are located in this direction," Friday

said. "No alien race lives out here. There's no group of stars with planets to live on."

"The threat isn't coming from within this quadrant. It's coming in from *outside* the galaxy."

Both Friday and Emma swung around in their seats to stare at Bettie, who looked up at them, her eyes haunted.

Emma couldn't imagine "outside the galaxy." Even with her sleep training, she was barely grasping being in space as it was.

"Oh, shit, you aren't kidding," Friday said.

Bettie just shook her head as both Friday and Emma turned back to their stations.

"Distant images coming in from scout ships," Bettie said.

Emma wasn't sure what she was seeing at first; then, it slowly became clear. It was a ship in the shape of a big metal ball. It didn't seem to be spinning, but it still looked like a disco ball there on the screen.

"It's the size of Jupiter," Bettie said. "Bigger than many small suns. And on its current course and speed, it will plow right through the Earth system in just under a year."

"How soon until it reaches our position?" Friday asked as Emma stared at the information flowing over her screens.

"Six hours until it reaches the edge of *League* space," said Bettie.

"Any sign of life?" Emma asked.

"Nothing so far."

"Where did it come from?" Red asked.

"If it has not changed course," Bettie said, "it has been traveling from the direction of the Andromeda galaxy for just over three million years."

Bettie took a deep breath. Silence filled the bridge for a moment.

"Our orders are to destroy it, stop it, or divert it," Bettie said.

"Of course they are," Friday said, shaking his head.

He sat for a second, then said, "Captain Dakota, Commander Mason, you are with me. Commander Daniels, I want the heads of engineering and weapons systems to meet us in the mess. Stay at your station and relay to us any research information that comes in."

"Understood, sir," Bettie said.

Without another word, Friday rotated up and out of his chair, his mind clearly focused, leaving Red and Emma to follow in his wake.

Clearly, this was not a normal first mission. She doubted there was anything normal about stopping a planet-sized alien ship before it destroyed Earth. But she knew for a fact that their ships would be like fleas on a dog's back compared to that monster coming in.

CHAPTER SEVEN

Friday sat next to Emma in the mess, a room of about thirty tables surrounded by chairs, all magnetically secured to the floor. The place had a faint coffee odor and was empty except for the five of them. For a fleeting second, it reminded him of the lunchroom at the nursing home, with Emma feeding him. But only for a second.

As they got settled, more information came in about the giant sphere. It was mostly hollow, with a stationary outer shell and a moveable inner shell. From the looks of it, the aliens who had built it lived on the inside of the sphere. Clearly, at one point, the inner shell had been spinning, creating a gravity on the inside of the sphere. Now it was completely dead, nothing was moving, and there was no atmosphere.

They all studied the new data from the scout ships for a moment. Then, Friday looked up at his command crew.

Across from him sat Henrietta Blend, the smartest engineer

he had ever had the pleasure to work with. She had long black hair and dark black eyes that seemed to just see everything around her. At her tallest, in heels, she was under five feet tall.

She had her head down, studying the computer tablet in her hand like she was defusing a bomb. Actually, she might be.

Friday's weapons expert was a short, intense guy who went by the name Helix. Friday knew he was from Mexico and seemed to love just about anything that fired a bullet or a beam or exploded.

"So any ideas?" Friday asked, glancing first at Helix, then Red, then Emma.

"We can't destroy it," Henrietta said without looking up. "Even if we could, all we would do is break it into massive chunks, and those pieces would do even more damage in the Earth system before we could break them up further."

"Does it have engines?"

"It did," Henrietta said. "But don't even think about trying to go in there and fire them up. Never seen this kind of technology before. Way, way out beyond us."

"Could we even blow a hole in the thing if we wanted?" Friday asked, glancing at Helix.

"No chance," Helix said, shaking his head. "At least not quickly. That thing, without shields, has been taking a constant rain of debris plowing into it for millions of years...and take a look at the surface. Even after all that, it's difficult to see a dent."

"So we stop it," Emma said. "Better than destroying it anyway and losing all that knowledge."

Friday looked at her for a moment. She wasn't kidding. He could tell.

"It's the size of Jupiter," Helix said. "In motion at a very high rate of speed."

"But hollow," Emma said. "A lot less mass if I remember some basic physics correctly."

She turned to Friday, who was trying and failing to catch up with her thinking.

"You said we have over a thousand ships this size out here, right?" Emma asked.

Friday nodded.

Emma turned to Helix. "You say our weapons won't hurt the outside, correct?"

Helix nodded, and Henrietta looked up, a frown on her face.

"What kind of thrust can one of these ships create against the force of a weapon firing on that surface?"

"And multiply that by all the ships in a pattern on the surface of the sphere," Friday said, finally catching up with where Emma was going with the idea.

"And use the big transport ships as well," Helix said.

Henrietta's fingers flew over the screen in front of her. Then, after a moment, she said, "It might work, depending on the actual mass of that sphere."

Friday clicked his com link. "Bettie, patch me in to Admiral Saber."

They all waited in silence for a moment until a clear voice came over their coms.

"Captain Franks," Admiral Brian Saber said. "What do you have?"

Friday had spent a lot of time with Saber and his wife, Dot. They were permanently stationed on the frontier and were two of the best people he had ever met.

"We think that if all of our ships are in a formation directly in front of the sphere, firing weapons and using full thrusters, we might be able to slow down and eventually stop it completely."

Silence greeted his statement, so Friday went on. "We would need exact calculations of the mass of the sphere and the speed and also the total force that all the ships out here, plus the transports, could generate against the sphere."

"Might work," Admiral Saber said after a moment. "Give me one hour to get the scout ships taking better measurements and the engineers crunching the numbers."

"Understood," Friday said, and the line went dead.

"Red, you and Helix figure out what level of weapons fired against the side of the sphere we can maintain to hold us away from the sphere while thrusters are firing."

"Going to have to be a perfect balance," Red said, "or we'll end up paste against that thing."

Friday nodded.

"Henrietta," Friday said. "Keep crunching the numbers as they come in."

Friday stood and indicated that Emma should follow him. "Captain, well done coming up with that idea. Now we've got some courses to calculate right down to the inch."

Emma laughed. "We can get it closer than that I'm sure. But we forgot something."

Friday looked at her intense blue eyes.

She smiled. "From all the information pouring into my brain while I slept, I seem to remember a fighter like this carries two small one-man fighters, two scout ships, and two crew transport ships for ground missions."

Friday realized what she was saying, and Henrietta just shook her head.

Friday tapped his com. "Connect me with Admiral Saber again. We have something to add to the mix that just might make this work."

Emma smiled that wonderful smile Friday had come to love over the last week. Now if they both didn't die over this crazy idea, he might even get to dance with her.

· · ·

CHAPTER EIGHT

Emma stared at the screens, both where they were in relationship to the massive metal sphere, and where they were in relationship to the other over eight thousand ships of various sizes that were moving into position.

In front of them, the big sphere no longer looked like a big sphere, but a wall of metal. Captain Friday had matched their ship's speed with the sphere, then moved them into position not more than fifty miles ahead of it before launching their six smaller ships.

From a distance, the *League* ships looked like a swarm of insects against a flat wall, spreading out over thousands of miles of the surface to make sure their push didn't buckle anything inside the sphere.

But Emma knew, and had checked the calculations herself twice, that the force of all the weapons of the *League* ships, combined with the thrust of the ships behind the weapons, would be enough to slow the big ball.

Thankfully, the thing was hollow, or this would never work. And even then, it was going to take time. Each ship was going to have to maintain a fine balance between the weapons and the thrust holding them away from the wall. At the engine thrust that each ship would be applying, if a weapons system holding them away suddenly failed, the ship would smash almost instantly into the big metal wall.

That was the problem. Time.

And no one was sure if the weapons systems could maintain such constant firing.

The engineers had worked out that each ship would fire for one hour, then cut thrusters and weapons, back away, and do a complete check of everything for one hour before resuming fire for another hour.

That would take them a lot longer to slow the big ball, but it would work.

At that moment, Bettie said, "Admiral Saber."

His square-jawed image appeared on Emma's screen. Emma knew he was on every screen in the fleet at that moment.

"We have another two hundred fighters headed to join you, and ten large transport ships," Saber said. "Start when you are ready, do the best you can, take no unnecessary risks. Good luck to you all."

With that, the Admiral vanished, and Captain Franks said to the entire crew, including those on the six extra ships, "Begin when ready. Abort and back away at the first sign of trouble."

Then, he turned to Emma and smiled. "An adventure, that's for sure."

She smiled back. "Wouldn't have missed it for the world."

Friday nodded, then said, "Fire weapons at will. Steady fire. I'll take the first shift of holding us in place."

At that, on Emma's screen, she saw photon beams streak from the *Disco Dancer* and form an orange hot area on the metal surface, seeming to do no damage at all.

Friday expertly kept his ship steady as the force of the weapon pushed into the big metal wall in front of them.

"The League really needs to figure out what that metal is," Red said. "Nice if all of our ships were covered with it."

As Emma watched, along the massive alien metal wall, more and more ships started to fire.

They were nothing more than ants pushing at a giant rock. But with over eight thousand of them, and more coming, it might actually work.

As Emma watched, she shook her head. All the people back home on Earth knew nothing about what was happening out here. If they managed to stop this thing, no one on Earth would ever know.

She just felt so lucky to be a part of this. All of this.

CHAPTER NINE

Friday sat alone in the big mess hall, eating a ham sandwich slowly, enjoying the flavor of the soft wheat bread and the mustard. "Operation Big Push" had been going on now for eight days, and a thousand more *League* ships of various sizes had joined in.

They had either been resting for an hour, or he or Emma were at the helm. It had been a grueling time, but they had survived it.

The *League* had lost over a hundred ships smashed against the metal wall, hundreds of good people whose families, when this was over, would be greeted with their loved-one dying in their sleep of old age instead of being honored as the heroes they really were.

But they were winning the battle. The big alien ball had slowed tremendously, and with each day it got slower and slower, and the danger to the Earth system was now a century away instead of mere months.

Saber said that a few hundred ships were being built and fitted with the structural ability to actually rest against the metal and push, without the use of the weapons fire to hold a ship at bay. Those tug-like ships would take over the last bit of slowing and finally stopping the giant metal ball far inside *Earth Protection League* space so it could be explored and studied.

There was a part of him that wished he could be part of the team to explore the big alien sphere. But that was a few years away. They had to get it stopped first. And then figure out a way to get inside it.

So he finished off the sandwich, then headed back to the bridge. Emma was holding the ship steady against the weapons fire as she had done so well for so many hours. She had turned out to be a fantastic pilot, maybe almost as good as he was. And he had a hunch that given time, she might be better.

Friday dropped into his chair and said, "Let's shut this down."

"Gladly, Captain," Emma said, easing back on the speed as Red brought down the weapons fire, the exact same careful routine they had done every hour for days. Yet this was the last time, thankfully.

"Captain," Friday said to Emma, "pull us back and away to a nice safe distance. Bettie, have our secondary ships rejoin us and dock."

"With pleasure," Bettie said.

One hour later, everyone was back on board, repairs were being done where needed, and the sounds of laughter echoed through the ship.

Friday and Emma were headed down the hallway toward the mess.

"You did great," he said, smiling.

"Thank you, Captain," she said. "So now what happens?"

"We have two or three days of repairs, and it will take that long for the transports to get ready to take us home as well. Maybe a little longer."

"And we will arrive back in our old bodies about fifteen minutes after we left?"

"Yup," Friday said.

"Longer is better out here," Emma said, smiling.

"Can't argue with that," said Friday. "So how about we go get cleaned up, take a nap, and then I'll meet you for a nice dinner in two hours? I'm buying, and you don't even have to feed me."

"I would love that," she said, laughing. She beamed at him, that smile that he had come to really enjoy back on Earth and now even more over the last week.

They stopped in front of her cabin, and he faced her, trying to look serious.

"Just remember one thing," he said.

She frowned and nodded. "What?"

"You promised me the first dance, and after dinner, the dance floor and bar will be open."

Again, she laughed and said, "I'm hoping for a lot more than one dance."

He laughed and said, "So am I. So am I."

Considered one of the most prolific writers working in modern fiction, *New York Times* and *USA Today* bestselling writer **Dean Wesley Smith** has published far more than two hundred novels in forty years, plus hundreds of short stories and non-fiction books. He has more than twenty-three million copies of his books in print. At the moment, he produces novels in four major series, including the time travel *Thunder Mountain* novels set in the old west, the galaxy-spanning *Seeders Universe* series, the cold case mystery series *Cold Poker Gang*, and the *Poker Boy* superhero series. During his career, Dean has also written dozens of *Star Trek* novels, the only two original *Men in Black* novels, Spider-Man and X-Men novels, plus novels set in gaming and television worlds. For more information about Dean's books and ongoing projects, visit his website at www.deanwesleysmith.com.

ACKNOWLEDGEMENTS

ROBERT JESCHONEK

This project could not have come together without the hard work and dedication of the entire *Space: 1975* crew. That crew consists of numerous teams and individuals, all of whom deserve a round of applause.

At the heart of the project, the all-star author team served up the written content, accompanied by the cover and story illustrations by top-flight artist Ben Baldwin. Author Marc Scott Zicree deserves special recognition for providing extra guidance and support in making the book even more incredible and complete.

In support of the authors, the editorial team at IE Books/Pie Press Publishing provided invaluable support, led by Kendra McConnell and Sonia Beltz and including Evelyn Burd, Sara Caskey, Karel Clark, Eyza Hamdani Hussain, and Caitlin Mobley. The Pie Press social media team, including those editorial personnel plus Sylvie Arnold, Jacquelyn Benoit, Ingrid Miller, Julianna Poljak, and Cassie Zhu, spread the word far and wide during and after the Kickstarter campaign that launched the project.

Speaking of the Kickstarter campaign, author Dean Wesley

Smith offered extensive guidance in shaping and executing it, as did Loren Coleman, who was part of the original author team until "life rolls" forced him to step aside.

Then there are the 241 backers of the Kickstarter campaign, without whom this project would never have gotten off the ground. Each and every one of them deserves a round of applause for bringing this book to life and making it so extraordinary with their financial support in these difficult times.

And, of course, thank you to all the writers, actors, designers, technicians, musicians, and filmmakers who created so much wonderful space opera (on the printed page, TV screen, and movie screen) that made the 1970s such an amazing time for fans like me and changed our lives for the better in countless ways. (Cue Freddie Mercury singing the theme from *Flash Gordon...*)

Finally, thanks to you readers as well, one and all. Without you, there would be no place for the tales we spin, and the world would be darker and more joyless because of it. *You* are the bright stars in the black firmament of the universe, lighting the way for us all, and each other, to find meaning and hope in the stories we all share.

Johnstown, Pennsylvania, December 25, 2020

BACKER HALL OF FAME

Thank you to all these backers for making this book a reality!

$150 Level

K.G. Anderson

Stacey Anderson

David Brown

Francis Bruno

Joe Cron

DebT222

Michael J DiMenna

A Friend

Karen Fonville

Katharina Gerlach

Jim Gotaas

Patrick Helmuts

Gordon Horne

Kari Kilgore and Jason Adams

Adrienne Lecter
M. Mahar and Thomas Strich
Deb Miller
Terry Mixon
Heidi Moone
Ronald E Mueller
Sonja Myers
Mary Jo Rabe
Rachel E. Robinson
Johanna Rothman
John Senn
Richard Schneck
Shadowfall
MJ Silversmith
Lesley L. Smith
Louisa Swann
Stephannie Tallent
Melissa Taylor

$100 Level

Susan Beltz
Diana Buhl
R.J. Hanson
Craig Martelle
Dan Shoemaker
Carlos Valcarcel

$75 Level

Dr. Joe Homan
Mark Leslie Lefebvre

. . .

$50 Level

Robert B. Battle
Todd Chamberlain
Todd Kranhouse
Matt Lamb
Thomas Leap
Michael Warren Lucas
Jefferson Nunn
Thomas Sturm
Jason A. Thees

$40 Level

ABeltz
Ron and Joan Brzana
Mary Gaitan
Ronald H. Miller
David Schmoker
Nathaniel Y. Sims
Benjamin Smith

$30 Level

Leslie Berger
Bill Erickson
Stevan & Alma Chavez-Fagg
Gary D Henton
Chrishaun Keller-Hanna
Jenn Mitchell
Ronald A Sanders

.   .   .

$20 Level

Atthis Arts
Doug Atkinson
Stephen Ballentine
E.W. Barnes
Thomas Bither
David Bruns
Tom Campbell
Mike Carlin
Kristi Chadwick
Chris Chastain
Thomas M. Colwell
Shimmy Comics
Fen Eatough
Joseph Evenson
Steve Ferrebee
Teddy Garrett
Kevin M. Glover
Elisabeth C. Haithcock
Douglas Jeffreys
Rob & Donna Kodalen
James Latzer
John J. Leen
Gary A. Leicht
Meredith Loughran
Brea Ludwigson
Donald H Mark
John Markley
Kendra McConnell
Kevin Forest Moreau
Brooks Moses
Jordan Nelson

Dan Ross
Richard Sayer
Steven Scherbinski
Caroline Schmitt
Bryan Smart
Dean Wesley Smith
Diane L. Smith
Willard T Wagener
Mark A. Woolsey

$10 Level

Brad Ackerman
Aethon Books
Rob in AUS
Teri J. Babcock
Bahof
Jennifer Flora Black
Richard Blackburn
Edmund M.S. Boys
Elizabeth Bridges
Penny BroJacquie
Michaela Cocker
Divadiabeetusdawg
Bonnie Elizabeth
Michal Frackowski
Christine "Mirintala" Forshner
Bernard John Alexander Galpin
Bruce Glassford
Marian Goldeen
Robert Greenberger
Timothy Greenshields

Nathan Haines
Jessi Hammond
Richard Heck
Hanji Hemiha
David H Hendrickson
Fred Herman
James Husum
Charles Isaac
Scott J
Michèle Laframboise
Meenaz Lodhi
Eugene Lloyd MacRae
maileguy
Jonathan Martin
Josh Medin
Scott Murphy
Scott Neil
Lisa Owen
Scott D. Parker
Emilia Marjaana Pulliainen
Friedrich Roehrer-Ertl
Carolyn Rowland
Damon Schofield
Jeff Sigmund
Erik Spigel
Raja Thiagarajan
Simon Walker
Chris Wuchte

$5 Level

AA 1874

alicat
Andreas
Robert J Andrews II
Michael Barbour
Charles Barouch, HDWPbooks
Thomas Bennett Jr.
Andy Benoit
Alexandra Brandt
John Four Owls Buell
Joanne Burrows
Michael A. Burstein
Tony Calder
Dr. James Caplan
Gabriel Casillas
Robert Claney
Paul T. Davies
Drew
Diana Deverell
Mike R. Doehler
Amy (A.K.) DuBoff
N. Engel
David Etherton
Ryan A. Fleming
GeoffM
Barb G.
Chris Halliday
Ryan Harron
Dave Hermann
Eva Holmquist
Chad V. Holtkamp
S. Jonda
Andrew Kaplan

Jim Kosmicki
Brian D Lambert
Warren Lapworth
Lianne
Céline Malgen
Nick Marone
Todd McCaffrey
Robert J. McCarter
Tod McCoy
Meyari McFarland
Jonathan Mendonca
John Robert Mead
Caleb Monroe
Debbie Mumford
Ergo Ojasoo
Gary Olsen
Mark O'Neill
The Professor & The Poet
Joseph D. Procopio
Jason Prugar
Cat Rambo
Iain Rockliffe
Sharon Scarborough
Jay Scarson
Lawrence M. Schoen
Adam Selby-Martin
Travis Siegel
Mike Southern
Deanna Stanley
SwordFirey
Hope Terrell
Robert W. Tinsley

Laura Ware
Gwen Whiting
Ryan M. Williams
Cliff Winnig
Risa Wolf
Tieg Zaharia